I, GRACIE

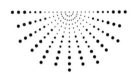

SHARON SALA

This book is for my Little Mama and me.
For the god-awful journey we took together.
For the hard times, and the bad times.
Because I loved her, and she loved me.
Parts of this we lived.
And parts of this are all Gracie and Delia's story.
But they will forever be entwined within my heart.

CHAPTER ONE

 t was the tenth of July—one day after Gracie Dunham's twenty-ninth birthday, and just before midnight—when Gracie called Brother Harp, the preacher from their church.

The hospice nurse she had been expecting had had a wreck on the way to their house. The hospice nurse was okay, but otherwise indisposed, so Gracie called the preacher to stand witness to Delia's last hours instead.

And he came with his wife, Ramona, and they sat with Gracie, listening to Delia gasping, choking, struggling to breathe.

Gracie was white-lipped and silent, sweat running down the middle of her back, her hands folded into fists in her lap, willing her mama to stop fighting the inevitable. Silently begging her to just give up the ghost and go find Daddy.

Brother Harp's prayers were long, loud, and vocal, as he prayed for Delia's soul to be delivered to the Lord, while Ramona patted Gracie's knee in cadence with the rise and fall of her husband's voice.

Just as the sun breached the horizon, Delia gasped, briefly opened her eyes, and pointed toward the foot of the bed.

"Hallelujah! She sees the angels come to carry her home," Harp cried.

Ramona turned, staring intently in the direction Delia had pointed, but all she saw was her husband's shadow on the wall, reflected by the rising sun.

Gracie, however, was beyond hallelujahs and prayers. The past nine years of Delia Dunham's dance with dementia had worn the life clean out of her. She was holding her breath, giving the air in the room to Mama, so she could take what she needed to let go. And then when she finally did, all Gracie could think was, *Finally, Lord.*

She was too worn out to cry, so Ramona cried for her. It was enough drama to wear Gracie slick. And because no one else seemed led to do it, Gracie got up and pulled the sheet over her mama's face.

At that point, Brother Harp noticed the beads of sweat on Gracie's upper lip, and the exhaustion in her eyes. She must have looked like she was about to pass out, so he thought to offer further aid.

"Gracie, can we call someone for you?"

"If you care to let Decker Funeral Home in Sweetwater know Mama passed, I would appreciate it," she said.

Ramona wiped her eyes, blew her nose, and gave Gracie a strange look.

Gracie suspected the woman was bothered by her lack of grief, but she was too numb to cry. There was nothing left of the woman who'd loved and raised her, and it was likely going to take the rest of Gracie's life to get past the memories of what these years had done to both of them. She barely noticed when Brother Harp went out into the hall to make the call, leaving the women alone.

"Bless her heart," Ramona kept saying, then stood up and moved closer to the bed, staring down at the sheet-covered body.

Gracie eyed the preacher's wife without judgment, noting only what she saw. The constant frown and lips always pursed with disapproval. The dyed black hair, and black dress she was wearing—hovering like that at her mama's bed—made her look like a turkey buzzard perched up on a fence, just waiting its turn.

Gracie shuddered.

"I'm going to get some fresh air," she said, then bolted out of the room, past the preacher, and straight out the back door into the rising heat of another day.

She was wearing yesterday's clothes, and her long, dark hair was still in the braid from the night before, but it didn't matter. Not yet. Later, she'd have to clean house and clean up. People would be coming, whether she wanted them or not. It's how things worked when someone died, even though they hadn't had a soul inside this house since the Sunday Mama had thrown a knife at their neighbor for coming to their door to tell them they had a steer out on the road. And they hadn't owned cattle in over six years, so they'd been on their own a long time. Still, she expected a few would come by, if for no other reason than curiosity.

A crow flew between the sunrise and Gracie's line of sight. The empty corrals and the drying pasture were vivid reminders that more than mama's good sense had disappeared from this place.

There were so many things she had to do now when all she wanted was to lock all the doors and sleep. There were her siblings to notify, not that they deserved it. They'd gone AWOL on her years ago, but she still had to call them and let them know. Delia was their Mama, too.

The screen door squeaked behind her, and then Brother Harp was beside her. He was a stout man with green eyes, a weak chin, and a big booming voice.

"Willis Decker sends his sympathies and said to let you know they will be here within the hour."

"Thank you," Gracie said.

"Is there anyone else you—"

"Not at the moment. I'll deal with all that later," she said.

Brother Harp nodded. "As you wish. The church calendar is open right now, so you just pick the day and time that best suits you, and we'll make it work, okay?"

"Yes, sir."

Brother Harp gave Gracie a sharp look, and as he did, Gracie saw a glint in his eye she didn't like. Then he smiled and cleared his throat.

"Now that you're free of your burden of health care, we'll be expecting to see you back in church...after a decent time of grieving, of course."

Gracie blinked.

"Brother Harp, I thank you and Ramona for coming. I called you here because it was something Mama had asked of me before she went and lost her mind, and because there was no one else to call after the hospice nurse wrecked herself outside of Abilene. I'll be in touch about the services. As for going back to church...that's gonna take some time. The last seven years of our lives were nothing short of hell. Neither you, or Ramona, or any of the congregation, chose to visit us during all these years to see if we were in need, so I'm not of a mind to return the favor."

Brother Harp turned red, and then he paled. "But we were told that she'd gone crazy. That it wasn't safe to be around her, and that she didn't know people anymore. Everyone in Sweetwater felt bad for the situation, but—"

Gracie cut him short. "I understand. You didn't want to get involved. She was crazy. But she didn't know it. And she didn't mean to be. However, I wasn't crazy, and I was hurting, and we were in need, but I was raised not to beg. So, I didn't. No thank you for the invitation to return to the fold. I appreciate you coming, and please thank Ramona for me. I'll let you two see yourselves out."

He looked like he couldn't believe he was being asked to leave. "What about the funeral home coming for the body?"

Gracie stared him down. "They know the way here. All I have to do is open the door."

Brother Harp had been dissed and dismissed with about as much class as he'd probably ever been party to, and he had enough dignity to not make excuses, or be angry with a truth.

"Yes, ma'am," he said. "I'm sorry." And then he went back into the house.

Gracie was still standing on the porch when she heard them drive away, but she had no qualms about what she'd said, and they knew their way back to Sweetwater.

She thought about what he'd said—about people in town being

4

afraid of Delia. She'd acted out a lot in the first two years, which was why Gracie had quit taking her to town. And after that, Gracie had gone on her own. People had sent their best wishes to Delia, but they'd never asked Gracie if she was in need. There was a difference.

Gracie thought about her mama lying there in that room all alone, and then looked out across the prairie and knew Delia wasn't here anymore. She was out there somewhere, dancing through heavenly bluebells with Daddy. The thought made her heart hurt. But instead of crying, she went back inside, washed her hands and face, got a cold Coke out of the refrigerator, and turned on the box fan standing behind the table.

She needed caffeine, but they'd been out of coffee for a week. At least Mama had had the grace to wait and die until her social security check hit the bank. Otherwise, Gracie would have had to give it back, and she was going to need it.

Mama's death was not a shock, and had been a long time coming, but at the same time, Gracie couldn't remember what it felt like to be free, or what it was like to know someone had her back. But she remembered their last happy family gathering nine years ago, like it was yesterday.

It was just after Easter dinner.

James and his wife, Darlene, were sitting side by side on the sofa. Their two kids, Caleb and Joanie, were outside with Mamie's husband, Joel, who was hiding eggs for them. James, the eldest and only son, was holding court, and the conversation, as if he were king.

Gracie's older sisters, Daphne, who'd never married, and Mamie, who had chosen to remain childless, were sitting in the two blue recliners, talking in unison and laughing without finishing their sentences, just as they'd done when they were kids.

Gracie had just graduated college in January and was about to move to Denver, Colorado for her new job.

"Are you excited?" Daphne asked.

"Oh, yes," Gracie said. "Getting hired as an event planner for that big

hotel will never be dull. The scope of the events will keep everything exciting. And I'm looking forward to mountains and lots of green trees."

James frowned. "We have trees here."

Mamie snorted. "Says the man who moved to flat-ass Houston, where it floods with less than an inch of rain. We have scrub brush and tumbleweeds here," she said, and everyone laughed.

Delia was sitting quietly in the loveseat beside her youngest daughter, seeing herself and her Tommy in all of them. Loving them so much, and at the same time, aware she was in possession of a bomb that was about to explode in all their lives.

Gracie was only slightly aware of her mother's unusual silence, but looking back, she would remember that the expression on her mama's face was something between pride and regret.

And then Delia cleared her voice and reached for Gracie's hand.

"Kids, there is something I need to tell you, and there's no need to keep putting it off. I have been having memory problems for almost a year. Last month, when I was leaving Sweetwater to come home, I forgot where I was going. I forgot about home, and I was halfway to Abilene before I realized what I'd done."

Gracie noted the looks of shock on all her siblings' faces, but it was the hidden horror in her mother's eyes that touched her most.

Mama was scared, and Gracie's heart hurt for that fear. "Oh, Mama! Oh no! You must have been so scared!" Gracie said, and tightened her grip on her mother's hand.

Delia squeezed it gratefully, then took a quick breath and kept talking.

"I remembered my granny. She'd lost her mind real young, and I knew stuff like that can run in a family, so I went to the doctor. After weeks of testing, they diagnosed me with fronto-temporal dementia, which means, I will not only forget people and things, but I could have a change in personality, too."

All of a sudden, the easy camaraderie they'd been sharing was gone.

Mamie was crying. "Does that mean you're gonna go crazy?"

Gracie frowned. "Oh, for the love of God, Mamie! What a thing to say!"

Daphne kept waiting for James to speak up, but he looked like someone had just poked a stick up his butt, while his wife, Darlene, was blinking back tears.

"I'm so sorry, Mama D., but we're all here, and we'll be there for you when you need help," Darlene said.

"Oh, it's okay," Delia said. "I just needed to get it said, and since we're all here together..."

She let her voice trail off as she kept searching her children's faces for something...anything...and it made Gracie mad.

"No, ma'am. It is not okay," Gracie said. "What can we do? What do you need?"

Tears welled then rolled down Delia's face.

"I don't know what to do. I don't know what I need. I hate this. I hate being a burden. I just wanted you all to know now, that I am okay with being put somewhere. Because when the time comes for it to happen, I might not be in my right mind. I might not be able to say those words."

"I can't stay. I have a job and family in Houston," James said.

"I can't move away and leave Joel in Austin all alone. My duty is to him, first," Mamie said.

Daphne, who was a realtor and lived in Dallas, was still looking at the floor.

Gracie felt them pulling away.

Her dreams and her future were going up in smoke, but she knew she would hate herself for the rest of her life if she didn't do the right thing.

"I'll stay with you, Mama."

The moment she said it, it was as if someone had just opened a window and let in fresh air. Her siblings were suddenly smiling and nodding and making promises to help.

Delia moaned. "Oh, Gracie...honey... your life is just beginning. I don't want this for you."

"And we don't want this for you, Mama. You have done everything for us all our lives. It is our honor to give back to you," Gracie said. "Your children are going to make sure you don't ever get lost again, okay?"

Delia threw her arms around Gracie's neck. "Thank you, baby girl. Thank you."

. . .

7

THE SOUND OF A PASSING VEHICLE PULLED HER OUT OF THE MEMORY. That was then, and this was now. Her siblings had managed to show up at Christmas for two years after Mama's revelation, but at the last visit, her erratic behavior had made them uncomfortable, and they'd never come back. That was the year Gracie had put away her resumé and accepted the fact that her dream job as an event planner in Denver was as lost as Mama's good sense. Gracie had understood their fear of Mama, but she'd never thought they would quit *her*. Like Brother Harp, they had a lot to answer for, and she didn't accept excuses.

She popped the tab on her can of Coke and drank long and deep— even though it brought tears to her eyes—even though it burned all the way down.

There were three stale cookies still in the cookie jar. She ate one with the rest of her Coke and called it breakfast. By the time the hearse arrived, she was as mentally prepared as she was going to be.

And then they were on the porch and knocking.

She opened the door, eyeing them through the screen. She recognized the short man with white hair.

"Good morning, Miss Dunham. I'm Willis Decker. On behalf of Decker Funeral Home, you have our deepest sympathies."

"Thank you, Mr. Decker. You can call me, Gracie. If you'll follow me."

Willis Decker held the door as two other neatly dressed men came inside with a gurney, then they followed Gracie down the hall to her mama's bedroom.

Willis Decker was trying to get over the shock of their level of living. Between the heat, the dust, and the utter lack of comfort, it hurt his heart, but he was here to do a job, and so he turned to Gracie.

"If you'd like to step outside, we'll just—"

Gracie stood her ground. "Thank you, I'll stay. Mama is past suffering indignities, but as long as she's still under this roof, she is my responsibility."

Willis nodded. Gracie Dunham was obviously all business, and he admired a woman with grit.

"Yes, ma'am," he said, and then began directing his helpers.

Within a few minutes, they'd managed to get Delia's body onto the Gurney, covered up, and strapped down.

"These are the clothes she wanted to be buried in," Gracie said, and handed him a paper bag with everything carefully folded up inside.

Willis took the bag. "Yes, ma'am," he said, then they started through the house, going room by room, then out onto the porch and down the steps to the hearse.

Gracie watched with an aching heart.

Mama was gone from this house.

Willis came back and handed her his card.

"We'll let you know when the body is ready. We won't put her in a viewing room until you are satisfied with her appearance."

"You have the casket she wanted?" Gracie asked.

"Yes, ma'am, we do. Everything will be as she asked. We won't let either of you down." He paused, then added, "We'll need you to come in and sign some papers so we can set a date and time for the service."

"I'll be in later today," Gracie said.

"Yes, ma'am. Again, we are so sorry for your loss."

Gracie watched from the porch as they loaded Delia up into the hearse. When they closed the doors, her gut knotted. She'd just given her mama up to strangers. Somehow, it all seemed so wrong, but she stayed on the porch, watching until they left the property, then went inside.

It was time to notify her siblings. She went to look for her cell phone, hoping she could get a good signal from their satellite service today.

She got out Delia's address book with all the names and addresses and sat down at the kitchen table to make the calls, but each time she punched in a number, it came up as disconnected.

First James in Houston, then Mamie in Austin. And then it hit her. These numbers were their old landline numbers! Most likely, they'd done away with them and only used cell phones now.

None of them had called her. They'd used the old landline in the house to call Mama until she'd forgotten who they were, and then they'd quit calling. Now that phone was gone. She had not heard their voices since that last Christmas seven years ago, when they'd all said goodbye.

Her last hope was Daphne, who lived in Dallas. When she turned the page to Daphne's name, and saw one number had been marked out, and another added below that. She had hopes it would be to a cell phone, and it was.

It rang, and it rang, and just when Gracie thought it was going to go to voicemail, Daphne answered in a breathless voice, as if she'd been running.

"Hello?"

"Daphne, it's me, Gracie. Mama died this morning," she said without preamble. "I tried to call James and Mamie, but their numbers are disconnected. If you want them to know, you'll have to tell them."

"Oh no! Gracie, I'm so sorry. Are you okay?"

"No. I am not okay. I haven't been okay for the past seven years. I will let you know when the service is held. Kindly do not show up here at this house before the services and pretend you are still part of my family. You will go straight to the church for the funeral and the dinner, and when it's over, you will all come to the house. There are things that have to be settled."

"But—"

Gracie hung up in Daphne's ear, then put her head down on the table and cried from frustration and rage.

She was a woman on fire, and for the past seven years, not one person had cared enough to even throw a little water on her, let alone put it out.

After the tears, she felt better. But it was moving on toward 10:00, and since Gracie had told Willis Decker she would stop by, it was time to get moving.

She showered and washed her hair, then began making a mental list of what she had to do in town as she tried to find something decent to put on that still fit her.

~

DAPHNE'S PHONE CALL TO JAMES CAUGHT HIM OFF GUARD. SHE RARELY ever called, and never at work. When he saw her name come up on Caller ID, he hit Save on his work screen and picked up.

"Hello?"

"James, it's me, Daphne. Gracie just called. Mama died. She tried to call you but got a disconnected number for both you and Mamie."

"Oh no! Oh man...I knew this day would come. What do we need to do? Does she—"

"She doesn't want shit from any of us. I've never heard such cold rage in someone's voice in my life. She will let us know the time and date later. We are not invited to the house early. We go straight to the church for services and dinner, and then go to the house only after it's over. She said there are things to settle."

James felt bile in the back of his throat and had to swallow hard so he wouldn't puke.

"Did you ever call her? I mean...after that last Christmas?" Daphne asked.

"No, but—"

"Neither did I. Did you ever check on them?" Daphne asked.

James's eyes welled. "No. I guess I thought if Gracie needed us, she would call."

Daphne's voice was shaking. "Except your number was disconnected. So, who the hell knows if she ever tried?"

"Oh my God," James said. "How will we ever make this right?"

"Just prepare yourself for the wrath, because I could feel it in my bones with every word she uttered. I'll text you info later, although you could call her yourself. She still has the same number from college."

Then the line went dead in James's ear.

He was a whiz as a CPA, but he'd fucked up his marriage. He'd fucked up his responsibilities as a father, and now it had come home to him what a sorry-ass son and brother he'd become.

He got up from his desk and went into his boss's office in a daze.

"Hey, Ralph, uh...my sister just called. My mom died."

Ralph Corrigan looked up, saw the devastation on James's face, and was immediately sympathetic.

"Oh man...James...I'm so sorry. My sympathies to all of you." He stood and shoved his hands in his pockets. "Where did she live? You'll need time off, of course. We can work around your schedule just fine. What days do you need to be gone?"

Ralph's kindness just made James feel worse because he deserved none of the sympathy. He would have felt better if Ralph had punched him in the face.

"She lived out on the family ranch not far from Sweetwater. I'm not sure about services, yet. As soon as I get a day and time, I'll let you know. For now, I just wanted to give you a heads up."

"Of course," Ralph said. "Listen, why don't you take an early lunch and then go home for the rest of the day."

"Are you sure?" James asked.

"Absolutely. Just let me know the name of the funeral home, and we'll send flowers. What was your mother's name?"

"Delia. Her name was Delia Dunham," James said and walked out.

TODAY WAS MAMIE FREEMONT'S WEEKLY LUNCH DATE WITH HER THREE best girlfriends. They were going to the Salt Lick just outside of Austin, and she was already anticipating the restaurant's famous mouth-watering barbecue.

Going out was one of Mamie's favorite pastimes, and today was no different. She had her white-blonde hair pulled up on top of her head, leaving the carefully coifed curls free to dangle. She was in skin-tight jeans that showed off her shapely ass, and a low-cut top that showed off her big boobs. And, as always, she was wearing all five of her diamond rings, because a Texas girl never had hair too big or too many diamonds.

Her husband, Joel, was on one of his business trips. This time back to Portland. Or was it Seattle? She couldn't remember. But it didn't matter. Mamie had the most fun when Joel was gone. She didn't exactly cheat on him. She'd never do that. But she liked to flirt when she was out with the girls, and today, she felt fine enough to flirt.

She was trading lipstick colors in her purse when her cell phone rang. A quick glance put a smile on her face. It was Daphne! She and her sister were only thirteen months apart, and as close as twins.

"Hello, sugar!" Mamie said.

"I have bad news," Daphne said. "Mama passed."

For a second, Mamie felt like someone had punched her in the gut, and then she took a deep breath.

"Oh no."

"That's not the worst," Daphne added. "You need to know Gracie is pissed. We are not invited to the house early. We are to go straight to the funeral home the day of the services. Dinner will be there, and when it's over, we are all to go back to the house to settle things. Her words. Not mine."

Mamie's eyes welled. "Well, that's just awful. That's our home, too. She can't—"

"We abandoned her, Mamie. Don't deny it. She tried to call you personally to let you and James both know but got disconnected numbers."

"Oh my God," Mamie muttered. "I guess I let time slip away from me after Mama couldn't talk on the phone anymore."

Daphne sighed. "Did you ever call Gracie?" Daphne asked.

"Well, no, I don't guess I did. But Mama always said she was busy, or—"

"Oh, for the love of God, Mamie. Mama lost her mind. Why would you believe anything she said then? She told the same story over and over, and then forgot who we were. I didn't call Gracie because I didn't want her to ask me to come stay. I didn't want to take care of Mama. Not even for a weekend, especially not after she got scary, talking all crazy. I will admit it right now. I sacrificed my baby sister for my own selfish life. I didn't want to know how Gracie felt living with Mama's crazy shit every day, because I didn't want to do it. I hate myself for that, and now I have to live with it. But I don't imagine time slipped anywhere for Gracie, so just be prepared for a cold shoulder when we get there."

Mamie didn't like being called down for anything, and she didn't want to talk about her failures, so she cut the call short.

"I'm just sick about this, but I have to go or I'm gonna be late. I'm meeting the girls for lunch. Let me know the details when you get them."

"You could call and ask her yourself," Daphne said. "She still has the same number."

"I guess," Mamie said. "But you let me know anyway," and then disconnected. She dropped her phone back in her purse, gathered up the rest of her stuff, and headed out the door.

She didn't feel quite as flirty as she had. In fact, she was feeling a little sick to her stomach, but she probably just needed to eat something. And staying home by herself wasn't going to solve seven years' worth of sins.

CHAPTER TWO

Gracie went into the funeral home to sign papers, then set the date for the service on Friday at 10:00 A.M.—three days away.

"Will you have a family dinner at the church? I'm asking because people always want to know," Willis said.

"Yes, and I remember from Daddy's service that Mama needed copies of the death certificate, so I need to order some."

"Do you think five will be enough?" he asked.

"I will only need one, so I assume so. If anyone needs more, they can order them, right?"

"Yes, ma'am," Willis said.

"Then, are we done here?" Gracie asked.

Willis nodded. "I'll call you tomorrow when she's ready for viewing."

"Thank you," Gracie said.

After Willis escorted her out, she drove straight to the bank and walked in with her sunglasses on, her long dark hair swinging down her back. The t-shirt and shorts she wore showed off the long legs she'd inherited from her daddy and hid a body just a shade too thin.

She withdrew a little over one thousand dollars from her mama's checking account, leaving $55 dollars in the bank, which would cover the $37.27 automatic withdrawal for her mama's life insurance policy one last time.

It was a bittersweet comfort to know she wouldn't be homeless *and* broke, but it was all due to Delia's need to make things right that the life insurance policy even existed.

It was the day after Easter. Everyone had gone home. Gracie was cooking breakfast when Delia came into the kitchen, insistent that they go straight to Sweetwater after they ate.

"To take care of business," Delia said, and so they did.

The first place they went was to her insurance agent to change the beneficiaries of her small life insurance policy from all four of her children to Gracie as the sole beneficiary.

"For you, and what you're about to give up," Delia told Gracie.

Then they went next to Delia's lawyer. Delia knew she was going to lose her good sense, but she wanted to put her affairs in order before it happened. So, she signed over her power of attorney to Gracie.

Gracie remembered then the feeling of life spinning out of control. This was all happening too fast. She hadn't thought—she didn't know—she should have—but it was already too late.

The last place they went that day was to Decker Funeral Home.

The whole trip there was, as Gracie thought of it later, a fucking out of body experience. She was standing at her mother's side, watching her pick out her own casket, and then sitting at her mother's side as she paid for her own burial expenses. Delia already owned the plot where her husband, Tommy, was buried, and her name was already on the headstone beside his. That's when Gracie finally gave up and cried, and Delia had just patted her hand.

"Don't be sad, baby girl. It's just me takin' care of business."

AND NOW, BABY GIRL WAS TAKIN' CARE OF BUSINESS FOR MAMA.

No one challenged Gracie's right to withdraw the money when she went into the bank, because her name was on the account, and she never blinked an eye when she pocketed the cash and walked out.

Her next stop was the florist, and her choice of flowers for mama's casket was swift and simple. Pink carnations. Always pink carnations.

When they were kids, their daddy used to dance Delia around the kitchen, singing old songs from the fifties. "A White Sport Coat and Pink Carnations" was her favorite and never failed to make her smile.

As soon as Gracie paid for the flowers, she got in her car and headed for the Sonic Drive-In. Dirty house or not, Gracie had to get something in her belly before she passed out.

As she pulled into the stall to order, it occurred to her that this was where she and Mama had come to eat the day Mama had picked out her own casket.

That day, Delia hadn't remembered tater tots, and they'd been her favorites. Gracie had ordered them for her anyway, and Delia hadn't remembered what the hell they were until they'd arrived on their tray. After that, she'd laughed at her forgetfulness and dunked every one of them in ketchup.

Gracie's eyes welled again as she lowered the window to order, but she knew in her heart what she was going to choose when she pressed the button.

"Welcome to Sonic. What can I get for you today?"

"I want a chili-cheese coney, an order of tater tots, and a large Coke," Gracie said.

"Will there be anything else?" the boy asked.

"No. That's all," Gracie said, rolled up the window, jacked up the air conditioner, then called the preacher.

He answered on the second ring. "Brother Harp speaking."

"This is Gracie Dunham. I've set the service for this coming Friday at 10:00 A.M., with the family dinner at the church after we come back from the cemetery. Will that work for you?"

"Yes. I'll notify the Ladies Aide so they can make plans to provide the food. Do you have any idea how much family will be coming?"

"Less than ten, counting me," Gracie said. "One other thing. If you would, please inform the congregation not to bring food to my house.

There won't be any family here ahead of time. I don't have a working deep freeze, and it'll all go to waste in this heat."

"Yes, ma'am, I will certainly do that," he said. "Do you have a eulogy written? If not–"

"Mama wrote her own. I'll drop it by the church in a day or so. She also picked out the songs she wanted sung, so I'll bring the file with all her last wishes. You can plan the service around that."

"Well, I'll say," Brother Harp said. "Delia was—"

"Always in charge," Gracie said. "She took care of business."

"Yes, that she did," Brother Harp agreed.

Gracie disconnected, then sent a text to Daphne, giving her the date and time of the service and the funeral home where Mama was being laid out.

She didn't want to talk to her. She wished she never had to see their faces again, but that was running away from trouble and wasn't Gracie's style.

She had money waiting when the carhop brought out her food. As soon as she was alone again, she opened a packet of ketchup, squirted it all over the tater tots, and then picked one off the top.

"Here's to you, Mama," Gracie said, and popped it in her mouth.

She ate slowly, savoring the food, the comfort of eating where it was cool, and the luxury of not having to stuff it in her mouth on the run like she had at home. And when she had finished eating, she headed for the supermarket. She needed cleaning supplies and enough food to last for three days.

A couple of hours later, Gracie was home and putting up groceries when she heard a knock at the door. As she walked back toward the front of the house, she saw a delivery van from the florist parked in the drive and opened the door to a man she'd gone to school with.

"Delivery for you, Gracie."

"Hello, Kenny. I'm not accepting flowers here. If you don't mind, please take everything to Decker's Funeral home."

"Uh...well, I..."

Gracie shut the door and caught a glimpse of herself in the hall mirror on her way back to the kitchen, then paused and moved closer.

She still looked like her daddy—dark eyes, black hair, and high cheekbones. But where her daddy's jaw had been square and sharp, Gracie's had a soft curve leading down to a very stubborn chin. She saw defiance and anger in her eyes—two emotions she had a right to feel.

Then she leaned closer, then closer still until she could see the pores in her skin and the glisten of sweat on her forehead and stared straight into her own eyes—as if she was facing down her worst enemy and didn't like what she saw.

She closed her eyes, took a slow, deep breath, and when she opened her eyes again, there was nothing left to see but pain, and that would fade with the passing of time.

Glancing down, she saw the dust on the floor, and on the hall table, and absently traced her name in it, as she had done so many times before as a child, writing, *I, Gracie,* as if she was just getting ready to swear to some kind of vow.

And then she smiled, remembering her mother's sharp tone every time she'd done it.

"Well now, Gracie Jean... since you saw fit to call attention to this ever-present west Texas dust, then I suggest you get a dust rag and the furniture polish, and start wiping it off."

"Yes, ma'am," Gracie would answer, and run to get the lemon oil. It was still one of her favorite scents.

She looked down at the name she'd just scribbled and could only imagine what a stir her refusal to accept flowers at the house was going to cause. But stirring was a woman's prerogative, and her days of careful silence were over.

It occurred to her then that notifying the other florists in Sweetwater about her decision might be prudent, so she sat down and did that, then finished putting away groceries.

Her next task was cleaning and laundry, so she headed straight to her mama's bedroom and began stripping the bed and putting everything in to wash. Then she did something she'd been wanting to do for years and began pulling down the old rotting curtains in Mama's room. She stuffed them in a garbage bag, then began emptying trash cans all over the house.

When the laundry cycle ended, she threw the sheets in the dryer and put her own bedding in to wash. Next came the floors. She got out the broom, then followed up with a dust mop. When she was through, grabbed a dust rag and the lemon oil, began wiping down the tables and the chairs, then all the woodwork.

She'd prided herself on keeping the old house clean, even as it began to fall down around them, but the dust storm last week, and then these last four days of Delia's sudden deterioration, had made cleaning the last thing that mattered.

It was late evening by the time she'd remade her bed, but the floors were spotless, all the surfaces dust-free. The rooms smelled of Pine-Sol and lemon oil. The old house was as presentable as it could possibly be, but Gracie looked like hell.

She had the box fan on in the kitchen, and the one going in her bedroom. It didn't cool anything, but it did stir the hot air. She was tired and hungry, but too dirty to eat. So once again, she showered, then put on her PJs, and went to the kitchen. She made herself a ham and cheese sandwich, poured a glass of milk, and carried them outside to the back porch to watch the sunset as she ate.

In the old days, Daddy would have been out here with a cold beer at his elbow, playing his guitar and singing songs at Mama's request.

Sometimes, James would join him, adding his harmonica to the music Tommy Dunham skillfully coaxed from the old guitar. Daphne and Mamie would dance—sometimes a two-step, sometimes a waltz, and sometimes a line dance, interpreting it with steps of their own when they forgot what came next.

Then Daddy had been killed in a car wreck, less than a mile from their house, and after that, the music had died.

She finished her sandwich and milk, and then sat in sweet silence as the sky turned vivid shades of red and orange, two of Mama's favorite colors, before fading into dusk, then full-on dark.

She was tired and needed sleep, but she didn't want to go into that house alone, and so she sat, waiting for the first coyote of the night to let out a little yip. When it did, it was the signal for the chorus that followed.

Gracie closed her eyes, letting their song of the prairie fill her. She felt battered and sore, like she'd been in a fight. Her spirit was down—really down, and listening to the coyotes took her back to the good times, when Daddy had still been alive, and Mama had known their names.

Finally, the coyotes moved on, and when they did, Gracie got up and walked out into the yard, grateful for the gentle breeze against her clean skin. She looked up at the night sky, then out across the dark prairie. She'd never felt so small, or so alone. She needed to be heard. She needed people to know she was still here, thinking God needed a reminder, too, that she was still alive—still dreaming.

And so she tilted her head back and thrust a fist into the air, shouting aloud into the night.

"I, Gracie, am not the Dunham who died. Life did not beat me. Mama couldn't kill me. The war is over, and I'm still standing."

Then she turned around, grabbed her dirty dishes, and went inside. The ritual of putting the house to sleep was as familiar as putting her mama to bed. She began going through each room, locking all the windows and doors.

She was so tired, she was numb. She hadn't slept more than an hour at a time in the past thirty-six hours and wasn't sure she could unwind enough now to relax.

She kept thinking Mama needed her, and then would remember Delia had no need of anything on this earth again. Gracie was sad, but she was not going to cry because Mama was gone. She'd prayed too many nights for God to come get her.

She accepted that the tears would come when the need arose. She opened the windows beside her bed and turned the box fan toward her face. She sat down on the side of the mattress, pulled her long hair over her shoulder, and slowly braided it to keep it off her neck as she slept. And when she was through, she turned out the lamp, crawled between the freshly washed sheets and rolled over onto her side toward the open window, feeling the cool spot on the pillow against her face.

It would be heaven if the central air conditioner still worked. Even at night, summer in Texas was brutal. But she wouldn't be here much longer, and it didn't matter anymore.

She was just about to close her eyes when she remembered she hadn't notified her sister-in-law, Darlene. So she sent her a text, with the same info she'd given her siblings and then hit Send, and waited for an answer. It came within moments.

I'm sorry about Mama D. But I will not grieve her passing. It is a blessing for her and for you. You already know how much I loved her. And you know how much I love you. I just sent money via Venmo, as usual. Don't argue. The kids and I are fine. I don't want anything from James Dunham, and wherever you're going, you are going to need it. Love you.

Gracie sent a text through a veil of tears.

Love you, more. Thank you for saving us. You will always be my sister of the heart. Don't lose touch with me. You're all the family I have left.

She hit Send, put the phone back on the charger, found another cool spot on the pillow, and settled in.

As she shifted her shoulder, a pain shot through the muscles all the way to her neck, and for a moment, the memories that flooded put a knot in her stomach. Then she sighed and let it go. It wasn't anything but a remnant from living with Mama.

The last thing she remembered was the moonlight on her face as she closed her eyes.

BROTHER HARP ALWAYS SAID HIS BEDTIME PRAYERS ON HIS KNEES AT THE side of the bed, but tonight, he was struggling with a heart full of guilt. He could hear Ramona banging around in the bathroom. The ceiling fan over their bed was circulating the flow of cool air from their HVAC system, and his belly was full from their evening meal of fried ham and biscuits with gravy.

It was one of his favorite meals, but it hadn't set well with him tonight. Probably that third biscuit he'd eaten.

He kept thinking of how hot the old Dunham house had been, and how worn out everything looked—including Gracie. She was at least twenty pounds thinner than he remembered her, and he'd been shocked when she'd let them into the house last night.

He hadn't seen the dust on everything, or the circles beneath her eyes, until the next morning. She'd obviously devoted the majority of her time to the care of her mother, but he'd had no idea of how sparse their existence had become until sunrise. And he had no one to blame but himself.

Gracie Dunham had shamed him today, and he deserved it. But there was no way to fix his sin of omission, other than to ask the Good Lord to forgive him because he feared Gracie would not. So, down on his knees he went and spilled his guts to God.

By the time Ramona came to bed, he was lying on his side, pretending to be asleep. He did not want sex. He did not want to talk. He did not want to listen to her complain. He just wanted to forget what a pitiful excuse for a preacher he had become.

MAMIE RECEIVED DAPHNE'S TEXT ABOUT THE SERVICES WHILE SHE WAS still at lunch with her friends and went straight to the mall after lunch to buy herself a new black dress.

Once she got home, she'd amped up enough tears to call Joel, telling him about her mama's passing, soaking up all of his sympathy and basking in his promises that he would be on the next plane out of Portland.

That night as she was getting ready for bed, she decided to take the tags off her new dress. Joel didn't need to know how much it had cost, and she'd make it up to him with some good hot sex anyway, so it didn't really matter. Tomorrow, she would make an appointment to get her hair done, and then make a reservation for a Thursday arrival at the La Quinta Inn and Suites by Wyndham in Sweetwater. It had a pool.

It was going to be dicey, explaining to him why they were no longer welcome at the old house, but one lie at a time was how Mamie rolled.

～

BEING A REALTOR, DAPHNE HAD THE FREEDOM TO TAKE TIME OFF WHEN she needed, although she rarely did, because living as a single woman meant she was also the only one bringing in a paycheck.

She did well for herself, and her fancy Dallas townhouse was evidence of that. She'd notified the other realtors in the office about the death of her mother to make them aware of her upcoming absence for a couple of days. They were instantly sympathetic and loving, which made her guilt about Gracie even worse. She had a horrible feeling that no one was hugging and loving on her baby sister in her time of grief, and that made Daphne feel like throwing up.

She couldn't believe it was only this morning when Gracie had called. It felt like forever. After she'd heard her sister's voice and the news she'd imparted, a part of her had kept trying to turn back time.

She needed a do-over, but God wasn't about that. What He did teach was redemption, but she didn't know how to go about redeeming herself in her sister's eyes. What she'd done from the free will He had given her had turned into selfish choices, a horrific level of betrayal with a huge dose of shame to go with it.

She kept thinking about the times right after that Easter revelation when Mama had told them of her diagnosis. It had been a shock, but the reality of it had not set in until Christmas. That first one had been strange. Mama kept calling her by the wrong name, and then hadn't known what the foods were she'd been eating. She hadn't remembered she had grandchildren and kept asking who they were. But it was the second Christmas that had ended it for Daphne.

Mama had picked up food with her fingers. Told Mamie she looked fat and hadn't remember James's name. It had devastated him. And then she'd scared the grandchildren, and that had been the last time they'd set foot in that house.

She'd called home after that, but she'd always talked to Mama. Never to Gracie. And when Mama had finally forgotten who Daphne was, she'd quit calling altogether and had consoled herself with the thought that Delia couldn't miss talking to someone she didn't know.

Never once, had she let herself go there and wonder how Mama treated Gracie now that she didn't know her, either. She couldn't imagine Mama being mean, but she'd suspected she would be a handful. Still, Gracie is the one who'd offered to stay, and that's how Daphne had shelved her guilt, until now—when it was too late to matter.

She'd made a list of things to do tomorrow.

Book a room at the La Quinta.

Send flowers to the funeral home.

Buy a new dress for the service and get her hair done.

It would be hot as hell out at the cemetery, but she wore her blonde curly hair up, so a little heat and wind wouldn't ruin the style. And there was always hairspray to keep everything in place.

She finally went to bed because she couldn't focus on TV and was dreading the moment she closed her eyes, fearing she would see the people she had betrayed, wearing stern, solemn expressions.

And she did.

But in her dream, they turned their backs on her and walked away, leaving her the one abandoned, as she had done to them.

James had been home all afternoon and was a six-pack of beer into the wind, trying to get up the courage to call his ex-wife, Darlene. She needed to know what had happened.

He cleared his throat, pulled up her number, and then waited. It rang and rang, and he sighed. They didn't talk anymore. He just sent alimony and child support, and he'd messed up so many times on visitation days that his kids no longer wanted anything to do with him. She might not even answer.

When she finally picked up, and the sound of her voice brought tears to his eyes.

"What do you want?" she snapped.

"Uh...I called to tell you that Mama passed this morning, and to give you the day and time for the services."

"I already know. This has been a long, damned time coming. The children will not be attending the service. Caleb has to work, and Joanie will stay with Mother."

Then she hung up in his ear.

He laid the phone down on the bed beside him and stared at the floor. So, Darlene knew more about Gracie than he did. And his nineteen-year-old son had a job he didn't know about. And Joanie, his daughter, had hated his guts ever since the summer she'd turned thirteen, when he'd forgotten to pick her up after a soccer game. She'd had to call her mother to come get her, and by the time Darlene had arrived, Joanie had been the only kid left at the field. Neither one had talked to him for a year afterward.

He'd cheated on his wife with her best friend and lost his family. Then he hadn't called home since the Christmas his mother hadn't known who he was. He'd been so stricken and so shocked that he no longer existed in her cognizant world, that he'd balled himself up in grief, bemoaning how sad it was for him not to be remembered, when all along, he was the one who'd forgotten both of them.

He hated himself.

He hated what he had become.

He got up and went to get another beer from the refrigerator, only to realize there weren't any more.

As the eldest child and only son, he kept thinking there were things he needed to do and preparations to be made. But then he would remember he'd abdicated his throne and his rights for his personal freedom. So, he staggered back to the bedroom and passed out on the bed, fully clothed.

CHAPTER THREE

A storm was blowing up from the south, jacking up the wind coming through the open window by Gracie's bed and rattling the old blinds above it.

In her sleep, the rattle triggered a memory. She moaned and rolled over onto her back in a subconscious move to protect herself, but it was too late. The memory had downloaded the event into nightmare form, and once again, she was caught up in the matrix of the past.

Gracie stood at the kitchen sink, washing up their breakfast dishes. The radio was on Delia's favorite country station, and she could hear her mama humming along and mumbling a word of a song now and then.

It was a day just like all the others she'd had in the four years she'd been here, and she was thinking about making a grocery list. As soon as she gave Mama her medicine and put her down for a nap, she could make a flying run to Sweetwater for groceries, because it was no longer possible to take Delia with her.

Delia scared people with her loud voice and belligerent behavior. However, one of the medicines the doctor had her on now made her sleepy, and when she finally laid down to rest, she always slept for at least two hours, which gave Gracie plenty of time to get to town and back.

Gracie heard the chair scoot back from the table, and then the sound of feet shuffling around on the old wood floor. Mama was dancing. She often danced when music was playing.

Gracie turned around and smiled. Mama was dancing with her eyes closed, probably dreaming of Daddy. Gracie picked up a handful of flatware and carried it to the table for mama to put away. Delia liked to feel useful, and she still remembered how to sort the flatware into the sideboard.

Delia stopped dancing and snatched them up.

"Here you go, Mama," Gracie said, and pulled open the drawer where they stored the flatware then turned around to go back to the sink.

She didn't see the light go out in Delia's eyes, nor the panic that ensued.

Gracie was halfway to the sink when she heard footsteps behind her. Before she could turn around, Delia was screaming, "Get out of my house! Get out of my house!" and stabbing her in the back, over and over.

At first, Gracie was in shock and barely registering the pain. But blood was flying, and she was begging, "No, Mama, no!" and trying to take the knife away. Then as Gracie turned, Delia began stabbing at her chest, too.

It was Gracie's instinct for survival that saved her. With her last bit of strength, she knocked the knife out of her mother's hand, and then doubled up her fist and hit her square on the jaw.

Delia reeled backward, dropped down onto the floor in her daughter's blood, and started crying and rocking where she sat.

Gracie staggered to the phone and dialed 9-1-1.

"9-1-1. What is your emergency?"

Gracie was fading in and out of consciousness. She had to get this said, or she would die.

"Help. Help...Gracie Dunham... Mama stabbed me...crazy...dementia... blood everywhere... 10473 Highway West...Help me... I..."

GRACIE WOKE WITH A GASP, BATHED IN SWEAT, HER FACE WET WITH tears, and then realized it wasn't sweat. Rain was blowing in the window. It hardly ever rained in July, but it was raining tonight.

She flew out of bed and shut the window, then ran into the bathroom and grabbed a towel to mop up the floor. She was halfway down the hall to her mother's room to close her windows when she remembered Mama was dead, and she'd already closed them before she went to bed.

Her heart still pounded, but her shoulders slumped as she went back to her room. She stripped off her wet clothes and the bed sheets, then made it up again with dry ones. Weary, she took everything to the laundry and started it to wash before heading to the bathroom.

The lights blinded her as she flipped the switch, then she paused in front of the mirror, eyeing her nudity. Without thinking, she ran her fingers along the thin scars on her chest, and then turned sideways in the mirror, eyeing the thicker, ropey scars on her back and shoulders. She vaguely remembered the voices of paramedics speaking in loud, frantic tones. They'd called for another ambulance to take Delia to the psych ward. Hours later, she'd woken up alone in a hospital, hooked up to machines with a continual beep, bandaged all over her upper body and frantic about her mother's welfare.

Gracie shuddered, then washed her face and grabbed a clean nightgown before going to the kitchen. She got a cold can of Coke, popped the top, and went out onto the back porch.

The rain was blowing beneath the overhang. The air had finally cooled, and so she sat down on the porch swing facing the prairie. With the rain blowing in on her feet, she drank her Coke and watched the storm.

But the dream from before wouldn't let go. She kept remembering going home from the hospital alone, and then spending hours trying to clean up the blood. But too much time had passed, and it had long since soaked into the old wood floors.

As the days passed and she began gaining strength, she gathered up everything sharp in the house, and then searched through the barn and even in the old chicken house, collecting anything that looked like a knife, then took it all up into the attic and put it in her great-granddaddy's old army trunk beneath his uniform. And still, she hadn't felt safe. So, she'd pushed the trunk into a corner and had piled it high with boxes.

After she was finally well enough to cope, she'd begun checking out places where she could put her mother for permanent care.

The shock came in finding out that none of the good places would accept Medicare or Medicaid. They wanted money. And lots of it. The care patients got in the ones that did accept it were on a level of horror she could not abide.

She couldn't sell the ranch to pay for Mama's care. It wasn't hers to sell. It wasn't even Delia's to sell. It was in a trust for James, who would inherit it all upon Delia's death. Only the heir had the right to sell. Delia had the right of occupancy for the length of her life, but ownership passed down through blood to the eldest son. The one who'd abandoned them.

Anger at the injustice of their lives had fueled her decision. She quit trying to figure out what to do with the woman who had tried to kill her and just brought her home, putting her back in her bedroom as if nothing had ever happened.

After that, she'd cooked things that hadn't needed to be peeled or cut up. They'd eaten instant mashed potatoes, or she'd baked potatoes whole. She'd bought meat already cut up from the meat department and used bagged carrots that already peeled. When she'd needed to chop up an onion, she'd used the old grater, and when she'd wanted to dice up peppers or celery, she'd cut them up with the side of a fork, or just broke them up with her hands and cooked it. She'd slept with her door locked at night and had never turned her back on her mama again.

THE STORM PASSED LONG BEFORE MORNING, AND BY THE TIME THE SUN was up, humidity was at soul-suck level without a breath of air stirring. It was like trying to breathe beneath a pile of wet blankets. Flies were sticking to the screens like ticks on a fat hound. Just another hot summer day.

Gracie opened all the windows in the house, turned on the box fan in the kitchen, and put it in front of the open window, hoping something would stir up a breeze. Then she made herself a bowl of cold cereal and a cup of coffee.

Daphne sent her a text while she was eating to let her know they would all be in Sweetwater by Thursday and staying at the La Quinta on Georgia Avenue.

Gracie read it but didn't answer. She didn't care where they were and wished to God she didn't have to ever look at their faces again.

She got a text from Darlene telling her that she'd see her at the services, and then she asked, was there anything she needed.

Gracie sent back a response.

All I need is a hug.

A couple of minutes later, Darlene replied.

Count on it. Love you.

Gracie blinked back tears.

Love you, too, she replied, then finished her cereal and put her bowl in the sink.

She had things to do today, but it wouldn't take all that long to pack because she didn't own much in this world. Everything in this house was part of the estate, but there were a couple of things going with her anyway: the quilt that had been on Mama's bed and the cuckoo clock from Gracie's room. Both had belonged to their grandmother, and now they were going to belong to her. She dared any of them to argue about it.

Today was Wednesday.

Sometime this morning, the funeral home would probably call to let her know her mother was ready for viewing. She'd have to go into town and deal with that, but in the meantime, she was thinking about her future.

She needed a new place to be, and she was going to need a job.

After getting suitcases from the attic, she began to pack. She didn't have a lot of clothes that she could wear anymore. The majority of what she'd brought home from college fell off her now. So, she started with her winter clothes, and as she was pulling down sweatshirts from a shelf, a piece of paper fell out from between them.

She picked it up, unfolded it, and then frowned.

I, Gracie, lost my mother today.

"Oh my God. I don't even remember writing this," Gracie muttered. But she damn sure remembered it happening.

Today was hot as hell, but the day she'd lost Mama had been cold as a well-digger's ass and promising snow.

It was mid-afternoon. The sky was gray, the clouds low and heavy, weighted down, like Gracie, with a burden they needed to let go.

Delia was having a bad day. Gracie didn't know what had set her off, but her mama couldn't settle. She'd paced the house all day, refusing to eat, cranky with Gracie, and having a few childish fits of pique at being redirected from what she wanted to do.

Finally, Gracie got her down for a nap, covered her up with the old patchwork quilt and tucked in with the heating pad on her sock-covered feet, then hoped for the best.

As soon as she saw the even rise and fall of her mother's chest, she tiptoed out of the room and went down the hall to clean the bathroom. It took less than fifteen minutes, and when she finished, she stopped by Delia's room to peek in on her, but she was gone.

Gracie sighed, put up the cleaning supplies, and then went to run her down, wondering where she'd gotten off to now. But her frustration soon turned to panic when Delia was nowhere to be found. Not anywhere in the house. Not in the cellar below the kitchen floor. Not in the attic above. Not hiding in a closet. Not anywhere.

Gracie grabbed her coat and headed to the barn, running now and calling out.

"Mama! Mama! Where are you?"

But the barn was empty.

The chicken house was empty.

Gracie turned, her heart hammering as she stared off across the fields behind the house, thinking surely to God she would not go out there. She must have gotten on the road and started walking. But just to make sure, Gracie started running along the fence line between the yard and the pasture, looking for a sign that her mother might have gone that way, and still calling.

"Mama! Maammmaa! Where are you?"

And then she saw it...a tiny piece of blue and gray flannel caught on a hook of the barbed wire, and her heart nearly stopped.

Mama had been wearing a blue and gray flannel shirt!

She looked out across the prairie, and all she saw, as far as the eye could see, was a sea of brown, dead grass.

Without hesitating, she opened the old gate between the pasture and the house, then ran for the house to get her keys. Within moments, she was in her car and flying through the gate, bouncing over dried gopher mounds, sliding across ancient buffalo wallows, trying to imagine where her mother might have gone. When she realized there were tiny snowflakes beginning to stick to the windshield, she groaned. This was not fucking happening.

She started to call 9-1-1 but realized she'd left her phone in the house, so she just kept driving, desperate to find Delia before dark—before the weather got serious with its bad self and turned loose with real snow.

"Please God, please, help me find Mama," Gracie cried. She was caught between weeping in gut-wrenching fear, and angry enough to curse the hard-headed, crazy-ass woman who no longer knew the difference between up and down.

She was so far out into the pasture that she could no longer see the house, but still on their land. She drove in an ever-narrowing circle, praying she'd see her mama somewhere in the grass, when she thought she heard her Daddy's voice telling her to look up. And then it hit her!

This was Texas. If there was a piece of flesh on the ground, there would be buzzards in the air—if they hadn't already migrated south for the winter. When she spotted a pair circling high above in the gray winter sky, she gunned the engine in their direction.

Gracie saw the blue and gray shirt first, and then the woman wearing it, and stomped the brakes so hard she skidded, slammed the car into park, and got out running.

Delia was lying on her side, nestled down in the dead grass and curled up in a ball. Her socks were embedded with stickers and grass seeds, her eyes glazed, her lips as blue as her shirt.

Gracie thought Delia was dead, and then she blinked.

"Mama!" she cried. Gracie dropped to her knees beside her to check her mama's pulse and see if she was bleeding anywhere.

Delia blinked again, and then looked at Gracie.

"Cows got out."

Gracie groaned. "No, Mama. We don't have cows anymore. We sold them years ago."

Delia blinked. "Tired."

"Can you walk?" Gracie asked.

"Tired," Delia said again.

Gracie stood then dragged her mother to her feet. She slung Delia's arm around her shoulder and started moving her to the car, yelling and pulling her along with every step of the way.

"Walk, Mama! I can't carry you. Move your feet!"

"Tired," Delia kept saying.

Gracie screamed. "I'm tired, too, dammit! I'm tired all the way down to my bones. But you're gonna walk now! One foot in front of the other! Just help me get you to the car. We'll drive the rest of the way home!"

So, Delia walked, because Gracie was taking care of business.

GRACIE WIPED THE BEADS OF SWEAT FROM HER FOREHEAD AS THE memory faded, then she looked back down at the paper in her hand, tossed it in the suitcase, and threw her sweatshirts in on top of it.

She kept working until all her winter clothes were packed, and then set the suitcases against the wall in her room and went back to the attic to get more.

She was coming down with one in each hand when her cell phone rang. She turned loose of the bags, letting them slide as they fell, and sat down on the stairs to answer.

"Hello, this is Gracie."

"Hello, Gracie. This is Willis Decker. We have your mama ready."

"I'll clean up and be right there," she said, then ran the rest of the way down the stairs, picked up the bags, and carried them into her room.

She stripped out of her old work clothes and washed up, took down her hair and brushed it again, then pulled it up into a ponytail at the nape of her neck before getting out more clean clothes.

As she was dressing, it occurred to her that she didn't have anything to wear for the funeral. She sighed. One more detail she had to address. She was walking past the kitchen when she remembered she still hadn't taken Mama's eulogy to Brother Harp, so she dug it out of the roll-top desk in the living room and left the house.

It seemed weird to have the freedom to do this now—to just get in the car and leave whenever she wanted. It was going to be an adjustment, having only herself to take care of, and a little part of her felt guilty for the brief spurt of relief that came with that knowledge.

She drove with the air conditioner on and thought how good it felt to be cool. She wished she could just keep driving until she came to where she was next meant to be. But there was unfinished business here, and Gracie wasn't a woman who left anything undone.

By the time she got to Decker's Funeral Home, she had herself as collected as she was ever going to be. This was the last thing she had to do for Mama—making sure she didn't look as crazy as she'd become. Still, there was a knot in Gracie's gut as she got out and went into the funeral home.

The secretary saw her as she entered the office.

"Good morning, Gracie. Just take a seat, and I'll let Mr. Decker know you're here."

"Yes, ma'am," Gracie said, then eased down into the pale, blue wing chair and folded her hands in her lap as the woman picked up the phone.

A couple of minutes later, Willis Decker appeared in the doorway, neatly dressed in a light gray summer suit, with a white shirt and a red and gray striped tie. He looked like a short, *en vogue* version of Santa Claus, minus the beard.

"Good morning, Gracie. Are you ready?" he asked.

"Yes, sir," she said, and stood.

Willis gently cupped her elbow, guiding her through the lobby then two huge swinging doors into the back, past a display of caskets and all of their accoutrements, past a couple of offices, and then into a room with a single open casket, parked right in the center of the floor.

Willis was talking like a car salesman pitching the latest model as he led her up to the casket.

"The white pearl casket with the pink lining is quite beautiful. The pink carnation casket spray was a good choice, but I have to mention that the dress Delia chose is unusual. I can't say as how I've ever buried someone in a wedding dress before."

Gracie's voice shook. "Mama said she'd only worn that dress once when she married Daddy, and it seemed the sensible thing to do to get one more wear out of it."

Willis chuckled. "That does sound like the Delia I knew. She was one of a kind." He paused and looked Gracie straight in the eyes. "I wish we'd known what a hard time you were having. I wish you would have asked for help. But I commend you for standing by your mama as her health and mind failed her. I cannot imagine all you endured, but you were a good and faithful daughter, Gracie Dunham. All those years certainly put some stars in your crown."

"I didn't do it for stars," Gracie said, and looked down at her mother then, lying there so peacefully, her snow-white hair in the soft waves she'd favored. All the discolorations on her face and hands had been covered with makeup, and the faint brush of pink on her lips made it look like she was smiling. But it was the old white lace dress with the high neck and long sleeves Gracie loved most. She used to dream of getting married in that dress. But then she'd grown tall like her daddy and had given up her dreams to take care of mama. Now, it no longer mattered.

Gracie smoothed out a bit of lace at the yoke of the dress, and then reached for her mother's hand. But the skin was cold, and the flesh was hard, and she pulled back.

"She looks beautiful," Gracie said. "Thank you."

Willis beamed.

"Yes, ma'am, of course. So, is her appearance to your liking?"

Gracie nodded.

Willis signaled to two of his employees who quickly moved the casket through the halls and into a viewing room, where they quickly readjusted the casket spray and rearranged the flowers around the casket.

"Where did all of these flowers come from?" Gracie asked.

"They've been delivering them since yesterday," Willis said. "You can check the cards to see who they're from. I do know that the large one at the head of the casket and the two larger arrangements at the foot are from your brother and sisters."

Gracie eyed the elaborate arrangements of cut flowers with a jaded eye. Typical that they would think nothing of spending all this money on flowers Mama would never see and ignore all her birthdays and Mother's Days that had come and gone.

One arrangement—the one from James at the head of the casket— was made of white and yellow gladiola spears. The two at the foot were made of roses—one all white, and the other all pink. Gracie was neither impressed nor consoled by their presence.

Willis touched her shoulder. "I'll just leave you alone now. Stay as long as you want. Come back as often as you want. I know you did not set up a specific night for a family viewing, but we can—"

"No, sir, but thank you," Gracie said. "I'm following Mama's requests right down to the last period on the page."

Willis nodded. "Understood. Thank you for letting us serve your family. I had the honor of tending to your daddy, Tommy, and now I have had the honor of tending to your mama's service, as well. If I don't see you before, I will certainly see you at the church Friday morning."

And then he was gone, and Gracie was finally alone. Just her and Mama, the way it had been for the last nine years. She moved to the side of the casket, and then this time when she touched her mama's hand, she did not pull back.

"Well, here we are, Mama. We've had one hell of a ride, you and me, and as hard as it was, and as sad as it was, I need you to know that every step of the way, you kept showing me what it meant to be strong, reminding me how tough Dunham women can be. I love you, Mama. I was lucky to be your girl."

Then she took a deep breath, turned around, and walked out.

The moment she stepped out of the building, heat slapped her down, reminding her she was still in West Texas, and to get busy and finish what else she had to do before she melted where she stood. As soon as she got back in the car, she jacked up the air conditioning and headed for the Baptist church where her mama and daddy had gotten married.

The irony was not to be missed.

Same church.

Same dress.

Just different occasions.

CHAPTER FOUR

*I*t was a few minutes past twelve when Gracie arrived. She grabbed the file and her car keys, then headed inside on the run.

The interior was dark, the air conditioner laboring somewhere overhead, as Gracie walked down the hall to the pastor's office. She was halfway expecting everyone to be gone to lunch when she heard a voice and followed it.

The door was open. She called out.

"Hello?"

Moments later, Brother Harp emerged.

"Oh, hello, Gracie. I was watching the noon news. Guess I had the TV too loud."

"No problem. I brought the eulogy," she said, and put the file folder in his hands. "There is a list of songs in there as well. I'll see you Friday."

"Let me walk you to the door," he said.

"No, thanks. I'm fine," Gracie said, and went out the same way she'd come in, leaving Brother Harp with Delia's last words and wishes.

Gracie was hungry, but she didn't want to go trying on clothes smelling like French fries and ketchup, so she headed for Bealls on Broadway to get the shopping out of the way first.

All she wanted was a little black dress and some shoes to go with it. She needed new everyday clothes, too, but she didn't have money for shopping. Maybe after Mama's life insurance policy came through. So, she drove toward Broadway with heat waves rising above the pavement like ghosts doing the shimmy on Halloween night, found a place to park, and hurried inside, heading straight to Gordman's for ladies wear.

Within moments of her arrival, a saleslady approached. Gracie knew her, but in a town the size of Sweetwater, if you grew up here, you weren't a stranger to anyone. The saleslady's name was Jolene, and she'd gone to school with Mamie. Gracie eyed the turquoise tips on Jolene's blonde hair, distinctly remembering mousy brown hair, and then Jolene was at Gracie's elbow ending her muse.

Gracie sighed.

She's gonna want to talk about Mamie or Mama, and I don't want to talk to people. I just need to buy a dress.

"Gracie Dunham, I swear to goodness, girl, you look amazing. I wish I was that thin. Do you do Keto?"

"No, I don't do Keto," Gracie said. "I need a black dress and some nice shoes."

Jolene's greeting shifted to the opportunity for a sale.

"I heard about your mama. You have my deepest sympathies."

"Thank you," Gracie said. "Now about that dress."

At that point, Jolene did not mess around. A few minutes later, she had Gracie and seven little black dresses inside a dressing room.

"I'll be right out by the checkout counter. If y'all need anything, just let me know."

Gracie didn't bother answering because Jolene was already gone. So, she stripped down to her underwear and started trying on clothes. She had to give it to Jolene for picking out the right sizes. Gracie had lost so much weight, she wouldn't have had a clue that she'd gone from a size ten to a six.

She quickly discarded four of the dresses for being too short.

Women with legs as long as Gracie had to be careful about that. She could not go to Delia Dunham's funeral looking like a hootchie-mama.

Finally, she was down to two dresses, and the one she loved best also fit her perfectly. Everywhere. But it was sleeveless, with a scoop neck and back, which also meant most of the scars Delia had put on Gracie's body showed.

At the same time, she didn't see the need to try and hide them since everyone in town not only knew when it had happened but had seen Gracie at different stages of healing afterward. Just because her siblings were ignorant of her life didn't mean they needed their precious feelings protected.

And with that in mind, she chose the one she liked best and came out of the dressing room with it over her arm.

"I'll take this one," she said. Jolene promptly rang it up, then pointed her toward the shoe department.

"I don't know if they'll let me off for Delia's funeral, but give Mamie my love, just in case," Jolene said.

"Thank you for your help," Gracie said, grabbed her bag, and headed for shoes.

It took even less time there, because as soon as she found a pair that were simple and comfortable, she bought them, then left the store.

Her car was an oven inside as she slid into the seat, but when she started it up and turned on the air conditioning, it didn't take long for the car to be comfortable enough to drive.

She was, as she used to tell her mama, starving. And as her mama used to tell her, "No you're not, Gracie Jean. Poor people are starving, but you are not. Go get a drink of water, and dinner will be ready soon."

Gracie's eyes welled. She didn't have water to drink. She didn't have Mama, and she damn sure wasn't cooking a meal in that old farmhouse in this heat. So, she headed back to the Sonic because she could sit and eat in the car, and it would be cool.

As she drove through the familiarity of Sweetwater, she kept wondering where life was taking her next. Wondering if there would be Sonics where she was going. Wondering if she would ever find work. Wondering if, at the age of twenty-nine, she had already missed all the brass rings with her name on them.

She arrived at the drive-in and pulled into the stall to order, still teary and in a snit at the situation life had dealt her. She ordered a bacon burger, fries, and a chocolate malt, and then she sat there waiting with her money in hand.

Everything bothered by today, and then, as if life wasn't through poking her in the eye just to watch her blink, someone knocked on the passenger-side window.

She turned her head and stifled a groan.

Redford Beaudine! She'd graduated high school with him. He no longer looked like the star quarterback he'd once been, but he still thought he was all that, despite five kids and two failed marriages.

He knocked again, and then motioned for her to roll down the window.

She let it down enough to hear him.

"What?"

"I just thought I'd say hi," Red said. "Sorry to hear about your mama. I know you've been cooped up out there on that ranch with her for years. Any time you'd like to go out, I'm your man."

Gracie's eyes narrowed. She couldn't decide if she was pissed or just outright disgusted by his lack of sympathy and manners.

"I wasn't cooped up, Red. I was taking care of my crazy mama. You do know what she had runs in our family...don't you? You still want to 'be my man'?"

His mouth was open, but the smirk was gone. His eyes widened, and before he knew it, she was rolling the window up. He snatched his hand back just in time to keep from getting pinched and didn't bother waving goodbye.

And then there was another knock, but this time at the driver's side window. It was the carhop with her order.

She handed over the money and took her food, then rolled up the window.

"Sorry I called you crazy, Mama. But we both know you were, and you taught me never to lie. I love you. I wish you were here in your right mind, stealing my fries," she said, and then stuck a straw in her malt and unwrapped her burger, savoring every greasy, salty bite of the food, and the cold, thick, sweet of the chocolate malt.

Later, she stopped at the gas station on the way out of town to fill up, checked the air in her tires, and then headed home, back to the hot house and the silence.

GRACIE HAD BEEN HOME FOR HOURS, CLEANING AND SORTING AND packing, when someone knocked at the door. She wiped her hands on her shirt and then hurried out of her bedroom and down the hall to the front door. When she saw their nearest neighbor standing on the porch with his hat in his hand, she sighed.

Randy Jacobs. He hadn't set foot on this place since Mama had thrown a knife at him. Obviously, he thought it was safe to come back now. She opened the door.

"Uh, Gracie, I hope I'm not disturbing you, but I just came to pay my respects."

"Thank you, Randy."

He nodded. "I also wanted you to know that if y'all plan to put your place up for sale, I'd like a chance to bid on it. I would give you a fair price."

Gracie sighed. Randy was nice, but just like Red. One wanted in her pants. The other wanted what he thought she owned.

"I'll let James know," Gracie said.

Randy nodded. "Yes, ma'am. I know you had a real hard time here, and I'm sorry it turned out that way. Miss Delia was a fine woman. That Alzheimer's and dementia stuff is ugly business. My great-granny ended up like that. Ain't no one in this county who don't think you are one hell of a woman for ridin' it out with her."

With that, he settled his hat back on his head and walked away.

Gracie was gutted. It was the first genuine measure of sympathy she'd gotten, and it took her by surprise. She closed the door, and then headed back to her bedroom, but by the time she got there, she was shaking. She sat down on the side of the bed, stared down at the floor, and then burst into tears.

Finally.

Shattered by simple kindness.

She cried for all the times she'd been afraid, and all the times she hadn't known what to do next.

She cried for all the years she'd lost, and for what her mama had suffered. No one deserved a good life to end like that, and yet hers had.

Gracie's siblings had broken her heart, but they had not broken her. Tears weren't a sign of weakness. They were the release valve on years of pent up rage.

She cried until her eyes were swollen and her shirttail was wet from snot and tears. Then she rolled over onto her side, facing the fan, closed her eyes, and slept.

GRACIE WAS SWEEPING OFF THE BACK PORCH WHEN SHE HEARD THE SCREEN *door squeak. She turned just as Delia shuffled out with a frown on her face, holding her hands out and shaking them, like she was trying to rid them of water.*

Gracie knew that look.

"What's wrong, Mama?" Gracie asked.

"You're gonna have to get me some new butter. Mine's gone bad. Just look at this mess. My fingers are all sticky, and it doesn't smell right!"

Gracie smiled. Butter was the only word Mama could remember for lotions and hand creams, and lately, she'd been using quite a bit. She walked over to where Delia stood and felt of her mother's hands. They were *sticky!*

She lifted one to her nose to smell and stifled a grin.

"Your butter didn't go bad, Mama. You just got the tubes of hand cream and the toothpaste mixed up. That's toothpaste on your hands, and you don't stink. You're just minty fresh. Let's get you back in the house and all this washed off. Then I'll put some hand cream on you, myself. How's that?"

Delia nodded, walking back into the house in Frankenstein fashion—stiff legged, with her arms straight out in front of her, still frowning.

It wasn't until they got in the bathroom to clean Delia up that Gracie realized the other half of the story had yet to unfold.

As she leaned over Delia's arms to turn on the water, Gracie saw something white at the corner of her mouth. When Gracie wiped it off, it didn't feel right, and so she smelled it, then rolled her eyes. Lilacs?

Lord have mercy. Mama had just brushed her teeth with the floral scented hand cream, and the confirmation was Delia's toothbrush. It was slick with the stuff.

Gracie's shoulders slumped.

And just like that, one more cog had slipped within Delia's comprehension. She could no longer be trusted to brush her own teeth. One more worry added to Gracie's list, along with the knowledge that Mama was slipping further away.

THE DREAM FADED, AND THE SUN WAS SETTING WHEN GRACIE AWOKE.

She sat up, then staggered to the bathroom to wash her face. Her eyes were red-rimmed and still swollen, but she felt lighter. The weight of responsibility was almost gone.

Afterward, she made her way to the kitchen through the darkening house and turned on the light as she entered the room.

As usual, the screen door was covered in flies. She doused them in fly spray, and then shut the door as they were dropping.

"Supper a la Raid," Gracie muttered, and turned on the fan to disperse the smell.

She got out a plate and the bread, then opened the refrigerator. She had two choices of meat with which to make her sandwich. Ham or pickle loaf. She chose some of both, along with a slice of pepper jack cheese, and made her sandwich, slathering it with mustard. Ice cubes crackled in the glass as she poured in sweet tea, and then she sat down to eat.

It was Wednesday night. Whatever was on TV would be summer reruns. She turned it on and opted for a game show because it took no concentration to follow. She didn't give a shit as to who won, or who lost.

She was still eating when she heard the coyotes yipping. They were out beyond the house and running in the pastures. But there were no calves, dogs, or barn cats left on the premises. She was the only prey on the place now, and she wasn't their type.

She finished her sandwich and took her plate to the sink, then thought about something sweet. That's when she remembered the honey buns she'd bought and got one from the pantry. She was peeling off the wrapper when a commercial for toothpaste came on TV. Gracie stopped, then turned around and smiled.

"Hello, Mama. Yes, I was dreaming about you, but as you can see, I am taking care of business and doing just fine."

THE GOOD CRY AND LATE NAP HAD MESSED UP GRACIE'S SLEEP RHYTHM. It was after midnight before she went to bed, but she couldn't get easy. Two more nights, and then she'd never be here again.

Like Mama, Gracie thought. Delia had exited under her own terms by finally giving up the ghost, which left Gracie free to choose her own escape. And it was time. As uncertain as her future seemed, anything would be better than where they'd been.

When sleep still wouldn't come, Gracie gave up fighting the bed, and as was her habit, stepped into a pair of slippers, grabbed a cold can of Coke, and went out on the back porch.

The moonlight was bright enough for her to see where she walked, which mattered when you were out for a moonlight stroll across your porch.

West Texas was rattlesnake country, and snakes were night crawlers with a partiality to rodents, which meant there might be a snake under their old porch, because they never had mice in the house. Rural living had its own rules and environment, and while Gracie was all about taking care of business, she also abided by rules. Out here, snakes had the right of way.

She sat down with her Coke, feeling the condensation soaking through the fabric of her nightgown, and then held the cold can against her cheek for a few seconds before taking another sip. When she pushed off in the porch swing, it set the chain to creaking.

Back-squeak. Forth-squeak. Back-squeak. Forth-squeak—like a rocking chair on a loose floorboard.

As she looked out across the moonlit vista, she caught a glimpse of motion from the corner of her eye and saw an owl taking flight from the old barn. Likely the squeaking had disturbed its peace. It flew across the roof of the long-empty chicken house, and in that moment, sitting here in the dark, she remembered the night she'd awakened to the sound of Delia's footsteps long after she'd put her to bed, and then panicked when she'd heard the screen door slam.

GRACIE WAS DREAMING ABOUT BISCUITS AND SAUSAGE GRAVY WHEN *something woke her. Immediately, she was alert and listening. Was it Mama? Stupid question. It was always Mama.*

And then she heard footsteps. Sliding steps. It was *Mama. Gracie laid there a moment longer, hoping she'd just gone to the bathroom and was on her way back to bed. But when Gracie heard the squeak of the screen door, and then the slam as it went shut, she threw back the covers.*

Holy shit! Mama was out of the house! She'd never done this at night before!

Gracie was in a panic as she felt around for her shoes, and then she grabbed a flashlight from the drawer and bolted.

By the time she exited the house, Delia was nowhere in sight. She flashed back to the day she'd found Mama out on the prairie and was already running toward the fence, thinking she couldn't have gone far, when she passed the old chicken house and then stopped and turned around.

The door to the chicken house was open, and it shouldn't have been. Mama had killed all the chickens one day, wringing their necks like they'd done in the old days, because she thought company was coming, and they needed a lot to eat.

Gracie swung the flashlight toward the doorway, caught a glimpse of movement inside, and breathed a quick sigh of relief.

Whatever she was doing in there, at least she wasn't lost.

Gracie didn't want to frighten her, so she started calling out her name and aiming the flashlight toward the ground as she walked, just to make sure she wasn't about to step on a snake.

"Mama! Mama! Where are you?" she called but got no answer. "Delia! Delia, honey! Where are you?" she called again, and then swung the flashlight around the dark interior. She saw her mama all the way at the end of the building, slowly walking along the wall of built-in cubbies, where the hens had always nested.

"Hey, sweetie," Gracie said, as she slowly approached. "What are you doing?"

"Gathering eggs," Delia said. "I need to gather in the eggs."

"Can I help you?" Gracie asked.

When Delia paused, Gracie saw her whole body stiffen. And then Mama ducked her head. "Do I know you?"

Gracie's eyes welled. "Yes, ma'am."

"Well, then," Delia said. "Come on along. But pick up that egg bucket. My hands are full."

"Yes, ma'am," Gracie said, and then leaned over, picked up an imaginary bucket, and moved up beside her, making sure to shine the flashlight in every empty nest, just to make sure it was still empty of critters, too. And so, they went along the wall, with Delia gathering imaginary eggs and putting them in the imaginary bucket, until they ran out of nests.

"Am I through?" Delia asked.

"Yes, you are," Gracie said.

"I'm tired," she said. "I believe I'll sit down a spell," and started to drop where she stood.

"Oh, wait, wait," Gracie cried. "Let's go rest in the house. We can wash the dust off our hands, and I can get us something cold to drink."

"I might like a drink," Delia said.

"Me, too," Gracie said, and slowly cupped her mama's elbow, led her out of the chicken house, and back up the porch, then inside the house.

Delia was covered in dust, but Gracie knew this was not the time of night *to be concerned with clean feet and clean sheets. She poured them both a drink of water, and while her mama was drinking, Gracie knelt in front of her mama and began washing her hands and feet as best she could.*

"You worked hard today, Mama. It's time to sleep, now," Gracie said, walked Mama back to her bedroom, helped her settle in bed, then leaned over and kissed her forehead.

The skin was soft beneath Gracie's lips, and her mama's breath was warm against her face.

"I love you, Mama. Sleep tight."

"...don't let the mud bugs bite," Delia mumbled.

Gracie smiled. Mama had always said that when she put them to bed. Well, not exactly that, but close enough. Gracie pulled the sheet up over Delia's shoulders, then turned out the lights, and tiptoed out of the room.

A VEHICLE WENT FLYING PAST ON THE ROAD OUT FRONT. THEY MUST have had the windows down because Gracie heard faint sounds of music as it passed. It reminded her she was in the here and now—not lost in the past.

So, she finished off her Coke and went back inside, locking the door behind her. Even then, she still wasn't ready to go to her room. So, she poked around in the house, walking the rooms without turning on the lights, and remembering the holidays they'd had under this roof.

She'd been so little then, but she vaguely remembered the huge turkey Mama had roasted every Thanksgiving back when grandparents from both sides of the families were still alive. The house had been full of laughter then. They were all gone now. All of the Dunhams were gone, except for her and her siblings...but she remembered.

Every room was imprinted on her DNA.

Every creaking floorboard.

Every water stain in the ceilings.

Every windowpane that rattled when the wind blew.

She knew the house, and the house knew her. But it was time to say goodbye. She paused in the hallway, knowing if she stood in a certain spot, her voice would carry throughout.

"It's me, Gracie. I have come to say goodbye. I can't cry about this, because I wouldn't be able to stop, but I'll never forget you. You sheltered three generations of my family and me, from the time I was born, throughout every sad time and glad time of my life. I'm not leaving you behind because you'll be with me in my dreams. And the DNA of me is all over you. Thank you for holding it together, even when you needed more than I could give."

Then she paused. She wasn't listening for an answer. Not really. But she needed to feel the weight of her words settle before she moved. Then something banged outside. It sounded like it was in the back yard.

She sighed. "Damn wind," she muttered, and went back through the house, then to the kitchen windows to look out.

At first, she saw nothing. And then she heard it again. She peered across the yard toward the old chicken house and saw the source of the noise.

The door had come open and was banging in the wind. And just as she saw it, she felt her mama with her and laughed.

"Dang it, Mama. You're doing it again. Yes, I was remembering us out there in that damn chicken house in the dark, but you didn't have to get literal to let me know you knew. You could have just said, *Hello*."

Then she was walking out the backdoor. She laughed as the wind hit her in the face. She leapt off the porch, running headlong into the force, feeling it push against her body like an impatient lover, delineating her every curve with the nightgown she wore.

She got to the chicken house, slammed and latched the door shut, then paused in the moonlight and lifted her arms up toward the stars.

"Blow all you want, you damn wind, because my sweet mama is free. I, Gracie, am free! You can't blow me away because I'm already gone!"

CHAPTER FIVE

*G*racie woke up to sweat between her breasts and her nightgown plastered to her body. The dead calm outside was depressing. Even a hot wind was better than no wind at all, but since her siblings would be returning to Sweetwater today, maybe this was just God, holding His breath for the confrontation to come.

She got up and showered, dressing afterward in the least amount of clothes she could get by with wearing, and went to the kitchen. She turned on the box fan, then began opening up windows and spraying the fly-dotted screens. She was just about to pour herself a bowl of cereal when her cell phone rang. She glanced at Caller ID and frowned.

It was the bank.

"Hello, this is Gracie."

"Good morning, Gracie, this is Roger Cantor. I hope I'm not calling too early."

Gracie's frown deepened. The president of the bank was calling? Now what had she done wrong?

"No, sir. I'm up. Is something wrong?"

Roger chuckled. "On the contrary. I wanted to let you know that someone here in town started a fund for you on the day your mama passed, and then posted about it on social media. People have been donating to it ever since."

Shock rolled through Gracie in waves.

"What? Oh my God! I had no idea."

"It's quite amazing," Roger said. "There's over six thousand dollars in there at the moment, and there are still donations coming in."

Gracie gasped. "You're not serious!"

"Yes, yes, I am," Roger said. "And the way it's set up, it's solely in your name. When you can, I need you to come into the bank and sign a signature card so we'll have it on file. You're the only one who can withdraw money from it."

"I can do that this morning," Gracie said. "I can't believe this happened, but it is a godsend."

"I'm happy to have passed on good news," Roger said. "I think you're past due for some. We'll see you soon."

Gracie laid down her phone before she dropped it. She'd been so scared about tomorrow. It would be weeks, maybe even months before the life insurance police would be paid. And, with no idea where she was going, she knew she wouldn't have enough money to survive for long. But now she had this. It was the cushion she needed to find her place in the world.

She finally calmed down enough to eat some cereal, and then went to change. Nearly everything was packed, but she pulled a pair of slacks and a t-shirt out of the suitcase, used a belt to keep them up, and slipped on her sandals. After turning off the box fans, she locked up the house and headed for her car.

The drive into town was of no consequence, but she realized after tomorrow, she might never come this way again. She began marking the passing of houses and people as she went.

She knew every farmer and rancher in this area for miles around. She knew the color of their trucks. How many kids they all had. Which houses had mean dogs, and which ones housed the men who couldn't be trusted.

She'd always thought of herself as country girl, but Delia's death had cut the roots out from under her. Until she found a new place to be, she would be another Texas tumbleweed, and it made her sad. She didn't want to get lost like Mama, because there was no one left who'd come find her.

It was just after 9:00 when she reached Sweetwater and parked in front of the bank. She was a little embarrassed to be going in to claim what amounted to charity, but whatever pride Gracie had once possessed had eroded along with the ranch. And if people had thought enough of her and her mama to do this now, she was grateful.

She walked in with her head up, her shoulders straight, and that long braid swinging down her back as she walked.

Roger Cantor had been watching for her and came out of his office to meet her. He wished he could tell her that Willis Decker had been the one to set up the fund and had donated the first hundred dollars to it. But he couldn't because he'd promised not to.

"Good morning, Gracie. My secretary, Doris, is going to help you with the details."

"Yes, sir," Gracie said, and followed him. She took a seat at Doris's desk.

Thirty minutes later, she walked out with a brand new debit card, a pad of blank checks, and a little over six thousand dollars, and still counting, in the account.

She wanted to share her good news, but the only person in the family she still talked to was Mama. So, she headed straight to the funeral home.

One of the employees stood in the lobby directing visitors to the different viewing rooms and nodded at Gracie. Gracie pointed to her mother's room and kept walking.

The number of floral arrangements around Delia's casket had grown since yesterday, but seeing her mother lying there was still hard. No amount of flowers and ribbons could erase what Delia had suffered or what Gracie had endured. But she had news to share and laid her hand on her mother's arm.

"Oh, Mama, you will not believe what has been happening!" Then she sighed. "Well, that was a stupid thing to say. It just dawned on me that you probably already know. I'm talking about the money, Mama.

People in Sweetwater have been donating money to me at the bank. I was afraid of what was ahead of me, and now I'm not. Now before you start banging more doors to get my attention, I'm just telling you that I wouldn't take so much as a drink of water from your other children, even if I was dying of thirst. I know once you forgot they existed, their absence no longer mattered to you, but it mattered to me. It mattered that they forgot about me, too. And no, I do not have to forgive them. That's God's job, not mine.

"Anyway, I just wanted to share the blessing with you and to tell you that you look absolutely beautiful in that dress."

The old lace felt soft beneath Gracie's fingers as she patted her mother's arm, and then she walked out. The secretary was waiting for her out in the lobby.

"Gracie, I wanted to catch you before you left. People have been talking nonstop about Delia being buried in her wedding dress. It's had many a woman in tears at how precious that was, and how beautiful she looks. I thought you would like to know."

Gracie's eyes welled. "Thank you. I love knowing that."

"Of course," she said. "Y'all take care now."

"Thank you," Gracie said, and walked out.

Now that she had a little bit of money, she headed straight to Walmart to buy pants. They wouldn't cost much there, and she was in dire need. If she was about to venture beyond this little piece of West Texas, she needed her ass not to be showing while she did it.

JAMES DUNHAM WAS ON THE WAY TO SWEETWATER. HE'D LEFT Houston just after daybreak. He had been on the road for hours and had hours of driving yet to go, but making this trip alone gave him far too much time to think.

He kept remembering how he'd felt the day he'd left home for his first job in Houston. Straight out of college, cocky as hell, and almost as good-looking as his daddy, but a shorter, blonde version.

Tall, dark, and handsome, Tommy Dunham was a hard man to

emulate, but James sure had tried. He was as skilled at balancing a spreadsheet as his daddy had been with roping and branding steers. And James soon made a name for himself with his employer. He was one of their go-to men for big company audits, and the one who got the job done quickest.

James wasn't just smart; he was also quick-witted and glib. So glib that he sold himself to Darlene Sawyer on their first date, and then married her four months later. They'd eloped to Vegas, done the deed, and had enjoyed their lives of wedded bliss. And from that union had come two children—Caleb and Joanie.

And then he'd gotten bored.

Everything had leveled out. There was no more excitement in a marriage with two kids demanding all of his lover's attention. Darlene became responsible, then his mother's irrational behavior had embarrassed him and scared the kids. Delia hadn't known who he was and couldn't remember his name, and they'd never gone back. He'd used Delia as an excuse to rebel, and he'd gotten away with it for a long time. But he would never forget the look on Darlene's face when she'd found out.

THEY WERE IN THE MIDDLE OF MAKING DINNER. JAMES WAS PEELING potatoes, and Darlene was getting hamburgers ready to grill.

Their phones were lying side by side on the counter. One phone signaled a text, and when Darlene saw Caller ID identifying her best friend, Shawn, she just assumed it was her phone and opened the text. It was a nude picture of Shawn, with a nasty little message that shattered her life and her world.

I'm hot, horny, and hurting. Come do me, baby.

That's when she realized she'd picked up James's phone, not hers.

"You sorry-ass, cheating little bastard!" she screamed, then spun and threw the phone at him.

James knew before he picked it up that he'd finally gotten caught. He saw the photo and the text and felt like he was going to pass out. He was sick that it had happened this way, but in a cowardly way, relieved it was out in the open.

Darlene just stood there. "You're not even going to deny it, are you? You don't care enough to even lie?"

JAMES SHIFTED LANES, ACCELERATING PAST A SEMI, REMEMBERING HOW her features had seemed to melt before his eyes, and then she'd gathered up their kids and left the house without saying another word.

He hadn't told any of the family what he'd done. He hadn't had to. Darlene had done it for him. Bitterly. Cutting cords and bonds. And that had been that.

He knew she would be at the services and didn't know how that was going to play out, but considering his track record with her and Gracie, he'd be lucky to get out with his hide.

MAMIE AND JOEL WERE ON THE WAY TO SWEETWATER. IT WAS A GOOD five plus hour drive from Austin, and the cool air blasting from Joel's Lexus kept the makeup on Mamie's face from melting.

She'd spun the story about deciding they should stay in a motel instead of out at the farm, due to her reluctance to stay where her sweet mama had died, and Joel had bought it.

But the real test would come with how much Gracie revealed back at the farm after everything was over. She didn't expect it would be pretty, but she knew how to turn on the tears. And she was sad about her mama's passing. It was just that Mamie had left home so many years ago, that she often forgot she'd ever been there. Her world was upscale now, and that's how she meant to keep it.

Joel glanced at his wife as they drove, ever conscious of her whims and needs, doing everything he knew how on this earth to make her happy because he loved her so much.

He knew she was flighty, but her inability to cope made him feel needed. He knew she was self-centered, but he fed the need with constant gifts and received the abundance of her attention as a result. They were what a guidance counselor might have categorized as "compatible enablers."

"Mamie, honey...do you need to stop for a potty break? Or get something cold to drink?"

Mamie sighed. "You are so thoughtful, darling. Yes. I would appreciate that."

"There's a big truck stop just ahead, and we're still over a couple of hours out of Sweetwater. So, we'll pull in there for a bit and stretch our legs."

DAPHNE DUNHAM LEFT DALLAS JUST AFTER 9:00 IN THE MORNING. IT was just a little over four hours to Sweetwater and arriving early served no purpose. She kept picturing friends and neighbors arriving at the old farmhouse to pay their respects and wondered how Gracie was explaining away their absence.

What they'd done to their baby sister was so awful and so wrong, there was no way to make amends, and she was the first to admit it.

But Daphne had also known her limitations. The last Christmas they'd all been there together, which was two years after Gracie had taken up residence as the caretaker, Delia had alternated between a faded version of their mama and a glassy-eyed stranger. It had scared Daphne in a way she still could not describe. All she had been able to think of was getting away. Going back to Dallas, to what was safe and familiar.

And now, she had to face the cowardice of that act and the ensuing years afterward. Basically, they had all hung Gracie out to dry.

Daphne had to apologize. She was going to admit her cowardice and say she was sorry. But she also knew it wouldn't mean shit to Gracie.

RAMONA HARP WAS IN THE BEAUTY SHOP GETTING HER HAIR DONE FOR Delia Dunham's service tomorrow. As the pastor's wife, she believed part of her job was her deportment.

Her appearance should be pleasing.

She should be the epitome of calm within a storm.

And she should always be on hand as the "hostess" at all the church functions.

When the dinner for the family began tomorrow, she would be in the background, making sure all was running smoothly, while her husband got all the attention and glory.

Sometimes it irked Ramona that everyone looked to him as their guide to heaven, because he was just as big a doofus and sinner as the next guy. But she'd understood when she'd married him that would be their life, and she'd jumped in with both feet.

So, this was why she was sitting in her stylist's chair, draped in a plastic cape, getting her white roots dyed back to black. It would be the height of poor judgment to show up for the funeral looking like a skunk.

GRACIE GOT HOME WITH FOUR NEW PAIRS OF SHORTS AND TWO PAIRS OF long pants, all of which fit, for under a hundred dollars.

"I will be Walmart chic and grateful for it," she said, as she stood at the washer, removing tags and tossing all of the clothes in to wash, then she went to her room to change into old clothes.

She was double-checking to make sure she had all of her personal papers packed when she realized she hadn't packed the papers for the life insurance policy. She headed to the living room and the roll-top desk. Everything of importance in this family had been kept in that desk, so she was sure that's where her mother would have put it.

And she had.

In the bottom drawer on the left, in a yellow file folder with Gracie's name on the tab.

"Thank you, Mama," Gracie said, as she reached in to pull it out.

When she did, she realized Delia had filed it inside another file—the one she'd brought with her from college—the same one with her old resumé and the contact information for the Colorado job.

She hesitated. What good would it do to even look? She'd already turned down that job when she'd decided to stay, and she had zero work experience since to put on a resumé.

But then she thought of James. He'd have his hands on everything left in this house, and that wasn't happening. So, she pulled it out, too, then sat down on the sofa, opened it up, and started reading.

There were contact names here. People she'd interviewed with. People she'd already met in person. People who'd thought enough of her then to offer her a job in their hotel.

She was still the same person, with the same education from before, but with nine years of experience in management and caretaking to add to it. Just because she felt useless, didn't mean she was. Maybe her situation wasn't as dire as she'd feared, but it didn't feel right trying to go backward. Colorado was from before. She didn't want anything to do with the past. It was time to move forward.

She'd have to update the resumé later. She didn't have a presence on social media and hadn't had her hands on a computer or a laptop since Delia had broken the one she'd had at college. She had a lot of catching up to do.

Her belly growled. She glanced up at the clock. It was well past noon, so she took the files to her bedroom and put them in the suitcase, then went to make herself some lunch.

There weren't any choices because she'd only bought enough food to get her through tomorrow. So, a cheese and mayo sandwich it was. But she did have potato chips left in the pantry. She began layering chips on top of the cheese, then spread a little mayo on the other slice of bread, laid it over the chips, and smashed it all with the flat of her hand, panini-style.

She had a few Cokes left and snagged one of them, then she carried her food to the kitchen table and sat down in front of the fan, turned on the TV, and watched a talk show as she ate. She was almost finished when she happened to look out the kitchen window and froze.

There was a lone coyote standing just inside the fence separating the prairie from the back yard, just staring at the house.

"What the hell?" Gracie muttered.

Coyotes weren't known to be active in the daytime, and to have one come this close to an inhabited house was suspicious. She hoped to God it wasn't rabid. That's all she needed.

She stood, and when she did, the coyote saw her movement inside the house and tensed. She walked to the open door. With only the screen door between them, she still felt challenged, and it pissed her off.

She pushed the screen door open and stepped out. When the door slammed, the coyote jumped and ran sideways toward the barn, then stopped and looked back.

"What?" Gracie yelled.

The coyote didn't move.

She walked to the edge of the porch.

"Get your mangy ass off my grass," she shouted, and raised her arms up over her head.

The coyote tucked tail, ran under the fence and out across the prairie, disappearing in the dry grass.

Gracie stomped back into the house, the screen door slamming behind her to punctuate her shock. And even though it was hot as hell, she shut the back door and locked it. Logically, she knew no coyote was going to try and break into her house, but she was unnerved that this had happened.

She cleaned up her lunch dishes, and as she did, she began to rationalize.

This damn place was all but empty.

There were no animals on the property.

And people rarely, if ever, ventured beyond the back porch.

With her mama gone, the nightly crazies had ended, and lights were out early. With Gracie coming and going so much the last two days, they could be excused for thinking the place was unoccupied.

It was curiosity, and nothing more, but it tempered the high she'd been riding—an omen of what would evolve here with the coming abandonment of their home.

After putting her load of laundry in the dryer, she carried all but one of the suitcases to the front door.

The only thing hanging in her closet was her new dress and shoes to wear to the funeral. She would wear a new pair of shorts and a t-shirt for traveling. Beyond that, she had no other plans than to get out of Sweetwater. Wherever she lived, from this day forward, there would be green and trees and water in abundance. She would be cool in the summer, warm in the winter, and do as she wished, when she wished.

She'd been thinking to go northeast, toward Missouri. It had mountains, and forests, and rain—lots of rain. Maybe to Branson. There should be jobs galore in a place that thrived on tourism. She nodded. That was her new plan.

~

DAPHNE ARRIVED AT HER MOTEL IN SWEETWATER A LITTLE AFTER 2:00. She would have arrived sooner, but she'd had to stop and throw up halfway there, and then pulled into the next truck stop afterward to get Seven-Up to calm her stomach.

Nerves.

She'd been this way her whole life.

If she had a crying fit when she was a child, she threw up afterward.

If she was anxious, or upset, she threw up.

And here she was again, not even the day of the funeral, and already losing her fucking mind. Lord, Lord, Lord, what sins she had wrought, her belly was paying for.

When she parked and got out, the heat enveloped her. She'd forgotten this—the feeling of being smothered—and made a beeline inside with her bag in hand.

As luck would have it, the clerk checking her in at the front desk was someone she'd grown up with. She braced herself for the recognition.

"Daphne Dunham. I have a reservation," she said, and slid her credit card across the counter.

"Well hello, Daphne. It's me, Andy Walker. I haven't seen you in years. My sympathies to you. We all heard about your mama's passing."

"Thank you," Daphne said. "I don't suppose James or Mamie are here yet?"

"I'll look," Andy said, and typed their names into the computer. "They both have reservations, but they haven't checked in."

Daphne nodded. "I'll see them later, then. I just want to get to my room."

"Yes, of course," he said, then ran her card and gave it back. "You'll be in room 420. Here's your room key. Our breakfast buffet hours are on your paperwork. Good to see you again. Enjoy your stay."

Daphne took the key and headed for the elevator. As soon as she reached her room, she dumped her bag, then went back down to her car and drove straight to the Sonic for a cold drink. She was afraid to eat for fear she'd throw up again. But she needed to settle her stomach before she went to the funeral home. There were things she needed to say to Mama that she didn't want overheard.

A few minutes later, she was sitting in a stall at the drive-in, sipping a cherry limeade, and absently watching the coming and going of customers, wondering why she felt it necessary to go to the funeral home to spill her guts. Her mama already knew what she'd done.

She took another sip of the sweet-tart drink and sighed. The truth of it was she needed to see Delia Dunham's face. To know she didn't have the wild, crazy look in death that she remembered of her in life. She needed her last sight of her mama to be something she could live with.

Finally, she'd had enough of the cold drink to ease the roll in her belly and left the drive-in. She didn't remember exactly where Decker

Funeral Home was, and missed the first turn, but quickly found it when she retraced her steps, then parked and went inside.

A man she didn't know approached.

"Hello? How can I help you?" he asked.

"Which viewing room is Delia Dunham in?"

He pointed.

Daphne took a deep breath and crossed the lobby, signed the guest book, picked up a memory card, then walked in, grateful there was no one else there.

The casket was surrounded in flowers. She saw the arrangement she'd ordered at the foot of the casket, slowly approached, and looked down in shock.

Her mother's hair was completely white! When had that happened? And what the hell kind of dress was she—

"Oh my God. Her wedding dress. Gracie was burying Mama in that old wedding dress!"

And then she stopped. She'd lost all right to complain about anything, and when she looked at Delia again, she began to cry.

"Sorry, Mama. That's not why I'm here. I came to apologize. I let you down, and I let Gracie down, and I can't change any of that. I was an ungrateful daughter, and a horrible sister to Gracie. I will say the same thing to her, but you needed to hear it first. You look beautiful. Say hi to Daddy for me. I miss us all...the way we used to be."

And then she turned around and walked out. She made it back to the car, grabbed what was left of her drink, and downed it. She felt like shit. Then she glanced at herself in the rearview mirror and sighed. She also looked like shit. West Texas had just melted the makeup right off her face.

CHAPTER SIX

*M*amie and Joel pulled into the city limits of Sweetwater just after 3:30.

"What's the address?" Joel asked.

Mamie entered it into his cell phone, and then popped it back in the stand in their console.

"Is there a plan for this evening?" Joel asked.

Mamie shrugged. "I'm assuming James and Daphne will join us for dinner later."

"What about Gracie?" Joel asked.

Mamie teared up on cue. "I don't know. I haven't spoken to her. She only notified Daphne about Mama and said to tell us."

Joel frowned. "What the hell? Why?"

She shrugged, carefully dabbing her eyes so she wouldn't smear her makeup.

"I guess Mama never did write down ours or James's cell phone numbers after we got rid of our land lines. Just Daphne's."

"But didn't you ever call Gracie?" Joel asked.

Mamie teared up again. "I don't guess I did. The time just got away from me and I—"

Joel gasped. "But honey! What the—"

"Joel! Don't fuss at me," Mamie wailed. "I'm just so sad about all this misunderstanding. I guess I thought if Gracie needed us, she would call."

Joel was grim-lipped and silent, trying to process the horror of what he was just now understanding.

"So, you're telling me that you haven't spoken to her since Christmas seven years ago."

Now was the time to sacrifice makeup. Mamie threw back her head, covered her face, and started sobbing.

"I guess that's my answer," Joel said. "All I know is you should be ashamed. And, while she's not my sister, I should have asked about her. I should have called. I just assumed you would be in contact when you sent them money."

Mamie wailed even louder.

The skin suddenly crawled on the back of Joel's neck.

"You did send money...didn't you? We talked about it. I just assumed..."

Mamie was bawling louder, and Joel's stomach suddenly turned. He was looking at his wife in a whole new light.

"We're almost at the hotel, so I suggest you suck it up. You're gonna look like shit walking into the hotel with mascara on your upper lip. Better dig out your sunglasses, girl."

"Joel Freemont! That is the most hateful thing you have ever said to me, and when I am at my saddest! I just don't know what to make of you. You have broken my heart," Mamie said.

"I doubt your devastation is in any way comparable to Gracie's," Joel said shortly, and pulled into the parking lot of the motel.

Mamie reached for a handful of tissues and began wiping her eyes and the mascara beneath them. Then she blew her nose and dug through her purse for the sunglasses. She'd never seen Joel like this. It was going to take more than a blowjob to smooth this over. It was time to go on the defense. A cold shoulder and a good dose of the silent treatment, coupled with a continuance of silent tears, should do it.

And if it didn't, well, then she had her share of the sale of the family home coming, and Joel Freemont could just kiss her ass and fork over monthly alimony if that's how he felt.

She pushed the sunglasses up her nose, then got out and, without waiting for Joel, walked inside.

Joel grabbed their bag and followed, equally pissed at what he'd just learned.

~

JAMES PULLED INTO THE PARKING LOT JUST IN TIME TO SEE JOEL entering the motel.

He parked, grabbed his bag, and hurried inside to catch up, wondering as he went if Darlene would be staying here. He hoped not. It would make everything that much more tense, but he had no say in what she did or where she went.

Joel was at the registration desk when James walked up, and it didn't take a genius to figure out Joel and Mamie were fighting.

Mamie had her nose in the air and was wearing sunglasses. Her lipstick was slightly smeared, and she stood with her arms crossed and her back to Joel. He didn't know who to speak to first, but blood was thicker, so he chose his sister.

"Mamie, darlin'," he said, and put down his bag and hugged her.

Mamie fell into his arms, sobbing.

"Oh, James. It's all just so awful," she said.

"I know," he said, hugging and patting her.

Joel picked up their room keys and then turned around.

James extended his hand. "Joel, I hope you had a safe trip?"

"It was a long one," Joel said, and picked up their bag, leaving James with his hand out. "Mamie, are you coming?"

"We'll talk later," Mamie said, and followed her husband to the elevator.

James checked in without comment, took his key, and headed for his room. So, here they were, back in Sweetwater to bury their mother, and face the judgment of their sins.

Basically, the next two days were going to suck.

⌇

Darlene had a reservation in Sweetwater at the Best Western Plus. The suites were nice but lacking in what her ex-in-laws would expect. She was absolutely positive that the Dunham siblings would be at the La Quinta Suites because it had a pool, and pool or not, Darlene didn't want to sleep under the same roof with James Dunham, even if there were hundreds of other rooms between them.

The only one left in that family she cared about was Gracie, and as soon as she checked herself into the motel, she went straight to Big Boys Barbecue and got takeout for both of them, bought a six-pack of Cokes, then headed out to the farm.

She knew Gracie was hurting. It had been a long time since they'd seen each other, but they'd never lost touch. She wasn't going to wait until tomorrow. She would, by God, see Gracie now. They would share food, and cry, and whatever else it took to help Gracie get through this last long day before they put Delia Dunham in the ground.

She headed out of Sweetwater, knowing Gracie had been struggling to keep a roof over their heads and keep Delia in one piece, but even she wasn't prepared for the sight.

The old farmhouse was sorely in need of paint. The corrals were rusty. The cattle, the tractor, and the farm truck were gone. Except for the backend of Gracie's car parked behind the house, the place looked abandoned.

"Oh, honey," Darlene whispered, then pulled up out front, grabbed her purse, the food, the present her kids sent for Gracie, and headed for the front door.

She knocked, then waited, listening for footsteps. Then knocked again. Moments later, Gracie opened the door. The screen door was between them, and then Darlene let herself in. She put her things on the hall table and wrapped Gracie up in her arms.

The heat inside the house was sweltering.

The aging furniture and limp curtains looked as sad as Darlene felt.

But it was what she was feeling beneath the soft fabric of Gracie's shirt that startled her. She was skin and bone, and her back was covered in scars.

"Gracie Jean...what happened to you?" Darlene said.

"Mama," Gracie said. "I am so glad to see you. I'm sorry it's hot, but the central air hasn't worked in four years. Come into the kitchen. I have a box fan in there."

Darlene picked up her things and followed.

"The kids sent you a present. I brought barbecue. We will eat. And we will talk. I have a room at the Best Western, but I had to come see you before you were surrounded tomorrow."

"That smells so good," Gracie said, as she got down plates and forks, then unrolled paper towels for napkins.

Darlene was still on the threshold, staring into the kitchen. There were dark stains in the wood floor that hadn't been there before. Part of the ceiling was blackened, and there were no knobs on the stove.

"What happened in here?" Darlene asked, pointing to the ceiling.

"Mama set a fire trying to cook something when I wasn't looking."

"Holy shit. How did you get it out?"

Gracie grimaced. "I threw a big pitcher of sweet tea on the ceiling. It put out that fire, and the tea that fell down landed on the burning pan and put it out, too. So...basically, God did it."

Darlene swallowed. She couldn't—wouldn't—let Gracie see the horror she felt.

"So, I guess that's why there are no knobs on the stove."

"Pretty much," Gracie said. "And now it's too hot to cook, so I had no need to put them back on. Come to the table. We can spread everything out here where the air is moving."

Darlene started across the floor, then paused, looking down at the dark splotches in the wood.

"Did it catch the floor on fire, too?"

"No. That's my blood," Gracie said.

The sack fell out of Darlene's hands.

"It's okay. I survived," Gracie said, then picked up the sack and carried it to the table.

Darlene wasn't a redhead for nothing. All of a sudden, her blue eyes were blazing and the flush on her neck had nothing to do with a hot room.

"What the fuck happened to you?"

"Come sit with me," Gracie said, and so she did.

"I'm sitting. Talk," Darlene said.

"I was doing dishes. Mama liked to put up the flatware, so I laid it on the table for her, then opened the drawer in the sideboard and walked away. Next thing I know, Mama is screaming at me and stabbing me with a knife."

Darlene was wide-eyed and shocked to the point her voice was shaking.

"What in the name of all that's holy did you do to get away?"

Gracie shrugged. "Basically, I knocked her on her ass and managed to call 9-1-1 before I passed out."

"Oh my God! Why didn't you call me? I would have come. I would have come. What happened to Delia then?"

"I was in the hospital a week, and they put Mama in the psych ward of the hospital for a month so I could heal. I came home, and after I was well enough and strong enough to cope, I started looking for a place to put her. But it didn't work out, so I got her out of the psych ward and brought her home. She didn't remember anything, and after she came back, she didn't really remember much about the farm, either."

"That's what I felt when I hugged you, isn't it? The scars." Darlene asked.

Gracie shrugged. "Yes."

"Do they hurt?" Darlene asked.

"Not anymore. One shoulder twinges when it's cold. Some nerves and muscles were cut, but I survived, and now she's gone and I'm free."

"I saw suitcases at the door. You're leaving here, aren't you?" Darlene asked.

"Tomorrow, right after my siblings and I have our 'Come to Jesus' meeting."

"Where are you going?"

"Where things are green, and rain is not a rare commodity. I wouldn't mind some mountains with it. I'm thinking Missouri."

"We don't lose each other," Darlene said. "Understood?"

Gracie nodded. "Understood. Now can we eat? I'm suddenly starving."

Darlene had a thousand more questions, but right now, none of them mattered. Gracie was too thin, and the shadows in her eyes broke Darlene's heart.

"They sent hot and mild sauces," Darlene said.

"Hot for me. Always hot," Gracie said, and liberally doused her smoked brisket sandwich, then took a big bite. "Oh my God, this is good. So good. Thank you."

"Of course," Darlene said.

They ate in mutual silence for a few minutes, and then Darlene finished and watched Gracie. She ate like she was starving. And she was so thin.

"Did you all go hungry?" Darlene asked.

Gracie shrugged. "It's over, honey. No need to drag up what can't be changed."

Darlene's eyes were blazing again. "I will say it now, and only to you, but your siblings have to be the most self-centered, selfish creatures on the face of his earth, and I officially hate them for what they left undone."

Gracie laid what was left of her food aside and looked up, emotionless, her voice calm, the words delivered in a stark, matter-of-fact tone.

"Hate was the first four years without them. After that, they ceased to exist."

Darlene shivered, then quietly stood and helped Gracie clean up before they both went out onto the back porch. The bleakness of the view put a knot in Darlene's gut.

She turned and gripped Gracie by the shoulders.

"Look at me, girl."

Gracie shifted her gaze.

"You are the strongest woman I will ever know. You have more honor in your little finger than your whole family combined. You will go far, and be happy, because you deserve it. Do you hear me?"

"I hear you. I just hope God's listening, because His attention has been otherwise occupied when it came to me and Mama for a long, long, time."

Darlene sighed. "Come inside. The kids sent you a present."

Gracie smiled. "They're not really kids anymore, are they? The last pictures you sent, Caleb looked like a man, and Joanie a young woman."

"I know, but they'll always be kids to me," Darlene said. "You sit. I'll get the present. She ran back to the living room where she'd left her things and grabbed it, then slid the box in front of Gracie. "They didn't wrap it, but Caleb said to tell you it's locked and loaded. All you'll need to do is set up your own email and internet when you get settled."

Gracie frowned as she popped the tape on the flat box, and then opened the flaps.

"Oh my God! Are you serious?" Gracie cried. "A laptop? Mama broke mine years ago, and I saw no need to get another. This is awesome," Gracie said, as she took it out and opened it up. "You tell my nephew and niece that they rock."

Darlene grinned. "I will. Caleb said you can't go job hunting without one these days."

Gracie sighed. "And I'm sure he's right. This is wonderful. Thank you so much."

A short while later, Darlene was gone, leaving Gracie with a belly full of barbecue, and something to think about.

She did deserve happiness, and she didn't have to settle for less ever again.

Daphne got a text from Mamie.

We're here. James is here. Do you want to go eat?

Daphne frowned, and responded.

Did you go see Mama, yet?

Silence. Then Mamie responded.

Did you?

Daphne rolled her eyes and shifted from text to call.

"Hello," Mamie said.

"Yes, of course I went," Daphne said. "It was the first thing I did after I got my room. That and throwing up."

Mamie sighed. "Oh sister, I'm sorry. I forgot how nervous your tummy gets."

"You guys go see her. And then I'll meet you wherever you want to eat."

"Eew, that will just ruin my appetite," Mamie said.

The tone of Daphne's voice shifted into high. "We are not here for a party, Mamie Leigh. There are rules and rituals to burying a loved one, and we've failed our sister. Let's try real hard not to dishonor Mama, too."

Mamie whined. She was still suffering the looks from Joel that scared her, and she didn't want her sister on her case, as well.

"I just don't know if I can do that," Mamie said.

"Then why did you even bother coming?" Daphne shrieked.

Mamie started crying. "I'm sorry. I guess I'm just not making myself understood. Of course I know that we will do this. I'm just afraid, that's all."

"I was afraid...and ashamed, too. So, get your ass in gear, and you three get to Decker's and see Mama, dammit. I haven't had an appetite since the day Gracie called, but I had the guts to go face her in a casket, and I expect you and James to do the same. We will eat later. Call me to let me know where you want to meet."

And then Daphne hung up and covered her face. "God, just help us get through this without killing each other. That's all I ask. We don't deserve anything more."

~

MAMIE HUNG UP AND LOOKED AT JOEL.

"We need to go see Mama at the funeral home, and then we'll call Daphne. She'll meet us wherever we want to go for dinner."

Joel nodded. He'd been thinking long and hard about Mamie and this revelation. He shouldn't have been so shocked. She'd always been selfish and self-centered. He'd just accepted and ignored it because he wasn't suffering from it.

But seeing that turned on Gracie had been eye-opening. He was ashamed of himself. He was ashamed of them. And Mamie, being Mamie, had just admitted the truth of herself to Daphne and didn't even know it.

Mamie was afraid—of everything. Of not being smart enough. Never having the confidence to get a job on her own. Living a shallow existence to keep herself busy when he traveled because she was afraid to be alone. He didn't hate her. But the shine was definitely gone.

"I'm going to call James," Mamie said. "He can ride with us."

Joel nodded.

A short while later, the trio was on the way to Decker's, and the silence within the vehicle was painful. It didn't get easier as they entered the funeral home. Being shown to the viewing room felt like walking a gauntlet. They signed the guest book, got the memory cards, and stepped inside.

Mamie gripped Joel's hand as they moved toward the casket.

Joel sighed and put his arm around her shoulders, then they were there, staring down.

"Her hair turned white," James said.

"She looks real pretty," Joel added.

But Mamie was staring at the dress.

"What the hell is she wearing? What was Gracie thinking putting that on her?"

"Mamie, for the love of God," Joel whispered.

And then Willis Decker walked in.

"Hello, I'm Willis Decker. I just wanted to pay my respects to the family. James. Mamie. It's been a while since I've seen you."

"Yes, sir," Mamie said. "This is my husband, Joel Freemont."

Willis nodded. "I won't bother you further, but I did want to tell you how touched all of the visitors have been seeing your mama in her wedding dress. It was Delia's wish to be buried in it, and as I told Gracie, I don't think I've ever had that happen before. But as I'm sure you also know, Gracie has been adamant about following Delia's last wishes. Your mama even wrote her own eulogy and picked out the songs for the service. She was something else."

Mamie swallowed, just nodding as if she'd known all along, but she couldn't talk for the lump in her throat. She'd just stood in front of her mother's body and disparaged her last wishes. This couldn't get any worse.

As soon as Willis left, Mamie walked straight up to the casket.

"I am so sorry, Mama. For everything. Gracie hates us."

James frowned. "Stop tattling. You were always the worst tattler. Gracie has a right to her feelings." And then he looked down into his mother's face and saw the woman who'd raised him. Her eyes were closed, and her face was so serene. The crazy was gone. Hell, all of her was gone.

"I'm sorry, Mama. We didn't do right by Gracie. She has every right to hate us. And I'm sorry we let you down, too. Just because you forgot us, didn't mean we had to let go of you. It was cowardly, and I am ashamed. I love you. And it's real easy to see why Daddy married you. You look beautiful in that dress."

Joel waited, standing back, and when they were leaving, he looked back, half-expecting Delia to sit up and give all of them a talking to. It would have made him feel better. But it was too late for all of them. They had to live with the guilt of what they'd left undone. They walked out, squinting against the lowering sun, and paused at the curb.

"Where do you want to go eat?" Joel said, and then glared at Mamie, daring her to play the victim card.

She shrugged. "You men pick, then I'll call sister."

"Let's get in where it's cool to talk," James said.

And so they did.

"We could do Buck's Steak and Barbecue," James said.

Joel nodded. "Works for me."

"I'll text Daphne to meet us there," she said.

THE SUN HAD GONE DOWN. THE FAN PULLED IN COOLER AIR FROM THE open window as Gracie stood in the kitchen. An old Zac Brown Band song called Roots was playing on the radio. The song spoke to Gracie. Her roots had always been with the land, but she was about to cut herself free.

She hummed along with the song as she worked, pouring up cereal and adding a little milk. She didn't like her cereal soaked down and always ate it fast while the flakes still crunched. She wasn't real hungry. The barbecue Darlene had brought earlier in the day had been filling. But she wanted something, and this was all she had.

She heard the coyotes tuning up outside, and out of spite, turned on the back porch light, just to let them know she was still here, then turned the radio off, and the television on. She watched it while she ate, wondering where the sanity of the country was going, and if she had the guts to venture out into the jungle it had become.

But then she could just hear her mama's voice, chiding her for the doubt. For letting in fear of the unknown, and so she changed the channel and finished her cereal.

It was time to go to bed.

Tomorrow was the finale to Delia Dunham's life on Earth, and Gracie intended to do it up right.

THE SIBLINGS ALL HAD AN AFTER-DARK SWIM IN THE MOTEL POOL, JUST because it was there. But there was no jovial atmosphere to add to it, and so they soon parted company.

James went to bed early, because there was nothing else to do, and left a wake-up call for 7:00 A.M. It would give him plenty of time to get down to the free breakfast, then get ready to leave for the funeral home.

He settled in bed and turned on the TV, but he wished he had someone to talk to. Not for the first time, missing the life he'd had with Darlene.

He fell asleep with the television on and dreamed he was out on the back porch at home, playing harmonica to Daddy's songs and watching Mama dance across the back porch.

JOEL AND MAMIE WERE IN BED, LYING WITH THEIR BACKS TO EACH other. The silence was brutal. Mamie wanted to say something but was afraid that whatever came out of her mouth would be wrong.

Joel was sick at his stomach. They'd had little spats before, but they'd never gone to bed angry. He was the man of the family. But Mamie had always held the reins of control.

And he'd let her, and now here they were.

"Mamie."

She rolled over. Devoid of makeup, she didn't look much older than she had when they'd married. Her eyes welled with unshed tears.

"We have to do better," Joel said.

Mamie sat up in bed, nodding.

"We will apologize to Gracie tomorrow, and mean it. She doesn't have to accept it. But it has to be said. Understood?"

She nodded more, the tears rolling now.

"I am disappointed in you, but I am also disappointed in me. Out of sheer selfishness and neglect, we failed two people we loved. That is unforgivable. Understand?"

Mamie was bawling now, her face buried against her knees.

"I'm sorry," Mamie said. "I'm so sorry. Don't hate me, Joel. I will die if you hate me."

Joel reached for her and pulled her down into his arms.

"I don't hate you, sugar. We'll figure this out as we go. Tomorrow is for your mama, and afterward is for Gracie. That's what we focus on."

Mamie nodded again and sobbed herself to sleep in Joel's arms.

CHAPTER SEVEN

 racie was dreaming.

"Mama, what have you done?" Gracie cried, eyeing the holes Delia
had chopped in her hair.

"I think I got lice. You have to shave off the hair to get the goop on 'em."

Gracie sighed, and carefully took the scissors out of her mother's hands,
wondering where the hell she'd gotten them. She thought she'd hidden everything in this house that could take mama's life.

"Why do you think you have head lice?" Gracie asked, as she slipped the
scissors in her back pocket and then covered them with the tail of her shirt.

"It itches," Delia said.

"Let me look," Gracie said, and began running her fingers through what
was left of Delia's hair.

At first sight, her heart skipped a beat. Delia's scalp was dotted with little
black specks. Holy shit! Maybe she did have lice, Gracie thought, and then
realized whatever it was, wasn't living. She leaned closer, sniffing, then
picked a few specks out with her fingers and smelled them.

"Mama...did you put something in your hair?"

"Medicine...to get rid of the lice."

"Show me," Gracie said.

Delia frowned.

"Mama, how can I make your head quit itching if you don't show me what you've already tried...right?"

"I guess," Delia said, and pulled a kitchen-size box of black pepper out of her pocket.

"You peppered your head," Gracie muttered. "Of course you did." Then she added, "I don't see anything on your scalp but black pepper. Let's go to the kitchen sink, and I'll wash the pepper and the lice right out. Then you won't be itchy, okay?"

"I guess," Delia said, and reached for her head, diligently scratching, then digging out the black pepper from beneath her nails. "Just look at them little buggers. I told you I had the lice."

"Well, lice aren't black, they're mostly white, but we're gonna wash them out right after I fix your haircut," Gracie said, wondering, at what time in her mama's life this had really happened. Because the reality of it now was her truth again.

She took Delia outside, set her in one of the old folding chairs, wrapped a tablecloth around her neck for a cape, then started cutting.

"Don't let those critters get on you, or we'll be cutting your hair off, too," Delia said.

"No, we will not be cutting anything more on me, Mama. Trust me," Gracie muttered, and kept snipping and combing, and running her fingers through Delia's gray hair, noticing as she cut, how white her hair was turning. Hardly any dark hair left at all.

She cut until the white cap of hair was about three inches in length. It wasn't the style she would have chosen, but at least the holes were gone. Then she shook off the cape and gathered up her tools.

"Now, let's go wash away that itch," Gracie said, and they went inside.

Within an hour of the shampoo, Delia had completely forgotten any of it had happened and crawling up onto her bed, she went to sleep.

Gracie confiscated the can of pepper and stashed the scissors up in the attic in great-grandpa's army trunk, with all of the other lethal weapons, then went out to the back porch to sweep up the hair.

The non-existent lice had been dispatched, along with a goodly amount of black pepper, and neither Delia nor Gracie had suffered. It was all she could ask on any given day.

GRACIE WOKE UP FROM THE DREAM. IT WAS A GOOD HOUR BEFORE sunrise, and it was Friday.

The day had finally arrived.

She threw back the covers and got up, padded across the hall to the bathroom, and when she came back, stripped all the sheets off the bed, folded them up and packed them. Then she got another set to go with them, added two pillows and some towels and washcloths to the box, sealed it, and carried it into the living room.

Tonight, the house would be empty, but looking after it was no longer her job.

She stepped into her slippers and walked through the rooms, pausing in the kitchen to get a Coke, then she got the last honey bun from the pantry and went out on the back porch to watch the sunrise one last time over the land on which she'd been born. By the time the eastern sky began coming to life, her honey bun was gone, and so she watched in silent rapture as it began.

Pale yellow wisps of cloud vapor slowly added in some soft pink, then began stringing across the horizon like a weaver carding cotton. The wisps grew into broad strands as the new day approached. Then just before the sun showed its face, the sky exploded, painting slashes of yellow, bright orange, and deep pink all across the sky.

Gracie blinked away tears.

"Oh, Mama...what a sendoff!"

Tomorrow morning when she woke, she would be in another place, looking at the world through a different window.

It was frightening, but she was ready to see what was waiting for her next. She glanced back at the sky. The sun was coming up now, and the colors were fading. It was the day to lay Mama to rest.

~

BREAKFAST HAD COME AND GONE. JAMES, DAPHNE, JOEL, AND MAMIE were dressed and ready to leave.

"We each drive our own cars," Daphne said.

"Agreed," James said. "I'll lead the way to the church and you all can—"

"We don't need a convoy, James. We just need to get there," Daphne muttered, and headed for her car.

Joel and Mamie got in their car, leaving James to trail along. So, being the eldest in the family did not hold water today.

He got in his car and left the motel parking lot, following his siblings to the church, accelerating to catch up, so they could at least walk in together.

~

GRACIE HAD BEEN AT CHURCH FOR OVER AN HOUR, EVEN THOUGH WILLIS Decker was in charge now. Organizing funerals was what he did, and Brother Harp said the words that laid the dead to rest. All she had to do was be present.

Gracie was not a fan of funerals in general, although she acknowledged they meant a lot to other people. It was their last way to honor a loved one, share their grief, and be comforted by the presences of friends and family.

To her, funerals were just ritual and drama in front of people you knew, so they could judge you on how much you did or did not spend, and how hard you were "taking it" when the casket was opened. But it was her mama's desire to do it this way, and so it was.

One of the classrooms in the church had been set aside for the family, and Gracie was pacing the floor, dreading the moment the others would arrive, when all of a sudden the door opened, and a fiery redhead in a blue dress came sailing in with her purse strap on her shoulder and the heels of her shoes clacking rhythmically on the old wooden floors.

"I thought you might need backup," Darlene said.

Gracie sighed. "I am seriously glad to see you."

Darlene eyed the black dress, and for the first time, saw the scars she'd felt last night, then looked away.

"You look stunning," she said. "Is there anything I can do for you, honey? Do you need some water? I have stuff for headaches and plenty of tissues. I come prepared."

Gracie smiled and hugged her. "There's already ice water over on that table. Your presence is enough."

"Do you need me out at the ranch afterward?" Darlene asked.

Gracie shook her head. "No. It won't take long to speak my piece, and then I'll be gone."

"Okay, then," Darlene said. "Just making sure." She glanced up at the clock. "It's after 9:30. They should be arriving soon. Just so you know, there will be no arguing between James and me today. In fact, I intend to do my best to ignore him. This day is for Mama D and you."

And then the door opened, and both women turned.

"Speak of the devil," Darlene mumbled, as James walked in followed by the rest of the family.

Gracie lifted her chin. Their shock in seeing Darlene standing beside her was obvious, and then they were looking at her as if she was a stranger.

She didn't move—didn't speak—and stared each of them down until they all had the grace to look away.

Daphne felt the chill, but she was so shocked by Gracie's appearance that she froze. The tall, thin woman in black, with her long dark hair hanging loose around her face was a female version of their father. And the fact that Darlene was here had undertones of something more. Apparently, their ex-sister-in-law had not abandoned Gracie.

Now she really felt like shit.

Mamie couldn't quit staring. She leaned against Joel, as if she were about to be attacked, and when she realized Gracie was staring at her, she burst into tears.

Gracie rolled her eyes, her focus shifting to James.

James started toward her, his mouth already open, when Gracie held up her hand.

"Save it. You do not get the luxury of unburdening yourself here. We will talk at home afterward and not a moment before. Say what you will to the people you talk to today but understand this. They all know more about Mama and me than you do, so be careful of what you say. You don't want to come off looking like a fool."

Joel blinked.

James gasped.

Mamie's tears miraculously dried.

And Daphne was about to throw up.

Gracie remembered Daphne's penchant for puking, saw the telltale white ring around her lips, and pointed, her voice as cold as the look in her eyes.

"Suck it up, sister. You're nearly fifty, for God's sake. Get a drink of water and sit down, but you do not throw up. Mamie always tattled. You always had to puke. And James never stopped talking. But not today, you don't. Not any of you. Not today."

Too shocked to argue, they sat. James got Daphne a glass of water, and Mamie stared at the floor.

Darlene stifled a grin. Gracie was going to be fine.

And then Brother Harp walked in.

"Ah, all of the siblings are together again. I would like to have a moment of prayer before the—"

"Save it for Mama," Gracie said.

Brother Harp was beginning to tune in to the stricken looks on their faces. Something was afoot, but it was obviously not his place to interfere.

"As you wish," he said. "They'll be coming to get the family in minute or so. It's time for the service to begin. There will be food served here for friends and family after you return from the cemetery."

As the preacher walked out, Willis Decker walked in. He nodded to the others but went straight to Gracie.

"It's time. I'll escort you down the aisle to the front pew, where you

84

will all be seated. Your mama's pallbearers are seated on your left. The family will be on the right side. Are you ready, Gracie, or do you need a minute?"

"I'm ready," Gracie said, and reached for Darlene. "This is my sister-in-law, Darlene Dunham. She will be seated beside me, and please seat the women next to her."

Willis nodded. "As you wish. If you'll all follow me," he said, and offered Gracie his arm.

She slipped her hand beneath his elbow, then looked back to make sure Darlene was right behind them.

Darlene winked, and they filed out of the room.

Gracie strode past her brother and sisters with her chin up, and that's when they saw the scars.

She heard them gasp. She heard a few murmurs, and then Darlene's voice.

"Shush it!" she hissed, and they did.

As they neared the sanctuary, Gracie could hear the low murmurs of conversation from the people sitting in the congregation, waiting for the ceremony to start.

Her eyes welled.

Help me through this, Lord.

Willis Decker paused at the doorway.

The pianist struck a chord, and then the congregation stood. As they started down the aisle toward the front of the church, everything hit Gracie at once.

Sunlight coming through the stained-glass windows had painted rainbows across the white pearl casket.

The people standing as Gracie passed, murmuring...

"Love you, Gracie... God Bless you, Gracie... Praying for you, Gracie..."

The lump in her throat was swelling to the point that she was either going to choke or cry to relieve the pain. She was grateful when they finally reached the family pew.

She sank down at the end nearest the aisle and felt comfort from Darlene's presence as she slid into the seat beside her.

From the corner of her eye, she saw Ramona Harp standing in the wings, her gaze sweeping the room before her. Likely making mental notes as to who was here and who was absent, Gracie thought.

After that, came Daphne, then Mamie, then Joel, leaving James at the other end of the pew on his own. It was Alpha and Omega. The oldest child at one end. The youngest at the other.

It wasn't until everyone was seated and the service began that Gracie looked up at the casket again, and then at all the flowers. It was a grand sight to see the love being shown to Delia, but the scent of all those hothouse flowers, that had been in the viewing room with Mama, was starting to turn. The water in the cut flowers was going bad. The flowers in the vases were on the verge of wilt. They were at the end of their time, too, and it was all a little sickening.

Brother Harp was saying a prayer.

Mamie was crying, and now so was Daphne.

Gracie's sympathy for them was nil, and she ignored them.

When he finished, someone began singing one of Mama's chosen songs, "Swing Low, Sweet Chariot."

Everything about this day was becoming surreal. But the moments in between the beginning and the end of the service were the memories Gracie would carry with her for the rest of her life—like the laughter rolling out across the congregation now as Brother Harp began reading Delia's personal, hand-written eulogy.

It's me, Delia, and if you're hearing this, I must finally be dead. Knowing how hard-headed I was, I probably outstayed my welcome. But going crazy isn't easy, and I expect my darling Gracie will attest to this.

I am not going to remark upon the dates of my birth and death because they're likely on that program you're holding, along with where I was born, my mother and father's name, and everything some genealogist might need to know to track down the people with whom you share DNA. If one of them is me, God help you. You're gonna need it.

Yes, I meant to be buried in my wedding dress. Part of that is vanity that it still fit, and part of it is the tightwad in me wanting to get a second wearing.

The laughter that rolled across the congregation filled Gracie's heart. It was medicine for the brokenness within her and made her laugh with them.

And then Brother Harp continued.

I will mention my children's names, because it hurt like the dickens giving birth to them, which, now that I read this, sounds like I'm tooting my own horn by having the guts to repeat that process four times.

Again, the titter of laughter and chuckles uplifted the mood, but they quickly quieted, anxious to hear more of Delia's story.

Thomas James is my eldest and only son. Daphne May, my oldest daughter. Mamie Leigh, my third child, and then my baby, Gracie Jean. I did not know it at the time, but Gracie Jean was aptly named, because she became my saving grace. I have a wonderful daughter-in-law named Darlene, and two grandchildren, Caleb and Joanie, who all survive me. At least I hope to God this turns out to be true, because if there is even one of you waiting for me upon my arrival, I'll be having a talk with the Good Lord for cutting any of those beautiful lives short.

I need you all to know that I am not sad to leave. I hope I have not destroyed my youngest child, but as I sit here writing this, I already know the diagnosis I have been given, and I fear for her path with me.

It says in the Bible, to honor thy father and mother, and Gracie did just that. She stepped up, sacrificing every plan she had for her own future, just to take care of me. I have no knowledge of what will transpire between us after I write this, but if I know my girl, she stood by me to the end. I have faith that all my children helped and stood by her, too, and I thank them.

Gracie had never read the eulogy, because it had been in a sealed envelope, but it was obvious Mama's words had struck at the heart of her siblings. She could hear all of them crying. Guilt was as painful as a slap to the face.

Brother Harp cleared his throat. Gracie guessed he was obviously remembering his own lack of attention to their plight.

Whatever.

And then Brother Harp kept on reading.

What I want all of you to know is how much I loved living among you. How dear your friendship was to me. How much your love meant to me when my Tommy was killed.

But don't you dare sit there and cry for me now because I'm with Tommy again.

Sing your songs for me today. Bury me deep enough that this West Texas wind does not uncover my grave. Eat some barbecue and baked ham for me. I'm going to miss deviled eggs. But that's your world, not mine.

Don't waste a minute of life because it's short. Just know that love is forever, and Tommy and I send ours.

Brother Harp sat down as a trio from the choir began singing yet another of Delia's chosen songs—this time, "Amazing Grace."

Gracie had heard the story all her life of being named for this song, except Mama hadn't actually named her Grace. She'd named her Gracie because Mama said she could tell by the look in my eyes when she first saw my face, that I was going to be a pistol, and that being burdened with a dignified name might become an issue.

Delia's song choices were comforting to Gracie, and because her mama had chosen them, they felt like messages she wanted to leave behind.

Gracie sighed. She was crying and didn't even know it until Darlene slipped her a handful of tissues to wipe her eyes.

And then the song was over, and Brother Harp moved back to the pulpit to speak to the congregation.

"At this point in every funeral I have ever preached, this would be my time to deliver a spiritual message to all of you...a kind of reassurance for the grieving. But Miss Delia requested this be the end. And I will read to you what she said."

Brother Harp, I know you always preach a little sermon at funerals, but I'd just as soon you did not at mine. The way I figure it, the ones needing saving aren't gonna hear the call on the day I'm being buried because they're thinking about pie and ham. And the others present who're already saved are probably needing a potty break.

The congregation roared.

Gracie grinned and shook her head. It was like hearing her mama's voice again—before all her good senses had abandoned her.

Brother Harp smiled, and then added. "I am to remind you, the burial will be at the Sweetwater Cemetery, and you are all invited back to the church for dinner afterward."

At that point, Willis Decker and his team began Delia Dunham's last reveal. They opened the top half of the casket, re-settled the casket spray back in place, and when they were satisfied that Delia was looking her deathly best, they stepped aside. The people seated in the back were the first to pass the casket, and then one by one, the sanctuary began to empty as people came down the aisle.

As was tradition in this part of the world, some paused by Gracie and her siblings to give personal messages, or their sympathies, before moving past the open casket—a simple gesture of paying their last respects to one of their own.

Gracie nodded, shook hands, accepted pats on the back, and the occasional hug. She said thank you in all the right places, but she was fading. This overload of sympathy made her ache in every bone. What she wouldn't give for a drink of cold Coke.

The lines seemed endless, and then finally the only people left within the sanctuary with the Dunham family were the Harps and the employees from the funeral home. This was it. The family's last chance to see their loved one's face.

One by one, her siblings stood, then gathered around the casket, holding onto each other in grief, and still Gracie sat.

"Honey?" Darlene whispered.

"I'll be along," Gracie said. "You go."

And when Darlene walked to the casket, the siblings parted for her arrival, then stood a distance behind her, as if in fear she might turn and decimate them for their sins.

Finally, Gracie stood, gripping the wad of tissues like a lifeline, and headed straight for Delia.

A peace enveloped her as she looked down into her mother's face, and then she laid a hand on her arm.

"We did it, Mama. You nearly killed me doing it, and I lost you twice, but I got you safe to Daddy. I won't say it was easy, but it was my blessing to have done this for you. You taught me two things in the past nine years that I will never forget. To never take life for granted, and to find strength within myself that I didn't know was there. I love you."

She pulled a pink carnation from the casket spray and tucked it in her mother's hands, and when she turned around, Willis Decker was there with the pallbearers.

They rolled the pearl casket out of the church and into a hearse, then ushered the family into a limousine for the ride out to the cemetery.

Still gripping the tissues, Gracie leaned back against the seat and closed her eyes, leaving Darlene to stare the others down.

They'd all heard what Gracie said at the casket. Now they were looking at those scars on her with new horror. Surely to God their own mother had not done that? Surely!

"I feel sick," Daphne mumbled.

"Save it for the cemetery," Darlene said.

Mamie had gone fetal. She hadn't let go of Joel since they'd entered the sanctuary, and now, sitting within the confines of the same vehicle, she felt Gracie's rage as if it were a living, breathing fire. She looked up at Joel with tear-filled eyes, silently begging him for forgiveness she didn't deserve.

James was struggling with the shame of what he'd ignored and denied, and what he'd left undone. Being this close to Darlene, after all these years, just made it worse.

The hardest part was hearing Brother Harp reading their mother's words, and her assumption that they had all stood by her and Gracie. He didn't know how their lives would play out from this day forward, but in his mind, he was forever branded as a traitor—forever changed because of shame.

THE SERVICE AT THE CEMETERY WAS POIGNANTLY BRIEF. LATER, THE cemetery workers would lower Delia's casket into the ground beside Tommy, but for now, it rested in quiet splendor, surrounded by flowers and sunlight, and the mourners who'd traveled with her to see her off.

The wind had laid, leaving them all sitting and standing in the torpid heat. Makeup was melting. Sweat was in abundance as Brother Harp read the Twenty-Third Psalm, then said a prayer, and it was over.

This time, when people came by to pay their respects to the family, the conversation was normal, and memories were briefly shared. It was very apparent to Delia Dunham's children that they were not the only ones who had been blessed by their mother's time on this earth.

Darlene was getting nervous. Gracie was too quiet and too pale. She rounded up the limo driver and herded Gracie inside where it was cool, which sent others to do the same.

They drove back to the church for dinner, and the moment they were inside, Darlene took Gracie to the ladies room.

"Go pee. Then come wash your face and hands and cool off. You look like you're going to pass out."

The ladies room only had four stalls, but Gracie was quickly ushered into the next empty one.

When she came out, Darlene had a wet paper towel waiting, and slapped it on the back of Gracie's neck like she was swatting at a fly.

"Don't pass out on me, girl," she said.

"I won't," Gracie said, and then stood at the sink sluicing her face with cool water until the feeling of nausea had passed.

"Lord have mercy, girl. You just washed off every bit of makeup you were wearing and still look like a million bucks," Darlene said.

The women who overheard them laughed, agreeing.

Gracie looked back at herself, then shrugged.

"All I see is Daddy looking back at me."

Daphne was in a stall puking, and Mamie was trying to repair the makeup on her face as Darlene took Gracie down to the dining room, seated her at a table, then headed to the kitchen where the church ladies were waiting to serve the meal.

"She needs to eat something. Now," Darlene said, as she grabbed a glass of iced tea and pointed to where Gracie was sitting.

One woman grabbed a dinner roll, tore it in half, and slapped a piece of ham between the bread, wrapped it in a paper napkin, then handed it to Darlene.

"Let her start with this and the cold drink. She can get a proper plate later."

"Thank you so much," Darlene said, and hurried to where Gracie was sitting. "Here, honey. The ladies in the kitchen got your back."

Gracie grabbed the tea, drinking thirstily, and then took a small bite. The warm bread and cold ham was heaven in her mouth, and slowly, the fainting feeling began to fade.

"Thank you," she whispered, as the room began to fill.

Darlene gave her a thumbs up, and then Brother Harp finally appeared, gave the blessing for the food, and the dinner began.

The entire Dunham family was seated at the same table by assumption that they would want to be together. So, the conversation there existed only when others came up to speak to them.

James was soon surrounded by people he'd gone to school with, and for a short time, he felt almost human again.

Daphne's stomach settled enough to make a plate, while Mamie and Joel stood in line at the buffet, filling theirs as the people moved along.

Later, as Gracie ate, she kept thinking how much Mama would have loved this. She loved a big gathering, and she loved parties. And even though she wasn't here for this, she was still the star of her own show.

Once everyone had settled down to eating, Gracie stood, and began walking among the tables, and once she knew she had their attention, she spoke up.

"If I could have your attention for a moment, I have a few words."

The room immediately silenced.

Gracie smiled. "Mama had her say today, didn't she?"

Laughter and comments ensued.

"So, I am, after all, my mother's child, and I have a little something I need to say to all of you while we're here together. It's about the fund that was set up for me at the bank. I only learned of this yesterday. I don't know whose idea it was, and I guess it doesn't matter. The shock came from how many donated. I can't say as how I've ever been more stunned, or more grateful. There aren't enough words to say how much I appreciate it, or how badly it was needed. I won't be able to send personal thanks to everyone, but if you would be so kind as to spread my sincerest gratitude for your love and generosity, I would appreciate it.

"Over the past nine years, I'd bet money that everyone of us here got a dose of Mama as she was coming undone. But I want you to know that I saw your patience with her, and how you excused her erratic behavior. I appreciated it, and I loved you for it. Mama was a strong-willed woman when she had her wits about her. But going crazy, she gave bad a whole new name. Yet, standing here in this place with all of you, I can honestly say I would not change a thing. I would do it all over again, just for the moments when I could still find her within the madness."

And then everyone was on their feet and clapping, and hugging Gracie, and she couldn't see for the tears blurring her vision.

CHAPTER EIGHT

*A*fter Gracie sat down, Mamie leaned into Daphne.

"What did she mean by Mama trying to kill her?" she whispered.

Daphne shrugged.

James frowned. "I doubt that she was being literal."

Joel stared at James as if he'd just lost his mind. "Then where the hell did all those scars come from?" he asked.

After that, conversation ceased.

Gracie knew they were whispering about her, but their time was coming. They had one more stop to make this day before they could scurry back under their respective rocks.

They had refused to come home while Mama was alive.

Now she'd given them no choice.

She'd picked at her food, eating all she could swallow, and then sat sipping iced tea and watching her family saving face, redirecting the locals' curious questions as to where they'd been, and basking in their moments of brief glory as they related their personal triumphs.

None of it mattered to Gracie. She was just waiting for her moment to slip away from the church. It finally came when Daphne and Mamie left to go to the ladies room, and James became involved in a conversation with an old friend.

At that moment, Gracie turned and gave Darlene a quick hug.

"Thank you for everything today. You are the best sister I could ever hope for. Thank the kids for my laptop. Tell Caleb he is a life-saver for loading it. Give me a thirty-minute head start, and then tell James and the girls I'm already gone."

"I will. Love you, Gracie. Call me when you get stopped for the night. I need to know where you are, and where you're going. I don't want to be worrying about you."

"I promise," Gracie said, and slipped out. She wanted to get home, change clothes, and load up.

As she was going out the back of the dining hall, one of the church ladies handed her a little sack.

"We know you're leaving Sweetwater. We'll miss you, but Godspeed, sugar. Here's a little something to take with you on the road."

"Thank you," Gracie said. "Dinner was delicious. Please thank everyone for me. I will miss you all, but life's been waiting on me for a really long time, and I'm already playing catch-up just to get started."

And then she was out the door.

Minutes later, she passed the city limit sign, heading west toward home. The ten miles seemed shorter. Looking in the rearview mirror as she drove, she could almost imagine the road rolling up behind her —giving her no other options but to keep moving forward.

The highway ahead of her was long, straight, and flat, and she saw home long before she reached it. One turn to the left, and she was on the driveway and headed to the house. She slid to a stop at the front porch and hurried inside, then went straight back to her bedroom to change.

She'd left out one of the new pairs of jean shorts and a blue t-shirt, and quickly changed, then packed her new laptop and what she'd been wearing, turned off the fan, and began carrying suitcases from the house to her car. The old quilt went in next, then the box with sheets and towels, and finally, her grandmother's cuckoo clock.

She locked the car, then went back into the house and headed for the old roll-top desk.

She dug out her mama's will, the key to the safety deposit box, the extra house keys, and carried it all to the kitchen table. Once she added her own house key to the pile, she was done. Now all she had to do was wait for the rest of them to show up.

She turned on the box fan in the kitchen, got the last cold Coke out of the refrigerator, and walked out on the back porch to toast the vista before her.

"To Dunhams, good and bad," she said, took a long drink, then sat down in the porch swing to await their arrival.

~

JAMES WAS THE FIRST TO NOTICE GRACIE WAS GONE AND LOOKED straight at Darlene.

"Is Gracie already gone?"

Darlene shrugged. "Likely."

"Why didn't she say something?" he asked.

"Say what? You've already heard what she said here. If you want to hear the rest of it, go home."

James glared at her, red-faced and angry, and began looking for his sisters, but Darlene didn't care about his attitude or him. Her job here was over, so she gathered up her things and left. She'd done everything she'd come to Sweetwater to do, and now she wanted to go home. Even if it would be way up into the night before she got there, she just wanted to be gone from this place. So, she went back to her hotel and checked out. She was southbound on her way back to Houston, while James, Daphne, Joel and Mamie all headed for the farm.

They talked nonstop all the way until they took the turn off the highway toward the house. At that point, shock set in.

"What the fucking hell happened here?" James muttered.

"We're about to find out," Joel said.

As they got out, they noticed Gracie's car was full of luggage, and the front door to the house was ajar.

Heat hit them as they pushed the door inward.

"Oh my God! Why is it so hot in here?" Daphne cried.

And on that question, Gracie walked into the living room.

"Because the central air died four years ago. No money to fix it. Come into the kitchen. There's a box fan."

And then she turned her back, leaving them to straggle behind her, eyeing the worn furniture, the limp curtains, and a faint and gathering layer of dust on everything.

James was already shedding his sport coat and tie, and so was Joel, but they all paused in the kitchen doorway, eyeing the blackened ceiling and stained floor.

"What the hell has happened to the place?" James asked.

"You will sit down to get your answers, or none at all, and never raise your voice to me again," Gracie said.

"I'm sorry," James said. "I didn't mean—"

Daphne pushed him forward. They all sat.

Gracie started talking, but her face and voice were devoid of expression.

"The condition of this property is on your heads. We had a two-year drought. The tractor broke. The farm truck died. We had no money to fix any of it. I sold cattle to pay property taxes and Mama's medical bills, and within three years, all of the cattle had been sold off because there was no hay left in the barn, and no money to buy any. Mama got a Social Security check every month. We lived on that.

"Five years ago, Mama freaked, thought I was a stranger in her house, and nearly killed me. I spent a week in the hospital, and she spent a month in the psych ward. When I got well enough, I brought her home."

They were staring at her now, their eyes wide with shock, too horrified to even cry.

Gracie pointed to the floor.

"That's my blood. It won't wash out." She pointed to the ceiling. "Mama set a skillet on fire. It caught fire to the ceiling. That's the end result. The knobs to the stove are hidden in the drawer next to the refrigerator, behind the stack of potholders. And, every knife, every object that had a sharp point or anything that would cut, is up in the attic in Great-Grandpa Dunham's army trunk, beneath his uniform."

Daphne jumped up and ran outside, throwing up off the side of the porch.

Gracie stood with her arms folded until her sister came back, washed her hands and face at the sink, then sat down again.

Gracie picked up where she'd left off.

"It wasn't easy keeping up with our mother once she lost her fucking mind. She wandered away from me twice. First time, I put her down for a nap and went to clean the bathroom. I came back to check on her, and she was gone. It was November...cold and threatening snow. After a frantic search all over the house and outbuildings, I found a piece of her flannel shirt on the barbed wire fence and realized she was out on the prairie. I searched for her for a long time in the car. It was starting to snow. And then I heard Daddy's voice telling me to look up. When I did, I saw turkey buzzards circling and drove toward them. She was curled up in the grass. She thought the cows got out and went looking for them. Only they'd been gone for years.

"The last time I lost her was in the middle of the night. I found her in the dark, in the chicken house gathering eggs. But the chickens were long gone. She killed them one day in some delusional moment. Wrung all their necks."

James looked out through the window behind Gracie, staring at the vastness of that land and saw the truth of what abandoning Gracie had done.

Mamie had her face buried against Joel's chest. He was the only one with the guts to still face Gracie.

Gracie took a slow breath. "Mama didn't just get crazy. She got mean. And we went hungry. If it had not been for Darlene, we would have starved. She sent us two thousand dollars a month, every month, for six years."

James's head came up. "That's the alimony money I send her!"

Gracie frowned. "I know all about what you did, and your 'hush money,' as she calls it. She said she'd never take anything from you for as long as she lived, and she gave it to us because we needed it."

Joel shifted in his seat. "Gracie, I am profoundly sorry that we weren't contributing to your welfare. I sincerely believed we were, but I also blame myself for not following up to make sure."

Mamie wailed. "I'm sorry, Gracie. I just let time get away from me."

Gracie didn't even look at her.

Daphne cleared her throat.

"I was selfish and afraid. I didn't call you because I was afraid of Mama and didn't want to stay with her. I am so sorry."

Gracie stared Daphne down, refusing to accept her lame excuse.

"Bullshit, Daphne. You think I wasn't scared? You think I *wanted* to stay? I was afraid of her, too. Especially after she tried to kill me, so I slept with my bedroom door locked at night and never turned my back on her again. The truth is, I don't care what any of you have to say. You no longer exist in my world."

Then she pointed at the papers and keys between them. "That's Mama's will. The land is in a trust. James inherits everything because that's what Great-Grandpa Dunham started—passing it down by blood to the eldest Dunham son. James can sell it, or not. It's his to do with as he wishes."

James turned red. "I knew nothing about this," he said, as his sisters shrieked.

Gracie ignored them.

"That's the key to the safety deposit box, and the extra keys to the house. Randy Jacobs offered to give you a fair price for the place if you decide to sell. He used to stop by now and then when the cattle kept getting out and the fences were falling down, but then Mama threw a knife at him, and he never came back...until the other day after she was gone. My time here is over, and if God is good, I will never see any of you again."

Then she palmed her car keys and strode out of the room, her steps long and steady. She paused once in the hallway, saw the dust already on the surface of the table again, and one last time, wrote her name.

I, Gracie, am gone.

They heard the front screen door slam behind her as she left, and then the car starting up. She drove away, slinging gravel out from beneath her tires and leaving a rooster-tail of dust to mark her passing.

She headed East with the sun at her back and her heart on fire. The pain of betrayal was choking. She hadn't just lost her last parent today. She'd lost the rest of her family.

Tears were rolling now, but she kept wiping them away. She wasn't a quitter. She was a survivor, and the only way she was going to get better was to get far, far away.

The faster she went, the more the tires began to hum, and within the sound, she heard a scream. And she answered back, screaming and screaming until she had no more breath.

She flew through Sweetwater with tear-stained cheeks, took the I-44 North, and never looked back.

GRACIE WAS GONE, BUT THE ENSUING FIGHT AMONG HER SIBLINGS WAS still ongoing. They had shouted and argued and cried until they were all red-faced and dripping in sweat, and then stopped as if someone had suddenly turned off a switch.

They stood, staring at each other across the old kitchen table, their hearts hammering, their disbelief at where they were suddenly coming to the fore.

Finally, James held up his hands in defeat.

"It may be in my name, but we'll share it three ways," he said.

"What about Gracie?" Joel asked.

"If we don't exist for her, then she doesn't exist for us, remember?" James muttered.

"Then we don't want any part of it," Joel said.

Mamie opened her mouth to argue, then saw the look on Joel's face and nodded in silent agreement.

Daphne sighed. "Gracie nearly died to keep Mama and this place. She bled to save it. I won't take blood money. I'm going home," she said, then walked out and drove away.

Daphne's departure prompted Joel and Mamie's exit, leaving James in the old house alone.

"I didn't ask for this," he muttered.

Then he picked up the will and the keys and left, locking the door behind him, thinking what a mess. What an ever-loving mess.

Joel drove straight to the bank with Mamie blubbering in the seat beside him, then got out and went inside. A short while later, he came out, and got back in the car.

"What did you do?" Mamie asked.

"We will not be going on our annual Christmas cruise this year. I donated the ten thousand dollars to Gracie's fund, instead."

"Oh no," Mamie moaned.

Joel glared. "Suck it up, Mamie. I will never get the images of that farm, or what Gracie endured, out of my head. Never. Be grateful for what you have now. There's no guarantee that it'll always be there."

THE MILES WERE LONG. THE STOPS FOR GAS AND FOOD BRIEF. GRACIE ate what they'd given her from the church and was still on I-44 when she finally reached Tulsa, Oklahoma. She needed to stop. She was so tired she was sick, but she kept driving, looking for a place that felt right, and then she saw an Embassy Suites just off the interstate and exited.

Everything she owned in the world was in this car, but as she pulled into the parking lot, the only thing she got out was her overnight bag. She'd already walked out of the wilderness and was leaving it up to God to watch out for what she had left.

Traffic from the nearby freeway drowned out the sounds of her footsteps as she walked toward the motel. It was creepy this time of night, being out in the parking lot alone. The closer she got, the faster she went, until she was almost running when she entered the lobby.

A clerk at the registration desk looked up as Gracie approached.

"I don't have a reservation, but I need a room for what's left of this night," Gracie said.

"Yes, ma'am," he said. "Are you traveling alone or will someone be joining you?"

"Just me," Gracie said.

A few minutes later, she exited the elevator on the fifth floor, oriented herself as to which direction she needed to go, and headed for her room.

She turned on the light as she entered, locked and turned the deadbolt, then staggered toward the bed.

The room was cool and quiet as she made her way into the bathroom. She came out nude, put her phone on the charger, pulled back the covers, then remembered she'd promised to text Darlene.

In Tulsa for the night. I'm going to Branson, Missouri to check out jobs and living options. I'll stay in touch. Love you.

And then she crawled between the sheets, found a comfy spot on the pillow, and closed her eyes.

THEY'D BEEN DRIVING FOR HOURS...GOING TO THE TEXAS STATE FAIR. *Gracie had worn out her welcome in the back seat with her three siblings, and at the last stop, they'd moved her to the front seat by Mama.*

She'd eaten her snack and had her bottle of pop, but now she was bored again. Daddy was singing along with a song on the radio, and James was in the back seat fighting with the girls.

Gracie leaned against her mother and sighed.

"Are we there yet, Mama?"

"Not yet, baby girl, but soon," Delia said. "Lay your head in my lap and close your eyes. It's going to be a really long day."

GRACIE WOKE WITHOUT OPENING HER EYES, AND FOR A FEW FADING moments could still feel the denim fabric of Mama's jeans against her cheek and smell the scent of her perfume.

"A dream. It was just a dream," Gracie said, and threw back the covers.

It was a little after 8:00 in the morning as she went into the bathroom to shower. The urge to get back on the road was like an outgoing tide, pulling her further away from what she knew into a vast unknown.

She dressed quickly, packed, and then sat down with her phone to check her balance at the bank. She couldn't believe what she was seeing.

The amount had jumped from a little over six thousand dollars, to more than twenty-one thousand. People were still donating? She clutched her phone to her breasts in disbelief, then headed downstairs.

The free breakfast buffet beckoned, and she ate all she could hold before checking out. After refueling and checking the air in her tires, she got back on I-44 north, sending up every positive prayer and vibe she could muster.

Gracie didn't want to be scared, but uncertainty had never been her friend. She was, at heart, a mover and a shaker, and for her, living within the status quo was like living with a herd all moving in the same direction, all bawling for someone else to feed them, care for them, and sell them to the highest bidder. Her fear of being lost in the crowd was a valid fear.

But as the miles passed, she felt easier. She had the same feeling of adventure that she'd had on their trip to the state fair when she was a kid, and an instinctual feeling she wasn't riding alone.

"Mama. Daddy. If you're here, buckle up. I, Gracie, am not messing around."

Then she stomped on the accelerator.

The same south wind in Texas that had dried up the ranch was now pushing her forward. She was barely hanging onto the speed limit, and the geography of Oklahoma was nothing but a blur.

CHAPTER NINE

*B*y the time Gracie crossed the border into Missouri, she was already in love. The Ozark Mountains called to her like a long-lost lover, beckoning her to come close—to move deeper into the ancient secrets hidden within the vast forests of green and the deep trenches of the shadowed valleys.

The energy around her was as strong as her heartbeat. She didn't know what fate had in store for her here, but it felt safe, and she hadn't felt safe in such a long time.

After a stop for fuel, and a to-go cup full of ice and Coke, Gracie was off to Springfield, then a slight jog east before heading back south to Branson.

She arrived just before noon, rolling into what had once been a small, mountain town long-since burst at the seams into the bustling, tourist-filled city it was today.

Gracie drove with one eye on the traffic, and the other on the sights before her. Signs advertising the daily music shows at their venues were everywhere, along with signs and arrows pointing the way to famous Silver Dollar City.

From the main roads, the winding streets that led up and down hills into older, quieter, neighborhoods were enticing, but something to see for another time.

She'd seen advertisements for the newer apartment complexes on the outskirts of downtown, but she would need to stand in the place to know if it was meant for her to be there, and that, too, would come on another day. Right now, she was just taking in the amazing mix of old and new and sensing the vibrancy of so many people coming and going. She would find a way to belong here. And somewhere, there was a job and a place here that would be hers to call home.

"I'm here, Mama. I made it," Gracie said.

But as she kept driving and seeing the hotel and motel parking lots full of cars, she realized it might not be as simple to get a room for a couple of days as it had been on the road. She needed a stopping place to reconnoiter. First thing was finding an apartment. It was time to get down to business or she'd be sleeping in her car to keep everything safe.

Because the name appealed to her, she pulled into Mel's Hard Luck Diner to get something to eat. The place had an old 50s-style vibe, with waiters and waitresses who kept breaking into songs from the era. She smiled. Singing waiters. It all reminded her of Mama and Daddy's music on the porch.

And the place was busy, which meant the food was likely good. They seated her at a small table against a wall, leaving her with a glass of iced tea and a menu to read.

When the waiter came back, she ordered a Hard Luck cheeseburger and onion rings, then got her phone and started pulling up hotel websites. After checking prices, she began making calls, and on the second try, she got a reservation for three nights with a 2:00 check-in at one she'd seen near the strip.

After that, she relaxed and glanced up, absently eyeing the other guests as the waiters and waitresses moved through the dining area serving food and refilling drinks.

It occurred to her as she sat there that she might wind up waiting tables, although not likely here. She couldn't sing good enough for a job like this, but she'd do whatever it took to pay the bills and be grateful for it. She'd already accepted that she was going to be behind the curve in work experience for someone her age, but it was what it was.

When her food came, she eyed the burger hungrily, tucked a strand of hair behind her ear, then picked it up and took a big bite, unaware she had become another diner's point of interest.

She ate until she was stuffed. She had almost come down from the high of her arrival when someone started singing an old Marty Robbins song.

"A white sport coat...and a pink carnation..."

She glanced up, and for a heartbeat, she was looking at her daddy. Then she blinked, and realized it was a waiter. The ache in her chest bloomed, rolling up her throat and blinding her with sudden tears. She was about to make a fool of herself and needed to get out of here.

JOHN GATLIN HAD BEEN EATING LUNCH AT THE HARD LUCK AT LEAST once a week for a good ten years—ever since he'd first come to Branson. He'd seen all kinds of travelers through the years, but not a one of them he could remember.

So, when he noticed the tall, dark-haired woman walk in leading with her chin, he thought, *Someone got lucky with that one. She's stunning.* But when no one joined her, his interest moved from appreciation to curiosity.

He kept eating his food while keeping an eye on the clock. Even though he had a landscaping company and was his own boss, he had been running all over town getting parts to repair equipment that was down and couldn't be late getting back to the shop to get it all fixed.

A group at a nearby table was celebrating a birthday. The singing waiters had gathered around it, and the birthday girl giggled as they began to sing. Before long, everyone in the dining room was singing "Happy Birthday."

John noticed the woman glance up as the singing started, but he could tell by the look on her face that her heart was somewhere else.

Then her food came, and when she picked that burger up with both hands and took a big healthy bite, he grinned.

No dainty pretense there, girl. Way to go!

Two other things about her struck him. She ate without looking at the phone beside her plate, and she was leaning against the wall as she ate—like she was trying to withdraw from all the noise around her.

He glanced at the time again. He needed to leave now, but she was still here, and he wanted to know her name. Was she just passing through, or was she a resident? He couldn't just walk up to a total stranger and ask her stuff like that without coming across as a creep. And so he stayed, hoping for something that would give him an opportunity to at least make eye contact.

One of the waiters started singing another song, and within seconds, it was like she'd been catapulted out of her seat. He watched as she began throwing money on the table, then as she turned to leave, she ran into a waiter, who knocked her purse out of her hands, and at that point, shit went flying.

John came out of his chair and began grabbing at coins rolling across the floor, then a tube of lipstick, and finally, he chased down the phone sliding across the floor. When he turned around to look for her, she was on her knees, frantically stuffing items back in her purse.

"Miss? Are you all right?" John asked.

When she looked up, he saw her face was wet with tears.

"Not yet, but I will be," she said, and stood.

"You dropped these," he said.

She took a deep breath. "Thank you," she said, put the items back in her purse, and headed for the door.

"Wait," John said, but she kept walking. He ran back to his table to pay for his food, and as he did, saw a small silver angel charm that he'd missed picking up. He ran to catch up with her, but by the time he got outside, she was gone.

Without knowing what she was driving, he could only stare at the myriad assortment of vehicles coming and going around him in dismay. He shoved his hand through his hair in frustration and groaned. It made no sense, but he felt like he'd just lost something important.

"Well, hell," he muttered, then strode over to his work truck, chiding himself for getting locked into a fantasy, and then he realized he was still holding the charm. He put it in his pocket with his change.

He had mower parts to buy and a two new weed-eaters to pick up before he went back to the office. He made a quick call to check on his other crews and to make sure there weren't any more breakdowns today to throw them off schedule. But even as he drove away, he found himself looking for her in every car he passed.

Maybe it was the sadness about her. Maybe it had been the tears. But he was going to be a long time forgetting that face.

GRACIE WAS STILL RATTLED WHEN SHE CHECKED INTO THE HOTEL. SHE had all her suitcases brought into the room, and then she transferred the quilt and the other boxes from the backseat to the trunk.

The urge to lie down and sleep the day away was huge, but sleep would come later. Gracie was a nester. She needed a place to be, but she needed to let Darlene know she'd arrived. So, she sent her a text.

I'm in Branson. Just checked into a hotel for a few days. I'm going to start looking for a job and a place to live. Send all the good vibes you can spare.

Then she crawled onto the bed with her new laptop, set up an email account, and began searching for apartments.

Logically, she needed one that was furnished, but it soon became obvious that wasn't going to be an easy task. So, she began pulling up Realtor sites and making calls. She didn't need a fancy apartment with access to a fitness center and a pool. She just needed it to have functioning air and heat and to be clean and safe.

The next two hours were frustrating and depressing. She would have to be approved before anyone would rent to her, which meant filling out an application without having a place of work to reference her monthly wages. Nobody wanted to rent property to someone who had no job, and she had no idea what her credit rating was, or if she still had one.

"I didn't expect this to be easy, but this is ridiculous," Gracie muttered, then set aside the housing issue for now and began searching online for jobs.

JOHN GATLIN FINALLY HAD ALL OF HIS EQUIPMENT BACK UP AND running, and tomorrow's schedules posted, when the crews began coming in for the evening. With no complaints to deal with and no more equipment out of service, he closed up shop for the day and headed home.

There was always traffic in Branson, and at different times of day, it was worse than others. Going home from work traffic for locals coincided with going out to dinner traffic for tourists, and then there was the traffic for the music shows that began later.

All he wanted was to get home. He was too tired to stop and pick up food, so leftovers were calling his name.

As he drove, he caught himself looking at the drivers he met, and the ones that he passed, giving any female with long, dark hair a second look. Finally, he made himself stop.

Chances were, she was long gone from Branson and on her way to somewhere else.

But he'd seen her face and her tears.

And he'd heard her voice, *"Not yet, but I will be."*

He didn't know what had happened, but he'd seen the pain it had caused, and it had made his heart hurt.

If only he knew her name.

By the time Gracie went to bed, she had applied for jobs online at more than a dozen places. Now, she had to wait for them to respond.

It was a maddening way to job hunt. But she was at her destination, and while the shine had come off a little on her expectations, she was, by no means, defeated. She would find work, and she would find a home, and she would find a way to be happy again. All she had to do now was just rest and be grateful for air conditioning and the lack of blowing dust.

~

James Dunham didn't get to go home when everyone else had. He was still in Sweetwater, at the La Quinta Inn, floating in the pool, and feeling sorry for himself.

Tomorrow, he had to go talk to his mama's lawyer. The will had to go into probate, and he had to get a change of address for her mail to be sent to him in Houston so he would be able to pay the utility bills and every other fucking deal that came with being a long-distance heir.

But the longer he floated, the worse he felt. Bottom line—he didn't deserve the inheritance, and selling the ranch was just selling out his daddy's dream that he would be the fourth generation Dunham to run it.

James knew his limitations. He wasn't a rancher. He was an accountant who lived about as far away from Sweetwater as a man could live and still be in Texas. He was mad at himself for being an ass all these years, and mad at the first Dunham to own that the land, who had decided it would be just fine with other generations of his family to give everything to the oldest son. Thus, he'd set up a trust that held his future heirs' feet to the fire in the process.

James had some thinking to do, and maybe the lawyer could help him fix this mess. Joel and Mamie had already refused a share. Darlene had called it "blood money" and walked out on all of them. And Gracie was in the wind. The only person who likely knew where she'd gone would be his ex-wife, and the thought of having to deal with her in any way made him anxious.

But, by the time he'd floated himself into a sunburn, he knew what he had to do. He just wasn't sure how to make it happen.

~

GRACIE HAD BEEN IN BRANSON THREE DAYS WITH NOT EVEN ONE response on job searches or any responses from leasing companies about apartments that fell into her price range.

She'd given up on getting anything furnished, because they simply weren't to be had, and had made peace with buying a bed and a chair if she could just find a place to live.

She was by no means defeated, but reality was setting in. She'd already extended her stay at the motel another couple of nights and was trying not to worry.

And then she woke up to a text from one of the realtors she'd contacted days earlier, asking her to call him back at her earliest convenience. It was just after 9:00. She hadn't meant to sleep so long, but the last two days of job hunting had been exhausting. So, she sat up on the side of the bed, made the call, then waited for him to pick up.

"Wainwright Leasing Company. Sam speaking."

"This is Gracie Dunham. I got a text from you to call."

"Oh, yes! Gracie! We just had a new listing that made me think of you. It's a furnished, garage apartment in the historic district. The garage below the apartment is the parking space for the listing. I've seen the property before. It's old style—eclectic, but charming, clean, and well-taken care of. I've already spoken to the owner about your recent arrival and the need for a furnished apartment. She's willing to waive some of the restrictions if you're interested in renting her property."

"What's the rent?" Gracie asked.

"A thousand dollars a month. Can you swing that?"

Gracie didn't hesitate. "Yes. When can I see it?"

"It's being cleaned and will be available for viewing by 1:00 today. Since you're new to Branson, if you want to come by the office around one, it won't take but about fifteen minutes to get there."

"Then yes, I want to see it," Gracie said. "Can I ask you something?"

"Sure," Sam said.

"Does the landlord live on the property?"

"Yes, but in the big house on the property. The garage apartment is behind it. She's a bit eccentric, but in an adorable way."

"Okay, good. Then thank you for thinking of me because it sounds like the answer to a prayer. I'll see you at one."

"Yes, ma'am," Sam said. "One it is."

Gracie disconnected, then jumped up, tossed the phone on the bed, and did a little dance in the middle of the room.

After living in a house that had been set on fire and walking on floors soaked with the remnants of her own blood, she wasn't picky about ambiance and style. She was all about cleaning and lemon oil. If it was cool in the summer, warm in the winter, and she felt safe, she would take it.

And with that good news, she got dressed and went down to breakfast.

~

Lucy Bedford was having breakfast outside on the back veranda when her phone rang. She swallowed her bite of toast, and then picked up.

"Hello. This is Lucy."

"Lucy. Sam Wainwright here. I'm bringing a potential renter out to your property a little after one today. Is that okay?"

"Yes. Is it that same woman you mentioned...the one who just got into town?"

"Yes, ma'am."

"Good job," Lucy said. "You know I don't like for that place to sit empty. This is a swift turnaround. Oh...one other thing. What's her name?"

"Gracie Dunham."

"Gracie. That has a nice ring to it," Lucy said, and disconnected.

Sam grinned. She'd just hung up on him. Ah well, he had a good feeling about this. He sure hoped it all worked out. It would be another lease for him, which was good for business, and it might help set Gracie Dunham off on the right foot to a new life.

~

DAPHNE DUNHAM STILL HADN'T GONE BACK TO WORK. SHE'D CRIED more in the past two days than she had in her whole life and had finally taken a sleeping pill last night. She hadn't woken up when her alarm went off. She couldn't face the world, so she'd called in and said she'd be working from home today.

She needed a reset.

Mama was dead, and her youngest sister no longer existed in her world. Gracie had cast her family out like the garbage they were, and now Daphne had two choices: Accept it and move forward or start wearing sackcloth and ashes.

She chose to move forward, accept the punishment as fair, and not beat herself up for being an asshole since it seemed to run in the family.

So, she carried her laptop into the kitchen, made herself a cup of coffee, then called the bank in Sweetwater, got the info she needed to donate money to Gracie's fund, and transferred five thousand dollars into the account. Gracie wouldn't know where it came from, but Daphne needed to know she'd done it to be able to live with herself.

And once that was over, she began pulling up the email on her listings. Life had happened, and now it was time to participate in it again.

~

JOEL AND MAMIE WERE STILL FEELING THEIR WAY BACK TO A SEMBLANCE of normal, but right now it all felt fake.

Mamie was overdoing the considerate wife role, and Joel was

unusually silent. She was afraid to talk about the elephant in the room, for fear Joel would have made a decision about her she couldn't live with.

She didn't want to lose him. She adored him, and he was already all broken in just the way she liked it. Or at least he had been, until she'd shattered his image of her.

As for Joel, he hadn't gotten over what had happened to Gracie. In his whole life, he had never known someone could suffer to that extent and not die. She was as broken as a soul could be and still be functioning, and they were all responsible.

His conscience hurt, and every time he looked at Mamie, he was shattered by the reality of who she'd shown herself to be. If she would abandon her own sister when the going got rough, what would she do to him if they suddenly lost everything? Would she be the kind of wife who would stand by her man, in sickness and in health, or would she jump ship on him? He had to decide if they were going to work on this together or go their separate ways.

"We have a situation," Joel said.

Mamie burst into tears.

"Don't leave me. I will die."

Joel rolled his eyes.

"No, you won't, and tears won't solve any of this. But I don't know how to fix us. Are you willing to go to couples counseling?"

"Yes, yes! I'll do anything you say!" Mamie cried.

"This isn't about pleasing me, Mamie. It's about the lies."

Mamie shivered. "I never thought about it like that."

"Secrets are lies. You don't keep serious stuff from someone you are supposed to love."

"But I do love you," Mamie wailed.

"Maybe...but you loved yourself more, and now I don't know whether I should trust you with the rest of my life."

Mamie's tears dried up so fast it made Joel blink.

"I guess I don't know what to say about that," she snapped.

"Which is why I'm suggesting counseling. Are you in or not?"

"I'm in," Mamie said. "But I don't want to ever hear you say that again."

"Fine," Joel said. "But now that you know I'm thinking it, I won't have to."

Mamie wanted to be mad again, but instinct told her to suck it up and play nice or hunt herself up a lawyer. And she really, really didn't want to lose her husband.

Unaware of her ex-siblings' drama, Gracie was in survival mode, in the process of starting from scratch to house and feed herself again.

She dressed in a pair of her black Walmart slacks, a red knit shirt, and slipped on her old sandals. With her dark hair down and lip gloss her only makeup, she left the motel for the leasing company, following the GPS app on her phone, going up and down the winding streets until she reached the address.

She entered the office, hopeful.

The receptionist smiled. "Good afternoon. Can I help you?"

"I'm Gracie Dunham. Sam Wainwright is expecting me."

And then a man came up the hall with a smile on his face and his hand out. He reminded Gracie of a professor she'd had in college. She'd liked the professor. She was still reserving judgment on Sam.

"Good to meet you, Gracie. I'm Sam. Are you ready to go for a ride?"

"Yes. And thank you for remembering me. Finding a decent, furnished apartment appears to be next to impossible here."

"Oh...hey...my job is to help people find homes. I still had your info and didn't think it would hurt to let you know. Furnished apartments are not a common commodity," he said, then glanced back at his receptionist. "We're going to look at some properties. Call if you need me," he said, then escorted Gracie out to his red SUV.

"Fire engine red and roomy," Sam said as he opened the door for her to get in.

Gracie was grateful for the leg room as she slid into the passenger seat and buckled up. Sam got in, too, and started up the car, jacking up the air conditioner.

"Let me know if that's too cold," he said.

Gracie sighed. "It feels heavenly," she said, as the blast of cool air hit her square in the face, and then to make the ride perfect, Sam's radio was on country music.

"Do you like country music?" Sam asked, as he turned down the volume a bit so they could talk.

Gracie nodded. "I'm from Texas. I grew up on it."

"Ah...what part of Texas?" Sam asked.

"West Texas, about ten miles outside of Sweetwater."

"Whoa! The geographic opposite of Branson, for sure."

"It's why I'm here," Gracie said, and then sat back, absently listening to Sam as they drove.

"You said you're job hunting? What kind of jobs are you looking for?"

"I have a degree in business, with a minor in communications, and a year of internship with an event planner in Dallas, which was my chosen field. But that was nine years ago, so I'll probably wind up waiting tables. I'll take whatever I am offered, and with thanks."

Sam nodded, and kept driving, pointing out different businesses and points of interest as they wound their way further into what was obviously an older part of Branson.

"This is considered the historic area of town. As you see, we're in a pretty ritzy part of the city right now. Lucy Bedford's property is just up ahead. It's the white, two-story with the huge wrap-around porch. The garage apartment is at the back of the property. I think you'll like the privacy this offers. It's an apartment, but in its own structure. No upstairs or downstairs. No neighbors making noise."

Sam slowed down to take the turn, then accelerated up the sloping driveway, past the perfectly manicured lawn and shrubbery as well as the grand old home, to the apartment at the rear of the property.

"The bottom part used to be a carriage house and is now your private garage. It's built out of native rock. The apartment above was added to it about forty years ago."

"That's a plus," she said.

Sam nodded. "There's more. You can get into the apartment two ways. There are stairs inside the garage, which means you don't have to deal with the weather to get in or out of your car. And, then the obvious way—the stairs you see on the outside of the building." He pulled up and parked, and they both got out. He keyed in a code at the garage door. Lights came on inside, revealing a concrete floor and shelving, and then a set of stairs against the far wall.

"It's single file up those steps. After you," he said.

Gracie grabbed the metal handrail, went up the stairs in seconds, then stood at the landing, waiting for Sam to catch up.

"I'm slow, but steady," he said, and then unlocked the door and went in, turning on lights as he went, with Gracie coming in behind him.

Gracie smelled lemon oil and sighed. It already smelled like home.

"As you can see, it's all open up here. You walk right into the kitchen, which makes it handy to unload groceries. Then you have a perfect line of sight to the small living area and the television while you cook. Everything you need to keep house is here. Dishes, flatware, glasses, etc. The refrigerator is a newer model with the freezer at the bottom. Ice and water dispenser in the door. Lots of storage. There's a small pantry here, a dishwasher, and a full-size gas stove."

Gracie didn't know where to look first. The cabinets were natural wood, which she loved, as was the wide-planked flooring. The countertops were black quartz with gold veining, and the appliances were all stainless.

But it was the living room furniture that intrigued her. They were a mishmash of pieces all upholstered in velvet. One chair was in jade green, the other in gold. The sofa was a darker shade of gold with tufted upholstery and ornate carvings on the wood frame.

Gracie sat in one of the chairs and leaned back.

"I'm from the land of blowing dust, cattle, and coyotes. Sitting in a chair upholstered in velvet is a first, and it's very comfortable."

Sam grinned.

"A definite historical vibe," he said. "The fireplace is an electric insert. Works with a flip of the switch. You'd be surprised at what a difference it makes to the comfort in the winter months."

"I love it," Gracie said.

Sam led the way down the hall.

"Wait until you see the bedroom."

Gracie walked in, took one look at the old cherry wood canopy bed and a matching cherry wood dresser and sighed. Straight out of her childhood fantasy. Was this really happening?

"It's beautiful," she said.

"The single bath is directly across the hall," Sam said. "Check it out."

Gracie poked her head in the door, saw the claw-foot tub and a sink mounted in a cabinet similar to the ones in the kitchen, and fell in love.

"It has central air conditioning and heating," Sam added. "You pay your own utilities, which include water, sewer, and garbage pickup. Electricity is included in your rent. All the services are on right now. All you need to do is notify the city utility company. They'll set up your account and switch it into your name. The television has basic cable right now. If you want to add more, that's on you, and it's internet and WiFi ready."

"Besides rent, how much is the deposit?" Gracie asked.

"Ordinarily it would be the equivalent of another month's rent, but that's one of the things Lucy said she will waive. When we fill out the papers, I'll run a credit check and a background check. It's how we protect our clients," Sam said.

Gracie shrugged. "I have no idea if I even have a credit rating anymore. It's been so long since I worked at a paying job. But it used to be good. Will I be rejected because of the credit rating?"

"Not according to Lucy. She gets all huffy about our rules, and says they make everything too hard for people trying to get by. And since it's her property, she can pretty much call the shots. We do require automatic withdrawal for monthly payments."

Gracie nodded. "I can give you my banker in Sweetwater as a reference. He knew I was leaving town. He'll transfer my money to whichever bank I choose here. I was just looking for a place to live so I'd have an address before I set that up. I hope it's going to be this address because I want it...so much," Gracie said.

Sam clapped his hands.

"I had a feeling this place would suit you, and now that you've decided to lease it, Lucy wants to meet you."

"I'd like to meet her, too," Gracie said.

"Then follow me," Sam said. He turned off all the lights and led the way back downstairs. He punched in the code to lower the door. "Oh...there's a remote control for this door. It's at the office. You'll get it with the keys. Now let's go meet your new landlady. I think you're going to like her."

CHAPTER TEN

$\mathcal{L}$ucy had dressed to meet the girl. She believed first impressions were important. And showing your true colors was also important to Lucy, which is why she'd fluffed and sprayed the purple tips of her white hair starch-stiff. Her earrings dangled, and the floral caftan she wore ebbed and flowed as she moved.

But now she was at the window, watching Sam and her new renter approaching. Sam was talking non-stop, as always. The woman with him seemed polite and attentive, but Lucy saw the wall around that girl as plainly as if it had been brick and mortar. She was one of the walking wounded, and it showed.

When they reached the sidewalk and headed to the house, Lucy took off for the front door and was approaching the foyer when the doorbell rang.

"I've got it, Muriel!" Lucy said, and waved off the housekeeper, then opened to door with a flourish. "Sam! Come in, come in," Lucy said, then stepped aside as they entered the foyer.

Sam immediately made introductions.

"Lucy, this is Gracie Dunham. Gracie, this is Lucy Bedford, your new landlord."

Lucy beamed. "Oh, I'm so happy you liked the place. It's a little eclectic for some, but it pleases me. Come sit with me a bit. I know Sam's busy, but stay long enough to have something cold to drink, will you?"

"Sounds good to me," Sam said. "Gracie?"

Gracie nodded. "Yes, please."

"I have coffee, iced tea, and soft drinks? What's your poison?"

"I'll have an iced tea. Unsweet," Sam said. "I'm supposed to be watching my sugar intake."

Lucy nodded. "And Gracie, what can I get for you?"

"I'd love a Coke, if you have them. If not, anything cold is perfect."

Lucy beamed. "Do I have Coke? It's my go-to soft drink. We are simpatico! Get comfy. I won't be a minute," she said, and sailed out of the living room, yelling at Muriel as she went.

Sam looked at Gracie. "Well, what do you think?"

Gracie looked around at the interior of this house and knew exactly where the furnishings for the apartment had come from.

"I think she's amazing," Gracie said.

A few minutes later, Lucy returned, Muriel behind her, pushing a tea cart with drinks and enough snacks to feed a football team.

"Gracie, this is Muriel. Muriel, Gracie is going to be the new tenant in the apartment."

Muriel smiled, then began passing out drinks and putting little plates of sweet cakes and savories on the coffee table in front of them.

"Don't be shy," Lucy said. "If you don't help me eat these, I'll just have to walk farther on the treadmill tomorrow."

Sam laughed out loud. "What part of 'cutting back on sugar' did you not understand?"

Lucy grinned. "It's all on you, boy. Willpower or greed. Your choice." Then she pointed at Gracie. "This one needs some coddling. I like to feed people, Gracie. Please enjoy."

Gracie took one look at all the treats, picked up a napkin and a little plate, and loaded it. She popped a little ham roll-up into her mouth and chewed, savoring dill, cream cheese, and something else...something salty in the spread.

"It's capers," Lucy said. "You're tasting capers."

Gracie blinked. "How did you know what—"

Lucy giggled. "I experiment with foods. That fools a lot of people."

Gracie filed that taste away for future reference, then one by one, ate everything she'd put on her plate, sipping Coke in between. It was the most perfect day she'd had in forever.

And then they were gone—back to the leasing company—signing papers, calling her banker, verifying her information, getting surprised by a decent credit rating, and then finally, writing a check for her first month's rent.

Sam handed over her paperwork, gave her the keys and the garage remote, and then reminded her. "Any time you have an issue with the property, you contact us. That's what we're for."

Gracie nodded. "And I can move in now?"

Sam grinned. "Yes, ma'am. You're good to go."

Gracie dropped the remote and the keys into her purse, then picked up her paperwork, hugging it to her chest.

"Thank you for going out of your way to help me."

"Of course. It's what I do. Think you can find your way back there?" he asked.

Gracie nodded. "I've had people go missing on me before, but I've yet to lose me. I'll be fine."

IT WAS NEARING SUNDOWN WHEN GRACIE FINALLY PULLED BACK INTO the garage for the last time. She'd brought in all her luggage first, and then had left to go get groceries. She shut the garage door, then got out and began carrying bags up the stairs. It took three trips to get everything inside, and then there was the business of putting it all up.

She had yet to unpack her clothing or check her email to see if she'd gotten any responses on her job hunting, but there was time now. She began putting up the groceries, and when she came to the notepad and pen that she'd bought, she tore off the packaging, got out the pen and wrote—

I, Gracie, am takin' care of business. I have someplace to be.

LUCY BEDFORD WATCHED WITH DELIGHT AS HER NEW RENTER CAME AND went. She was building her nest, and that was a good thing. A person needed to touch things and move things in a place until it felt right. It was going to be a joy to get to know Gracie, but all in good time—and at her pace.

JOHN GATLIN WALKED OUT OF E.R., HIS LONG LEGS MAKING EVEN longer shadows on the pavement as he paused to remind himself of where he'd parked. Getting the call that one of his employees had gotten hurt on the job was part of being the boss. Fortunately, the injuries had not been serious, but he'd still had to make a flying trip to the hospital with all the insurance information. It did, however, leave him shorthanded, which meant tomorrow he'd be on the job with that crew. It had been quite some time since he'd been in the field, but he was looking forward to riding a mower. It was far better than riding a desk.

Once he located his truck, he jogged toward it. All he wanted now was to go home, take a shower, have a cold beer and some pizza.

He took the highway out of Branson toward Table Rock Lake. As usual, the traffic made the trip slower than it should have been, but he was used to it. It gave him a little time to unwind as he drove and to admire the beauty of the Ozarks.

Five years ago, he'd abandoned the city and bought a home near the lake. Even though the drive to get out here meant dealing with traffic, it had been worth it.

When he finally saw his turnoff ahead, he began to relax. The road leading home was always the Off switch to job responsibilities.

He saw the roofline first and was already envisioning the wide-open floor plan and his kitchen. He'd left dishes in the sink this morning and still needed to do a load of laundry, but all of that would be dealt with before he ended his day.

Right now, the sight of the two-story log home made him smile. He watched morning light appearing over the trees from the front deck, and the sun setting below them from the back. The grounds around it were laid out with greenery and native rock, and he'd laid a curved blacktop drive within the trees to keep from cutting any of them down.

He'd worked hard for what he had. A thriving business. A beautiful home. Plenty of friends. The only thing lacking in John Gatlin's world was someone to come home to.

He grinned as a rabbit hopped out of the front flower bed and slipped beneath the porch pilings. He liked being the sanctuary for wildlife. Sometimes there were deer in his back yard late in the evening, and rabbits and raccoons abounded.

His friends kept telling him he either needed to get a woman or a dog. But the dog would not abide the wildlife, and John didn't want to trade one for the other. So, the deer and the rabbits had won out.

As for the woman, John had already lived a life of merry-go-round dating, none of which had worked out. He was at the point where either fate would provide, or it would not.

He parked in the garage around back and got out, pausing briefly to check out the property, saw nothing amiss, and went inside.

Cool air met him at the door.

He took off his work boots in the utility room, and then padded through the house and up the stairs to his room and stripped. As he was emptying his pockets, he saw the little silver angel still with his change. He'd been carrying it ever since the day he'd seen her. He just couldn't turn loose of the hope that he'd see her somewhere again, and if he did, it was going to be his excuse to talk to her. He had never been this focused on a total stranger and was inclined to blame it on the solitude of his personal life.

His family lived in Kansas, but ever since he'd bought this place, he'd become the host for the family festivities at holidays. His parents, his sister and husband, and their two kids always came and stayed. It was unbridled chaos, and he loved it and them.

At least their visits were something to look forward to.

~

GRACIE HAD EMPTIED HER SUITCASES AND SHELVED THEM DOWN IN THE garage. The groceries were put up, and she was eating a cookie as she prowled through the rooms, opening doors, looking in drawers, finding out what she had to work with.

It had been a long time since she'd actually cooked on a stove, but this place was cool and clean, and the hardwood floors were smooth beneath her feet.

She had so many options for her evening meal that she couldn't decide on anything and wound up with a bowl of cereal and a can of Coke, because sometimes the familiar was what was needed to settle. She took her food to the little dinette table, turned on the TV, and ate watching the evening news.

As soon as she was finished, she took her laptop into the living room, and curled up on the velvet-tufted sofa to let Darlene know she'd found a place to live and was actively applying for jobs.

I found an apartment. It's as eclectic as Mama was. A little bit of everything from different generations. I love it. I'm sending you the address. Job hunting is in progress. Love to all of you.

She hit Send, and then pulled her laptop into her lap to check for replies from her job applications.

There were seven, but the first six were rejections. Either the jobs had already been filled, or she had lacked the experience required.

Disappointing, but not surprising.

She opened the last one, expecting more of the same, but to her surprise, the hostess job she'd applied for at a local steakhouse had a positive response. She had a request for an in-person interview tomorrow with the manager. That was a job she could do in her sleep, and the pay was decent. All she could do was hope.

Darlene sent a return text about an hour later.

Caleb and I have been in the ER. He smashed his thumb in the car door. Ugh. He's fine. Mama, not so much. Kudos on the apartment and thanks for the address. Happy job hunting. Stay in touch. We love you.

Gracie winced just reading it. Poor Caleb. Poor Darlene.

JAMES WAS BACK AT WORK AND DEALING WITH THE LEGAL ASPECTS OF the ranch long-distance. With the mailing address changed, he continued to pay the utility bills. He'd had the furniture put in storage, was having the home painted inside and out, and new flooring and appliances replaced in the kitchen. It shamed him that he was also putting in a new central heat and air system because it was going to sit idle in an empty house. After the misery his mama and Gracie had endured, they would so have appreciated it, but he also knew if he had a decent chance of selling it, the house needed to be habitable. Right now, there was nothing more to do until the will went through probate.

Unaware that his siblings had already donated money, he had also donated ten thousand dollars into Gracie's fund before he'd left Sweetwater. It had been the only way he'd known how to get money to her without her knowing where it came from. He'd thought it would make him feel better, but it hadn't.

When people got broken, it always caused pain, and there wasn't enough money in the world to repair the damage. He consoled himself by knowing that, wherever she was, she wouldn't be hungry or homeless. He needed to remember to say daily prayers for his immortal soul, because James was still on the "me first" track, and he really didn't want to go to hell.

LONG AFTER GRACIE WAS SHOWERED AND IN HER OWN PAJAMAS READY for bed, she walked through the darkened apartment, using night-lights and moonlight by which to see. It was a thing with her—the need to know her safe place by day and by night. What a person knew, she could not fear, and Gracie did not ever want to be afraid again.

And so she moved from window to window, looking out at the grounds, and the sky, and the lights of the city, and the security lights on the neighbors' properties. Soon, she would know what was normal, and what was amiss.

She was grateful tonight.

For a man named Sam, who'd thought to call her back.

For a woman named Lucy, who had a rebel heart and a propensity for not following rules.

But for them, she would not be here in this place.

Finally, satisfied that she was where she belonged, she made her way back to that four-poster bed and climbed in.

The central air was moving through the room, stirring the canopy above her. Moonlight came through the cracks in the blinds. She didn't hear coyotes, but she did hear traffic, and she could hear faint strains of music coming from somewhere. It was good enough to sleep to.

THE ALARM WOKE GRACIE FROM A DREAMLESS SLEEP.

She rolled over to shut it off, and then remembered she had an interview this morning and leaped out of bed.

The newness of her surroundings was still a total delight, and she dawdled in the claw-foot bathtub longer than she should have, then raced into the kitchen, popped a breakfast sandwich into the microwave, and made herself a cup of coffee.

Then because she could, she ate standing up at the kitchen sink, looking out the window at a blue jay catching hell from a squirrel in the same tree.

The trees, alone, made this place special. All the green, and the shade beneath them—she couldn't wait to see what it all looked like in the winter when it snowed.

As soon as she was through eating, she ran to get dressed. She didn't know what the dress code for hostesses at this steakhouse might be, but black slacks and a black and white top should be safe, and the blouse covered up all of the scars—something the average diner would not want to be greeted with. She put on the black heels she'd worn to the funeral, which made her appear even taller, left her hair down, and pulled out a red lipstick, giving her lips a quick swipe.

At that point, this was as good as she was going to get. The steakhouse wasn't in Branson proper, but out on the road toward Table Rock Lake. She didn't know how long it would take to get there, and didn't want to be late, so she decided to leave early. It was a little after 9:00 when she got her purse, opened the garage door from the landing, and took the stairs down to her car.

She was just about to get in her car when she saw a landscape crew off to the side of Lucy's driveway, obviously getting ready to work. One of the men was offloading a riding mower and happened to look up just as she stopped to watch them. Within seconds he had the mower on the ground, and then came out of the seat and started toward her in long, hurried strides. That's when she realized she knew him.

Then she corrected herself. She didn't "know" him, but she'd seen him before—at the Hard Luck Diner, when everything had fallen out of her purse.

Before, she'd been so rattled he had barely registered in her mind, but now that she had time, she could appreciate the view.

She liked his face. High cheekbones. A bit of a hawk-like hook to his nose. And a strong jaw. His shoulders were broad. His legs were long, and the closer he came, the more she felt like running, which was weird. Men didn't scare her. Mama had scared her, but she'd never met a man that gave her pause. So, she stood her ground, waiting.

CHAPTER ELEVEN

$\mathcal{T}$he Bedford property was the second stop of the morning for Gatlin Landscaping. Lucy had been one of John's first customers, and she had stayed with him through all his struggles getting his business started and continued to applaud his success and growth.

He liked Lucy, but since he'd quit going out on daily jobs, he rarely saw her. He was hoping he'd at least get to say hello, and was helping the men unload equipment, while keeping an eye on the house, just in case she came out. He was backing the riding lawn mower off the trailer when he happened to look up. Within the seconds it took for him to register the woman standing in the doorway of the old garage as the one he'd been looking for, he jumped off the mower, without looking where he was walking, and threw out orders as he passed.

"Go ahead and start cleaning beds and edging, I'll be right back," he said, and took off toward her.

He couldn't believe she was still here. This had to be a sign. *Please God, don't let her already be taken.*

He took heart in the fact that she was watching him as intently as he was looking at her, and he hoped she remembered him. Otherwise, this long-awaited moment could turn out to be a bust.

And then they were standing face to face, and John stopped, dug his hand into the pocket where he kept his change, and pulled out the little charm.

"I have something I think belongs to you," he said, then gently took her hand and laid the angel on her palm.

Gracie gasped. Mama had given that to her the day she'd gone away to college, and she'd never taken it out of her purse. She'd had no idea it was gone and would have been devastated to lose it.

"Oh my God. Thank you...so much," Gracie said, clutching it to her chest.

John smiled.

"I was afraid I'd never see you again to return it. My name is John. John Gatlin."

Gracie dropped the charm into her purse, then held out her hand.

"I'm Gracie Dunham."

Her handshake was firm. He didn't want to let go.

"It is entirely my pleasure. So, where are you off to this morning?"

"A job interview. It's hit or miss as to whether I get it, but I have to start somewhere."

"Well, if my opinion matters, you look beautiful."

Gracie almost smiled. "If you were hiring, it would."

John laughed. "In any case, good luck."

"Thank you," Gracie said.

John nodded, then cleared his throat.

"May I ask you a question?"

"I guess," Gracie said.

"Are you single?"

He wasn't laughing. He wasn't flirting. And Gracie would have sworn he was holding his breath for the answer.

"As the day is long," she said.

John nodded. "So am I. If I had your number, I would definitely call to ask you out for coffee...or lunch...if I had your number."

Gracie's eyes narrowed. Did she want to do this? Now? "Do you know my landlady?" she asked, avoiding his request for number.

"For almost ten years. She's one of my oldest customers," he said.

131

She frowned. "I'm going to be late for my interview."

Not deterred, John pulled out a business card.

"Then here's my number. No pressure, but I'd love to hear how the interview goes, so call me tonight if you want. That has both my business and personal number. It's been a pure pleasure to meet you, Gracie. I'll be looking forward to your call."

Gracie dropped the card in her purse. "Thank you for saving my angel."

"Meant to be," John said. "Good luck on your interview."

Elated, he turned around and jogged back to his crew as Gracie backed out of the garage and drove away.

She already had the address entered into her GPS app, so she followed the directions, wasting no time looking at scenery and sights. Being prompt mattered.

This morning, she'd been completely focused on this interview, and then John Gatlin happened. He'd helped her on her first day here, then gave her something today that she'd hadn't known she'd lost. She hadn't decided if she would call him or just let all this slide, so she set him aside for now to focus on where she was going.

Her heart began pounding when she finally reached the restaurant. She knew it didn't open until eleven, but the employees' cars were already on site, and they were inside setting up for lunch.

Waiting tables had been her college job until her senior year of interning. It wasn't the actual work here that made her anxious; it was the possibility of being rejected.

The front doors were still locked, but she'd been told to call, so she did. A couple of minutes later, a waitress showed up to let her in. She tried to give Gracie the side-eye, but Gracie was too tall to intimidate, so she locked the door behind them instead.

"I'm Karen. Greg is in his office. Follow me."

If waitresses here called the boss by his first name, this could be a sign he was good to work for, Gracie thought, and followed her through the dining area, past the public restrooms, and down another hall to the office.

Karen knocked on the door, then pushed it inward.

"Your 10:00 appointment is here," she said, and walked off, leaving Gracie standing in the hall.

So, that's Greg, Gracie thought, eyeing a handsome, well-dressed man with blond highlights in his hair.

Greg Lassiter saw Gracie, liked what he saw, and came to meet her.

"Come in, come in. I'm Greg Lassiter. Just have a seat, and we'll get started," he said.

He held the chair for her as she sat, then gave her shoulder a light squeeze.

In that moment, every aspect of Gracie's creep radar came on as he seated himself across the desk. She sat up straighter, her knees together, her feet tucked beneath the chair, and stared him straight in the face.

Too full of himself to see the warning signs, Greg flashed her a wide smile, then shuffled through the application and resumé she'd submitted online.

"So, Gracie, according to your resumé, it's been several years since you have worked in the public. Was there a specific reason or was that just personal choice?"

"I was a caregiver for my mother. I stayed with her until she passed."

"Oh. I'm so sorry. My sympathies," Greg said. "So, this was recent."

Gracie nodded. "Yes, but as you can see by my resumé, I'm more than qualified for the job you're offering."

Greg nodded. "I agree. I also see you're new to Branson. Just so you know, we cater more to fine dining here, therefore I like for my hostesses to dress in what I call, after-five chic. You know...sexy, but classy. You're very tall. Some men don't like a woman to be taller than them, but you have a pretty face. If you don't mind, I'd like for you to stand up, turn around, and walk toward the door and then back. You'll be seating guests, so I want to see how you look coming and going." Then he winked. "It never hurts to see what's in the caboose, right?"

Gracie was so enraged, she was shaking. She stood, walked all the way to the door, opened it so hard it slammed against the wall, and then turned around and let him have it.

"My daddy, if he were still alive, would have beat you to within an inch of your life for what you just said to me! You want to see my ass? Then you better look fast because that's the last thing you're going to see. I don't kiss ass to get a job. I don't show my ass to get a job. And I'm not going to work for an ass to do it."

Then she slammed the door shut so hard the window rattled. She strode past employees staring at her in shock. Past the tables. Past the front desk, and then walked up to hostess station, to Karen, the waitress who'd let her in.

"You! Unlock the door and let me out."

Like everyone else in the building, Karen was staring at Gracie in shock, unable to believe what she'd just heard.

"NOW!" Gracie shouted.

Karen jumped, and then went running toward the door and unlocked it.

Gracie hit it with the flat of her hand and kept walking.

"Son-of-a-bitch!" she muttered, and then got in the car and left rubber on the pavement of the parking lot as she drove away.

The abruptness of her exit had set a fire of its own inside the restaurant. The employees were whispering among themselves.

"Who was she?"

"Does anyone know her name?"

"Man... I wish we'd gotten that on video."

"He's had that coming for years."

"I wish I'd had the guts to say that."

And then Greg came out of his office, red-faced and furious.

"Get to work! All of you. We open in less than an hour." Then he pointed to a pretty blonde. "Jessica! You'll be working hostess today. Go fix your hair and put on some makeup. And tomorrow, wear something nicer."

Jessica paled. "Please, not me, Greg. Hostess duty doesn't get tips, and I need the extra money to—"

"Don't tell me, no! Do it, or you're fired!" he shouted.

Jessica burst into tears.

Karen was horrified and feeling sorry for Jessica.

"I'll do it, Greg."

He glared at her.

"Since when does staff start rearranging my scheduling?"

Karen flinched. "I'm sorry. I was just offering to—"

"You're both fired!" Greg shouted.

Now Jessica and Karen were both crying as they went back to the employee lounge to get their things.

"Then I quit," one waiter said, threw his apron at Greg's feet, and walked out.

"I quit, too," another said, and then another, and then another, until Greg Lassiter was in the dining room alone.

His heart was pounding. This had not just fucking happened!

When he began hearing doors slamming in the kitchen area, he ran back to look.

It was empty, and every appliance had been turned off.

The whole kitchen staff was gone, and it was almost time to open! He locked the front door, then ran to the office to call his boss, Henry Owens.

What he didn't know was that one of the employees had already called him, and by the time Greg called, Henry had already been warned.

Greg had a scenario all set up for himself as he made the call, and when Henry picked up, Greg added concern in his voice to the mix.

"Hello, this is Henry."

"Henry, it's me, Greg. We have a serious situation here at The Beef Master. The whole staff pulled a walk-out and—"

"I heard," Henry said.

Greg's heart dropped. Shit.

"You did? Well, uh—"

"Yes," Henry said. "I'm going to ask you some questions, and I would like direct answers. Yes or no will suffice."

"Uh, okay, but—"

"No buts," Henry said. "Did you have an interview for a hostess job this morning that went awry?"

"Yes, but it wasn't my—"

"Yes or no, remember?" Henry said. "Did your applicant actually say to you, and I'm paraphrasing, 'I won't kiss ass for a job. I won't show my ass for a job. And I won't work for an ass to get it'?"

Greg sighed. "Yes."

"Did you insult her?" Henry asked.

"No! Of course not!" Greg said.

"Then tell me exactly what you said to warrant her outburst, and I'll be the judge."

Greg took a deep breath, trying to even remember what all he'd been saying. "I was explaining that I needed an attractive woman for the position. She was very tall. I mentioned her height, because you and I both know men don't like women to be taller than them. And I told her we catered to fine dining for our clientele and would want someone dressing in what I called classy chic...and something about sexy."

Henry interrupted. "You said 'sexy'?"

Greg frowned. "Yes."

"Go on," Henry said.

"I asked her to walk to the door and back, because when a hostess is seating guests, their view is of her is her backside and I want—"

At that point, Henry lost it.

"You did not actually ask her to do that!"

Greg stuttered. "Well, yes, but—"

Now Henry was shouting. "Were you hiring for a hostess or a hooker? Is there something going on beyond fine dining at my restaurant that I know nothing about?"

Greg's stomach rolled. "No! Of course not. I didn't—I wouldn't..."

"But you did!" Henry said. "We'll be lucky if we don't get a sexual harassment suit filed against us. So, what the fuck else did you do to cause the whole staff to walk out? And don't tell me nothing because I don't believe for a second that they walked out in unity over a total stranger."

Greg's voice had gone from assertive to begging, and he didn't even know it.

"I guess I was in shock at the way that woman reacted. I mean, it came out of nowhere and—"

"Bullshit. We have already established that you insulted her, so no, it did not come out of nowhere. Have you been treating the rest of the staff like this?"

"Not that I was aware of," Greg said.

"Then what happened?" Henry snapped.

"I told one of the waitresses she'd have to work the hostess position. She refused, arguing that—"

"I'm sorry, but that's not what I was told," Henry said. "How about I tell you what I heard, and then you fill in the blanks. You told Jessica she was going to work the hostess shift, and she asked you to choose someone else because she needed her waitress tips. And you lost your temper and fired her. Then Karen offered to do it for Jessica, and you fired her for arguing with you. And right about then, the wait staff started standing up for their own people, and they all walked out on you. Does that sound about right?"

Greg sighed. "I might have lost my temper, but—"

"That required a yes or no answer, not an excuse," Henry said. "Jessica has worked for the restaurant since we opened. You have been working there for a little over five years. So, you're fired, and she is not. Lock up, and when you leave, drop the keys in the mailbox out front. I will be at the restaurant within the hour to contact the staff, myself. Now give me the name of the woman you interviewed and her contact info. I need to put out your goddamn fire before she sues us."

"You don't have to do this," Greg said. "I can—"

"Yes, yes, I do have to," Henry said. "Send me the info now, then get your stuff and get out," Henry said, and hung up.

Typing in the name Gracie Dunham made Greg shudder all over again. It felt like he was evoking the devil because she'd scared him that bad. And then he'd taken his shock out on the staff, and now here he was—leaving with his tail between his legs. Well hell, and all that went with it, he thought.

137

He got a sack from the kitchen, emptied his personal property from his desk into it, and walked out, locking the door behind him. He dropped the keys in the box, just like he'd been told. This incident would be all over the restaurant industry here before nightfall, so his chance of working somewhere else here was nil.

He'd always wanted to live and work in Vegas, and since he couldn't show his face here again without being laughed at, it might be time to get away before he got caught up in a lawsuit.

UNAWARE OF THE ENSUING FALLOUT OF HER INTERVIEW, GRACIE WAS ON her way back into Branson, too pissed to even think about crying. The reality of job hunting was setting in, and something told her she might run into more like that restaurant manager.

Shit happened.

And now she was over it.

She needed to find a bank and get her money transferred, and she needed to shop for clothes.

"What a son-of-a-bitch," she said, again, and kept driving. She knew there were outlet malls in the area, and she'd seen Chico's, White Barn, and some interesting boutiques. She had all freaking afternoon to work off the insult, and then maybe tomorrow she'd try somewhere else. But not today. Not while she still felt like taking somebody's fool head off.

She was all the way back in Branson and looking for a place to park at Chico's when her phone rang. She glanced at Caller ID and frowned. She didn't know any Henry Owens, but she'd sent out a lot of applications. She pulled in to the first empty parking spot she saw and answered.

"Hello."

"Gracie Dunham?"

"Yes?"

"Miss Dunham, my name is Henry Owens. I own the Beef Master Grill. I just learned of what happened to you today and wanted to call and personally apologize for the appalling way in which you were treated. I also want you to know that Mr. Lassiter is no longer employed with me. I hope you will accept my apology, and if you so choose, I would be honored to interview you, personally, for the job."

Gracie was stunned. "Thank you for the apology, but I don't want back in that work environment."

"Mr. Lassiter lost his cool after you left, and to make a long story short, the entire wait staff and kitchen staff walked out on him. At this moment, the place is closed. I'm trying to get the staff back for an evening service and will be taking Greg's place myself until I can hire a new manager. So I can assure you, there will be no hard feelings in that respect," Henry said.

"Good Lord," Gracie said.

"That's not what I said when I found out about it. I do not condone sexual harassment on any level. That will not happen again on my property, but it's your call. If it makes you feel uncomfortable, I understand, but I would still like to meet you...at your convenience, of course."

Gracie didn't hesitate.

"I'll meet with you, but that's all I can promise."

"Wonderful. Thank you for understanding. Do you want to try this again tomorrow...say 10:00?" Henry asked.

"Yes, I can do that," Gracie said.

"Excellent! I'll see you in the morning. Call this number when you get here, and I'll let you in, myself."

"Yes, sir," Gracie said.

"Thank you," Henry said. "And again, my sincere apology for what happened. By the way...I saw on your application that you are new to Branson. Have you found a place to stay yet?"

"Yes."

"Excellent," Henry said, and disconnected.

Gracie stared at her phone, then dropped it back in her purse. Talk about whiplash. She'd been furious only minutes ago, and then this happened! Not only did she have a second interview, but a big apology from the owner himself.

She could only imagine his stress level right now. The whole staff had walked out! That would have been something to see. But that was his headache, not hers, and right now, she needed wardrobe and shoes.

Chico's was first, and then she'd go from there.

JOHN WORKED ALL DAY WITH ONLY ONE THOUGHT IN MIND: HOPING Gracie would call him tonight. He was excited and hopeful, and trying not to make too much of a new thing. But he felt fourteen all over again, remembering the day the new girl in school just smiled at him, and when she had, he'd gotten so flustered, he'd walked into the wrong classroom and sat down before he'd realized he wasn't supposed to be there.

Gracie was the same, wild, excited, unknown.

He'd bombed out with the new girl, but he had a better feeling about Gracie. Fate had already put them together twice, without either one of them even trying. He was older and wiser, now. This time, he wasn't lost. He knew exactly where he was going.

When the workday was finally over, he stopped to pick up smoked ribs and sides, then headed home. As always, he began unwinding as he drove, and by the time he reached the cabin, he was at peace.

He ate ribs on the back deck while watching the deer coming out of the forest and the birds going home to roost. When he was through, he carried everything back inside, cleaned up the kitchen, and then went back out with a cold beer to wait for Gracie's call.

GRACIE HAD SHOPPED FOR CLOTHES, SHOES, AND EVEN UNDERWEAR, and as she was browsing through a mall, stopped in at a nail salon for a mani-pedi, then had to blink away tears at the luxury of having that done. It had been so long since she'd taken care of herself, that she didn't know how to receive it. She finally left the mall, dumped her bags in her car, and drove away. As she left the parking lot, she saw a Gatlin Landscaping truck pulling a trailer load of equipment, and thought of John. He must be something of a successful businessman to have his own company and multiple crews on the job.

She wondered about the wisdom of calling a total stranger and was still not convinced she should do it.

She was hot and too tired to go looking for a new bank. For a day that had started out good, then gone bad, then sort of leveled itself back out, she was ready for it to be over.

Tonight, she would cook. And she would hang up her new clothes, take a long, soaking bath in her tub, and sleep without fear. And that's all she would ask of this day.

She stopped at a drive-through on the way home to get a Coke, and by the time she pulled into the garage, she had cooled off, and the Coke was gone. She punched the remote, watching as the door went shut behind her car, and then grabbed her bags and went inside, announcing herself as she went.

"I, Gracie, am home!"

The place pleased her. Old velvet, hardwood floors, cool and clean, with a faint, but lingering scent of lemon oil.

She dumped all of her purchases on the bed, glanced up at the cuckoo clock she'd already hung on the wall. She changed into old clothes then began hanging up the new stuff and putting away new shoes.

She sat down in the easy chair beside the window to braid her hair, and as she did, looked up, then blinked. Just for a moment, she'd forgotten where she was and had expected to see the dry landscape and rusty corrals beyond the old farmhouse.

Her view, instead, was neatly clipped hedges, freshly watered flower beds, and huge trees casting long shadows upon the newly mown grass. And it was beautiful.

She finished braiding her hair, and then got her phone to check her balance at the bank. She hadn't spent a lot of money, but until she had a job and a paycheck coming in, spending anything felt like a risk.

To her shock, the twenty-one thousand plus balance that she'd had upon her arrival, was now a little over thirty-one thousand dollars.

"Oh my God," Gracie mumbled, unable to believe what she was seeing.

It never occurred to her than any of her siblings were responsible. She was just grateful for the added security, which gave her the leeway to find the right job.

She flipped the braid off her shoulder and headed for the kitchen. She hadn't eaten since breakfast, and all of a sudden, she was starving. She made herself some iced tea, then got out a skillet and a little package of pork chops. It had been such a long time since she'd had the luxury of cooking that it felt strange. But the familiarity of a lifetime of kitchen skills soon kicked in, and she was banging lids and turning the perfectly browned chops like a pro.

CHAPTER TWELVE

*T*he dishwasher was running, and Gracie was in the living room, kicked back in the blue velvet chair with her feet up on the matching hassock, watching TV.

The mindless luxury of no longer being responsible for Mama, or answering to anyone else, had become her reality. The weather alert for this area called for thunderstorms. Where Gracie came from, rain was money falling from the sky.

Then she remembered John Gatlin. She wanted to hear his voice again and ran to get his card, then called the number.

He answered so abruptly, she wondered if he'd actually been waiting for her to call.

"Hello?" he said.

"Hi, John. This is Gracie Dunham."

"Gracie! I'm so glad you called. I've been hoping you would. Have you had your dinner?"

"Yes. I'm full of pork chops and watching TV."

John chuckled. "We both went the pig route tonight. I had smoked ribs, and I'm watching two deer eating my grass so I don't have to mow it."

She had an immediate image of forest. "You don't live in the city?"

"No. I have a log home just outside of Branson. It's off the main road, back up in the trees. It's all green and peaceful here."

"That sounds amazing," Gracie said.

"It is. I'd love to show it to you sometime...if you'd like." Gracie was suddenly silent, and her hesitation was just enough to warn John not to move too fast. "So, how did your interview go?"

Gracie realized her silence had been taken as a no, but it was too late to go back and explain how rusty she was in the dating scene. His question was the perfect shift she needed.

"Using one of my daddy's favorite sayings...it was nothing less than a shit show."

John laughed, and then immediately apologized.

"Oh, God...sorry. I wasn't laughing because the interview was a bust. I was just appreciating your daddy's humor. He must be a pistol."

"He was," Gracie said. "He's been gone a long time."

John sighed. Another *faux pas*. "I'm sorry. Where was your interview?"

"At a place called The Beef Master Grill."

"I pass that place every day going to work and coming home. What on earth happened?"

"I had an interview for a hostess job. I'm beyond being picky about a position anywhere, considering how long I've been out of work. I've had a lot of rejections since I got here, and this was my first positive response."

"I get that," John said. "It's about ninety percent of why I started my own business. I couldn't even get hired to park cars when I first arrived."

"Well, that actually makes me feel better," Gracie said.

John chuckled. "Happy to oblige. So, what happened to you?"

"I arrive. The manager comments about my unemployed status for the past nine years. I reminded him why, which I'd put on the application, and I point to my resumé, reminding him of my work history along with my degree, and that I had more than enough qualifications for a hostess position."

"Can I ask why you hadn't been working? Or is that too personal?" John asked.

"Not personal. Just a fact of my life. My mother was diagnosed with dementia, and I turned down the job I had waiting when I finished college to stay home and take care of her until she died," Gracie said.

John took a deep breath. "For nine years."

"Yes."

"Whoa."

"That doesn't even come close," Gracie said.

"Sorry," John said. "So, back to your interview."

Gracie sighed. "This is where it went downhill. Bottom line, the only qualifications he was interested in were how I looked, what I wore, and if my butt was sexy enough for the job."

John was stunned. "Are you serious? Do women always have to go through that?" he asked.

"I don't know what the protocol is these days, but I'm not working for a jackass."

John frowned. "Are you okay?"

"Oh, I'm fine, and I got a phone call from the owner, Henry Owens, calling to apologize for what happened."

"I know Henry. I wonder how he found out?" John asked.

"Apparently, the staff told him the manager flipped out after I left. He wound up insulting some other employees, and they all walked out and called Henry. Then he fired the manager and was in the process of trying to get all the wait staff back when he called me. He kept apologizing, said he'd interview me himself tomorrow if I would want to reconsider."

"Are you going to?" John asked.

Gracie sighed. "I said I'd talk to him, but that's all."

John sighed. "What a horrible day you've had."

"Not as bad as the manager who got fired," Gracie said.

John chuckled. "True. I'd tell you about my day getting chased by a dog that got out of the neighbor's yard, but I don't think I can compete with your story."

"Oh no! Did he bite you?"

"No. He was chasing the mower I was on, just like he chases cars."

Gracie laughed. "Oh. That's a whole other scenario. Now that would have been a sight to see."

"You have the best laugh," John said.

Gracie was taken aback by the compliment. "I haven't used it a lot lately."

John thought back to the day in the Hard Luck when he'd asked if she was okay. *Not yet, but I will be,* she'd said. So now, he knew she'd been in exile with her mother, but he still didn't know what had happened. Something, or someone, had hurt her terribly.

"Will you go out with me sometime?" he asked.

Gracie's mind raced. There were times when you knew the words coming out of your mouth were going to change your life, and this was one of them.

"Maybe...probably... But I need to concentrate on finding work right now."

"No problem," John said. "Just knowing you're thinking about it works for me. Would it be okay if I wish you good luck again, or would you rather I keep my best wishes to myself?"

Gracie laughed. "I'll take your best wishes and say thank you."

"You're welcome. Sleep well, Gracie. It has been very nice talking to you."

"I liked talking to you, too," she said, and disconnected.

John didn't want to lose the connection, but she was gone. He had always been an all or nothing kind of guy, and he already knew he wanted Gracie.

Please God, let her want me back.

GRACIE WAS STILL RIDING THE HIGH FROM THEIR PHONE CALL AS SHE turned off the TV, then went to get her laptop and a Coke. She began checking email to see if there were any new job openings that had posted since she'd last looked.

There *were* two that were commission only, which she automatically rejected. Gracie knew her limitations. She didn't have a salesperson bone in her body. The bullshit genes in their family had all gone to Daphne and James. Then she shook off the thought and went back to filling out applications.

She was still working when the storm rolled in, bringing wind, then the lightning and thunder that came rumbling and grumbling through the hills on which Branson was built.

Gracie ran to the window to look out and was standing there when the rain hit, splattering it against the windows and rattling down upon the roof. Within minutes, she could hear water running through the gutters and downspouts.

"Oh my lord, Mama! Look at it pour!"

She stood, transfixed, watching the lightning off in the distance, feeling the vibration of the thunder within her while the rain poured, soaking into the grounds and running down the sloping driveway to the streets below.

Finally, she gave up and went to bed, set the alarm for tomorrow's interview, and then fell asleep, listening to money coming out of the sky.

And dreamed.

GRACIE WAS MAKING COOKIES.

Mama stood beside her, one hand cupped as if holding a bowl, the other curled as if holding a spoon.

When Gracie stirred, Delia stirred.

When Gracie added ingredients, Delia added ingredients, mimicking everything Gracie did. And every now and then, she would look up, see Gracie, and jump back in surprise.

"Where did you come from girl?"

"Sweetwater. I came from Sweetwater," Gracie said, and kept stirring.

"Do I know you?" Delia asked.

Gracie sighed. "Yes, ma'am."

"What's your name?" Delia asked.

"My name is Gracie," and then she dumped a package of chocolate chips into the cookie dough.

Delia stopped, and then walked away from the cabinet all the way to the kitchen door and looked out, and when she turned around, Gracie saw she was crying and ran to her.

"What's wrong, Mama? Why are you crying?"

"I think I lost my babies. I remember having them, and I don't see them anymore."

Gracie's heart broke. "We're not lost, Mama. We grew up. Your babies are all grown up now."

Delia wiped her eyes with the backs of her hands.

"They're not lost?"

Gracie put her arms around Delia and pulled her close, patting her back and rocking her where they stood. Mother and daughter had traded places. Gracie had become the parent, and now Mama was her child...her little mama.

"No, ma'am. They're not lost, and I'm here taking care of you. We're just fine, you and me. And we're making cookies, remember?"

"I like cookies," Delia said.

Gracie took her by the hand and led her back to the counter.

"Here, you stir the dough. I'm going to get the baking sheets."

She handed the spoon to her mother and made a dash for the baking pans before something untoward happened to the dough.

When she turned around, Delia had her hands in it, picking out the chips.

"Mama, what are you doing?" Gracie said.

"Picking out the weevils. The flour must of gone bad."

"That's chocolate, not bugs. Here, you go wash your hands, and I'll finish," Gracie said.

"Wash my hands," Delia said, and then sat down in the floor and started licking the dough from her fingers.

"Whatever it takes, Lord. Whatever it takes," Gracie said.

. . .

THE ALARM WENT OFF JUST AS GRACIE TOOK THE COOKIES OUT OF THE oven. She opened her eyes to the canopy over her bed and remembered.

West Texas was gone.

Mama was gone.

That Gracie was gone.

"That's then, and this is now, and I have prospects," she said, then threw back the covers and headed for the shower.

~

LAST NIGHT'S RAIN HAD PUT A HALT TO MOWING LAWNS, BUT LATER, John would send crews out to clip hedges and weed flower beds. Later, they would be planting shrubs and trees at a new home site.

He'd wanted to call Gracie this morning and then hadn't. Instinct told him to be mindful with her. She'd already dealt with a pushy, sexist asshole. He didn't want any part of his growing feelings for her to be misunderstood, so he went about his morning, making breakfast and then leaving for work.

The little rabbit was out beneath some shrubbery as John got in his truck.

"See you this evening, little guy," he called out, then drove away.

He thought about Gracie again as he passed The Beef Master Grill. He admired the stance she'd taken yesterday and knew it would take guts to go back there again. He also knew the interview today would be okay because Henry Owens was a good man. He hoped, for her sake, she got the job.

~

GRACIE WAS SEMI-SORRY THAT SHE'D EVEN AGREED TO THIS SECOND interview, but she'd said she would go, and she never went back on her word. But today, she was confident of the gray tailored slacks and a white blouse with three-quarter length sleeves she was wearing, and she'd put her hair in a braid. Her new shoes were flats, and her only makeup was lip gloss. She was as ready as she was going to be to do this again.

She had the window down in the car as she backed out of the garage. The air smelled rain-washed fresh, but she was uneasy—like there was something she'd forgotten to do. It made her antsy.

Just as she was about to drive away, her phone signaled a text. She put the car in park and read the message, then sat a few moments before responding.

Now she had one more interview today besides The Beef Master. An interview for a job at the concierge desk at one of the hotels. Options were good. She may, or may not, get a job offer from either, but this felt like progress.

It was straight up 10:00 when she pulled up in front of the restaurant, called Henry's number, and then waited, watching the front door. When he appeared, she got out, slung her purse over her shoulder, and headed for the entrance.

As she did, she shivered. That same, "didn't feel right" vibe was still with her, and then an older man with gray hair was holding the door open and smiling, and she let it all go.

"Good morning, Gracie. I'm Henry Owens. Thank you for coming. I've already spoken to the staff. They know I asked you back. They want you to know you are welcome, whatever you decide."

"Thank you," Gracie said.

"Of course," Henry said. "Let's go to the office to talk, shall we?"

Staff saw her entering and stopped what they were doing out of curiosity, maybe wondering if Henry would offer her a job. Or wondering if she would take it.

Again, Gracie sat in front of the desk as Henry took a seat behind it, then he looked up at her and smiled.

"I've already read your resumé. You are over-qualified for the job. We both know that, but I like to know my employees beyond just names. It makes for trust that works both ways. That's how I found out about what happened. My employees trusted me enough to call, so I could hear it from them as to why they'd walked out."

"I don't talk about myself much. Why don't you ask questions and

I'll answer," Gracie said.

Henry smiled. "I can do that. What caused your hiatus from the work force?"

"I was a caregiver for my mother. She had dementia. She recently passed."

The lack of emotion in her voice said a lot.

"I am so sorry," Henry said. "My mother had Alzheimer's. Our family called it the long death."

"It is that," Gracie said. "I didn't get to ask any questions when I was here before. May I?"

"Of course," Henry said.

She proceeded to question him about working hours, second shifts, pay scale, raises, and what, if any, benefits were attached to the job.

Henry answered without hesitation, answering all of her questions and concerns and ending with the rate of pay.

"Hostess positions pay fifteen dollars an hour, which comes out to $2100.00 a month for the shifts they work, or more if you wind up working extra hours for someone in an emergency."

Gracie nodded. She knew it would be less after everything was taken out, but considering her rent, and the fuel costs to drive out here and back every day, it would be tight.

"Just so you know, I am offering you the job," Henry added.

Gracie sighed, still feeling uneasy. "I appreciate it. I do have another interview today, so I will hold my decision until that's over."

Henry sighed. "I understand. I so wish you had not had such a bad experience yesterday, but I am grateful you trusted me enough to come back. I hope you decide in our favor." He stood. "Thank you for coming. I'll walk you out."

Gracie felt all eyes on her as they moved through the dining room but didn't look up. Yesterday had poisoned this place for her. She needed a positive vibe, and this wasn't it.

It was after eleven by the time she got back to Branson, so she found the hotel where her next interview would be held, and parked, but didn't immediately get out.

The concierge job would be dealing with the public. The pay wasn't great, but it could get her foot in the door to a better position, and the drive from home to work would be short. She wanted to like it because she already knew she wasn't going back to The Beef Master Grill.

She was in the hotel on time and seated in an outer office waiting for her name to be called. There were two other young women, and one man, also waiting. Probably to be interviewed for the same job.

And then a door opened. A pretty young blonde came out and walked past them, her heels clicking on the faux marble floor as she left. The man behind her stood in the doorway and called the next name.

"Gracie Dunham."

Gracie got up and followed him inside.

Thirty minutes later, she walked out feeling absolutely certain she would not get a call back. Then she glanced at the clock. It was time to get an account set up at a bank so she could have her money transferred.

The sun was high and the temperature hot and steamy as she headed downtown to the bank she'd decided to use. She walked into the lobby, approached a young man at a nearby desk, and explained what she needed.

He began setting up a new account, then helped her through the steps of moving her money into it. Now her old account in Sweetwater no longer existed, and when she walked out, she had yet another new bank card, a pad of checks, and nearly thirty-six thousand dollars in her account. It was just another step in starting her new life.

SHE WANTED A COKE AND MADE A DETOUR INTO A FAST FOOD DRIVE-through on her way back to her apartment, then relished the cold tingle of it sliding down her throat as she drove.

She passed a Gatlin Landscaping truck, but John wasn't driving it.

She wanted to see him, and knew she was the only reason it hadn't already happened.

That night after her supper was over, she sat down to check email, and as she'd predicted, the concierge job at the hotel had been filled. They thanked her for applying, which reminded her she had left Henry Owens hanging. She sent him a text, thanking him for his offer as she turned it down, and her evening ended.

THE FOLLOWING WEEK CONSISTED OF MORE JOB EMAILS CITING "NOT right for the job" and "lack of experience." It all began to weigh on Gracie's confidence. She wasn't ready to quit on herself, but she was beginning to wonder if waiting tables would wind up being her last resort. The only thing keeping her upbeat were John's nightly phone calls, and she'd made up her mind that if he asked her out again, she would say yes.

She went to bed each night and dreamed of home...and Mama. Sometimes the dreams were sad. Sometimes the whole night was a dream that kept looping until she woke up bathed in sweat or tears.

It was becoming apparent to Gracie that distance had nothing to do with memories—and that no matter where she lived, her past would always come with her.

IT WAS ON THE THIRTEENTH DAY OF HER ARRIVAL IN BRANSON WHEN SHE got an email from another job application. She wasn't superstitious, but she also did not consider thirteen a fortuitous number.

However, the job *was* something she'd learned to do during her internship in college. It was something she had enjoyed and was surprisingly good at. As per the instructions, she called to confirm the appointment time, then, because she was at loose ends and lonesome, she called John.

CHAPTER THIRTEEN

$\mathcal{J}$ ohn was in his office, slogging through the business end of his job. He had an accountant, but he still had to get the information to her, and that's what he was doing when his cell rang. He was relieved to have a reason to stop and then elated to see Gracie's name come up on Caller ID.

"Hey, Gracie!"

"Hi, John. I hope I'm not disturbing you."

"On the contrary. You just saved me from the depths of hell, otherwise known as bookkeeping. How's the job hunting business?"

"That's why I called. I have another interview this afternoon at Majestic Floral Design. Do you know of it?"

"Oh yes. That florist does a lot of upscale events here in Branson."

"Good to know. I worked for an event planner my senior year of college. I got pretty good at the floral design end of it, and I really liked doing it. We'll see how it goes today."

"I'll be keeping my fingers crossed for you, Gracie."

"Thanks."

"You'll find your place soon enough, honey. I know it. In the meantime, I would love to take you to dinner. I don't know about you, but I get tired eating alone."

"Okay," she said.

John blinked. "Really? You just said 'yes'?"

"Yes," she repeated chuckling. "I would love to go to dinner with you."

"Is tonight rushing it?"

She laughed again. "No, tonight would be perfect."

"Awesome!" John said. "Where do you want to go?"

"You pick. I have no food allergies, and I like pretty much everything but sushi."

"How does a steakhouse sound?"

"As long as it's not The Beef Master Grill, I'm in," she said.

"Copy that. Is 6:30 good?"

"It's perfect," Gracie said.

"Good luck this afternoon, and I can't wait to see you again."

The husky sound in his voice made her shiver as she disconnected, but she was glad she'd called. She wanted to see him again, but she'd been hesitant—for no reason other than distrust. She was afraid to fall for someone who would let her down. Delia had left scars on her body, but her brother and sisters had left scars on her heart.

GRACIE ARRIVED AT MAJESTIC FLORAL DESIGN PROMPTLY AT 2:00 AND was surprised by the size of the storefront. It was double the size of the businesses on either side of it.

A bell dinged over the door as she entered, and she was assailed by cool air and a barrage of floral scents. As she walked past a display cooler with arrangements ready to purchase, silver-green spires of Eucalyptus caught her eye. Next to lemon oil, they might be her favorite scent.

A clerk approached as Gracie stopped at the register.

"Good afternoon," she said.

"I'm Gracie Dunham. I have a 2:00 appointment with Donna Franklin."

"Oh! Sure thing, Ms. Dunham. Donna is expecting you. Follow me."

Gracie followed the clerk through the workroom and then down a hall to the open door of an office.

"Donna, Ms. Dunham is here," she said.

Donna Franklin looked up. "Thank you, Reba," she said, then shifted focus to Gracie. "Good afternoon, Ms. Dunham. Excuse me for not getting up, but I am nursing a broken ankle. Please have a seat."

Gracie sat. "Sorry about your injury. I hope you're on a good road to recovery."

Donna rolled her eyes. "I'm on the road, but I am an impatient patient."

"Yes, ma'am. I tend to be that way myself," Gracie said.

"No, ma'am. Just Donna. Now, let's talk. I see on your resumé that you interned an entire year with an event planner in Dallas. What, exactly, did you do during that time?"

Gracie leaned back in the chair, immediately at ease.

"Basically, everything that goes along with that job, including the chaos of mistakes and disasters. One of the more memorable events I worked was a wedding where the groom failed to appear. The bride and her family got into a brawl with the groom's family on the other side of the aisle. It was a nightmare."

Donna burst out laughing. "Oh my God! What a cluster-fuck that must have been."

Gracie grinned. Apparently, Donna was not shy with her vocabulary.

"Pretty much. But, with regards to the floral aspect, which was my favorite part of the job, I went to flower market at least twice a week. I learned how to order supplies for floral design. And there was always floral work for big events and conventions. Some event planners sub that out, but the one I worked for was all-inclusive."

"I won't lie. I'm looking for someone with more experience, and I see you haven't worked in..."

"Nine years," Gracie said. "I stopped my life to take care of my mother after she was diagnosed with dementia. She recently passed, and now I'm trying to pick up where I left off."

Donna was listening carefully to everything Gracie said, but she was also focused on her body language. The moment Gracie started talking about her mother, her body tensed and her hands fisted in her lap.

"I'm sorry for your loss," Donna said.

Gracie blinked, unaware there were tears in her eyes.

"Don't be. I lost her years before she died. It was a hard, hard time for both of us. I'm still in jump and run mode, but I'm getting there—realizing that my time is my own again."

"Understood," Donna said. "I'd like to have you design a few arrangements if you're willing, just so I can see if your work is at a level I need. Reba will show you where everything is, and if you need something, just ask. We're working an anniversary party and a funeral right now. Let's go pull a couple of work orders. I'd like to see what you do with them."

"Of course," Gracie said.

Donna stood, grabbed a pair of crutches from the corner, and led the way out of her office back into the work room.

"Reba, honey. Will you please get a work apron for Gracie?"

Reba ran into the break room and came back with a clean, pink-bib apron.

Gracie put it on as Donna began going through the work orders for the anniversary party, then pulled one, and handed it to Gracie.

"This is for a twenty-fifth wedding anniversary party. They want a cut flower arrangement for the table where the cake and punch will be served, so it needs to be lovely and showy, without being so large that it's in the way. I think there is a height request on the work order."

"Got it," Gracie said, and laid it aside as Donna pulled one from the funeral and gave it to her, as well.

"The funeral is for a seventy-three-year-old man, and as you can see by what they paid, they want a big, showy basket of flowers in a three-sixty format."

Gracie took the last work order, then looked around. "Where is the cooler?"

Reba pointed.

Gracie nodded. "Okay...next question. I have no idea what the different prices per stem are for flowers, so I'll need to know that, to stay within the customer's budget," Gracie said.

"Reba, do you know where those charts are that I made up when they raised prices on us last year?" Donna asked.

"In the work drawers," Reba said, then opened the drawer in the table next to Gracie and handed it to her.

"Thanks," Gracie said. "And last question. For the twenty-fifth anniversary party, do they have a color scheme?"

"Oh...good call," Donna said. "Yes. Their colors for the party are the wedding colors, which were pale pink and mauve."

"Got it," Gracie said, and pointed to a worktable that was already equipped. "Is it okay if I work there?"

Donna nodded. "Yes. That's my table. Work away, and just send Reba back to get me when you've finished."

Gracie had the price chart in her hand as she headed for the cooler. She was going to do the funeral arrangement first, and after looking through what was available at the correct price range, she began getting a picture in her mind of what she wanted to create.

She came out carrying myrtle, silver dollar Eucalyptus, blue and lavender hydrangeas, green poms, and white peonies. Then she chose a large, white plastic standing basket and began cut and packing it with floral foam.

At that point, she began sorting and cutting hydrangeas, staggering the heights and colors as she placed them within the basket, then filled in with white peonies and green poms, then the shiny green leaves of silver dollar Eucalyptus and long stems of myrtle to add definition and height.

She stopped, stood back to look at it, then checked the price sheet, and went back into the cooler. She came out with a few stems of gold Peruvian lilies, dark yellow stock, and purple and yellow irises and began filling them in within the arrangement until it was a riot of color from every angle.

Then she paused. "Hey Reba, are bows expected on funeral arrangements?"

Reba stopped, frowning. "Well, usually yes. But as beautiful as that is, I don't know that it's necessary."

Gracie thought about it a minute, and then went to the ribbon shelf and pulled out a roll of ocean blue. She began cutting off six-inch lengths, notching them at one end and fastening each to a floral pick. She used them as filler around the base until she had finished it off. At that point, she filled it with water to saturate the foam, totaled up the florist's cost, and set it aside.

Then she picked up the work order for the Silver Anniversary. She chose a cut crystal vase from the supply shelf and walked back to the cooler for the peonies she'd seen in there earlier. She came out with lavender-pink peonies with feathery petals, two other varieties in varying shades of pink, and tree fern for the greenery.

Since the vase was clear, she was going to need clear marbles rather than floral foam to hold the stems in place.

Once the marbles were in place, she filled the vase part way up with water, then began adding flowers, keeping all the stems the same height and mounding them like a formal wedding bouquet, then she added a collar of tree ferns in shorter length around them.

With her vision of a bridal bouquet in mind, she grabbed two spools of silver ribbon—one wide enough to make bows and the other narrower to make streamers.

She hadn't made bows in years, but the skill came back the moment she started working. And when she was finished, she fastened it to a green floral pick and inserted it in between the stems. Now the arrangement, which had been a full three-sixty design, had a front.

She stepped back again, eyed the arrangement and smiled. It looked like a bridal bouquet. A gorgeous, pink and mauve bridal bouquet, the perfect height for the four-tiered anniversary cake noted on the work order. At that point she totaled the cost and stopped.

"Okay, Reba. You can go get Donna," Gracie said.

Reba looked up, her eyes widening, and then headed down the hall.

Gracie knew they looked good, but without seeing the level of work coming out of here, she had no idea if it would measure up. Then she heard the thump and scoot of Donna's crutches and turned as she entered the work room.

DONNA HAD HAD TO MAKE HERSELF STAY BUSY TO KEEP FROM PEEKING. Her other two employees had gone to late lunch, so they weren't here, and it was just as well. It wasn't easy to do your best work with people watching. She liked Gracie Dunham and really hoped she was good enough to hire. When she finally heard footsteps coming toward her office, she glanced up. If Gracie was through, she'd done two big orders in under an hour.

"She's ready," Reba said.

"What do you think?"

"You're the boss," Reba said.

Donna sighed. She didn't know what to make of that comment, so she got up and hobbled out of her office. Within seconds of walking into the workroom, she saw Gracie, then her work, and froze.

"Holy shit!" Donna said, and hobbled forward as fast as she could move toward the funeral arrangement.

"I love that ribbon fringe around the basket. I've never seen anything quite like that! It's stunning. The whole arrangement is gorgeous. And the anniversary arrangement! Oh my God. You turned it into a wedding bouquet. I know that couple personally, and this is going to blow their minds."

Gracie breathed a quick sigh of relief.

"I kept a list of what I used, and the total cost of each arrangement," she said, and handed over the list.

Donna glanced at it and nodded.

"Detailed *and* gifted. You, Gracie Dunham, are a find! Reba, honey, would you please put the proper cards on these two arrangements and get them in the cooler? Gracie, follow me back to the office, please."

Reba winked as they passed.

Gracie felt like dancing, and she hadn't felt like dancing in years.

"Have a seat," Donna said, and dropped back into her chair. "I was expecting to offer you the minimum starting salary if you were good enough, and you, my dear, are good enough. But I cannot, in all conscience, pay you a starting salary. You are very gifted, my dear. I am offering you this job at $3,500 a month."

Gracie exhaled on a slow, relieved sigh. "I'll take it."

Donna beamed. "Wonderful! I have a large clientele, and your experience with event planning is going to play a part in your job. We do weddings, funerals, corporate parties. We even do flowers for the musical shows on the strip, for the upscale hotels, plus all the usual floral customers. I have a thriving business, but it's working me to death. Your experience will relieve me of having to deal with event planners. They make my eyes roll back in my head."

Gracie laughed. "They're detail oriented. They have to be."

Donna shrugged. "I know, I know. So am I, but in a different way. Can you start tomorrow?"

"Yes."

Donna grinned. "You don't have to dress up. But you need to be neat, because at any time, you might work the front with a customer, especially until my ankle is better. We open at eight, and close at five, with an hour off for lunch, and we're open a half-day Saturday. We're closed on the usual national holidays. I pay by direct deposit, so I'll need your bank info. Always wear comfy shoes, and one of the girls will show you how to operate the register tomorrow."

"Thank you for the opportunity," Gracie said.

"This has worked out great for both of us," Donna said. "Let's get the paperwork finished, and then we'll be done here until tomorrow. There's a place to park in the back. I'll be here, so ring the bell. Someone will let you in."

"Okay," Gracie said, and then filled out the paperwork and handed it back.

Donna scanned it quickly.

"Okay, girl. We're good to go." Then she looked at the paper again and frowned. "Hey...that address is familiar."

"It's a garage apartment at Lucy Bedford's place," Gracie said.

"Are you serious? She hosts one of the hottest parties in town on New Year's Eve. She's the best. Tell her I said, hello."

Gracie nodded. "Yes, I will."

"Okay... I think that's all I need," Donna said. "Have a great evening, and I'll see you tomorrow morning. And thank you for such amazing work. Both clients are going to be elated with your artistry."

"That makes me happy," Gracie said, and then stood. "Don't get up. I'll see myself out."

"Much appreciated," Donna said, and then as soon as Gracie walked out, she let out a little whoop. This was her lucky day.

But Donna wasn't the only one celebrating.

Gracie was beside herself. She had phone calls to make and good news to share, but she was suddenly starving. She drove until she found a fast food drive-through, got a Coke and fries, and headed home, eating as she went.

BACK IN AUSTIN, JOEL AND MAMIE'S FIRST SESSION IN COUPLES counseling was proving difficult. Expressing their emotions and talking about what had gone wrong left both of them feeling vulnerable and scared.

Their counselor was a sixty-something woman with a no-nonsense attitude, which made Mamie anxious. While Joel was ambivalent about how she looked and what she said to them, he didn't care about any of that as long as she could get him and Mamie back to where they'd been.

They were on their way home from their first session and had been in the car for over thirty minutes navigating city traffic without having said a word to each other.

Joel finally broke the ice.

"You're awfully quiet. What are you thinking?"

Mamie shrugged.

Joel saw the jut of her chin and the red splotches on her face. She was pissed. He sighed.

"I'm not going to fight with you if that's what you're amping up to do," he said. "I was going to ask if you wanted to go out to dinner, but it doesn't appear to be a good idea."

Mamie blinked. "I would like to go out."

"Well, obviously so would I. But I don't intend to sit at a table with you if you're going to act like this."

Mamie glared.

"Act like what?"

"Sulled up like a pissed-off possum, is what," Joel said. "What I don't get is why you're mad at me. We both agreed to go do this."

Mamie sniffed. "You said terrible things about me."

"We were supposed to tell the truth," Joel said. "Nothing I said was a lie."

Mamie slapped both hands on her knees. "I know that!" she shrieked. "But maybe I don't want the world to know how awful I am."

Joel sighed. "Honey. You aren't awful. Your actions were appalling, but you're not a bad person. There is a difference. I didn't get mad at you when she asked you questions about me being gone on business so much. I knew you were probably lonely sometimes, but I had no idea to what extent. I didn't know I was making you feel abandoned."

Mamie sniffed. "Well, you do."

"I understand that now. So, the answer to that is I cut back on work, we cut back on our lavish lifestyle, and spend more time together."

Mamie's eyes widened. "Cut back on what?"

"Travel, expensive gifts, expensive clothes, fancy vacations," he said.

Mamie gasped. "But I don't want to do without that."

Joel resisted the urge to roll his eyes.

"Well, sugar, I cannot be in two places at once. Either I work to provide your ritzy lifestyle, or we cut back and spend more time together. This will be your choice now, and you can no longer feel abandoned if you are the one who decides if stuff is more important than us."

"Oh my God! That is so unfair!" Mamie cried.

"Or you could get a part-time job... or start volunteering somewhere to fill your days when I'm gone."

Mamie's eyes widened in sudden panic.

"I can't get a job! I don't have any skills."

Joel frowned. "That is so not true. You know clothes and style like the back of your hand. You could work at any upscale clothing store in Austin, and all you'd have to learn is how to ring up sales."

"Oh, I can't do that," Mamie said. "What would my friends say if they came in to shop and saw me working like that? They'd think we were hard up, and I'd be out of the lunch bunch in nothing flat."

Joel frowned. "That would be my sign to pick new friends."

"I can't. I won't," Mamie said.

Joel shrugged. "Then kindly discard your abandonment issues because you have none."

Mamie slumped in silence and said nothing for a few minutes more until she realized they were already in their neighborhood.

"I thought we were going out to dinner!"

"I've completely lost my appetite. I've chewed all the fat I care to tonight," Joel said.

"Well, you just hurt my feelings," Mamie said.

Joel shrugged. "And you hurt mine, which is why we're in the state we're in."

Mamie pouted.

Joel pulled into the garage, got out while the door was still lowering, and walked into the house, leaving Mamie to get out of the car on her own.

She didn't know how to act and sat there getting madder. Finally, she got out, slammed the door, then stomped into the house, and nearly fell over Joel, who was slumped on the floor in a spreading pool of blood. A masked assailant stood over him, holding a bloody knife and a duffel bag.

She screamed, and without thinking, grabbed the cast iron skillet off the stove beside her, and swung it just as he lunged. The assailant slipped in Joel's blood, and as he started falling, she swung the skillet like a hatchet, hitting him on the back of his head. He dropped like a felled ox over the lower half of Joel's body.

Mamie was still screaming as she hit him one more time for good measure, then dragged him off of Joel, grabbed a hand towel from the counter for a compress to Joel's wound, and dropped to her knees at his side, pressing the towel down with one hand as she called 9-1-1 with the other.

"9-1-1. What is your emergency?"

"I need an ambulance. An intruder just stabbed my husband. He's bleeding badly. Help! I need help!" Mamie cried.

"Yes, ma'am. I'm dispatching now. Are you safe? Where is the intruder?"

"He's on the floor, unconscious. I hit him with my cast iron skillet. I hope I broke his damn head," she cried, and started to shake.

"And your husband—where is his injury located?"

"His stomach," Mamie said. "I have a compress on it, holding it as tight as I can, but I'm not very strong." Then her voice broke. "Please hurry. He's bleeding so much. I can't lose him. He's everything to me."

"You just took out a bad guy with a skillet, so you're strong enough. Now stay on the line with me. Help is on the way. You need to unlock your front door."

"I can't leave Joel. He might bleed to death."

"Seconds, just a few seconds, and you can come right back," the dispatcher said.

Mamie bolted through the house screaming, "Don't die, Joel! Don't die!" at the top of her voice, unlocked the door, and raced back.

The assailant hadn't moved.

And neither had Joel. She dropped back at his side and pushed the folded-up towel back on his wound.

"I'm back. He's still bleeding!" Mamie screamed.

"What about your assailant?" the dispatcher asked.

Mamie moaned. "He hasn't moved. I'm afraid he's going to wake up!"

"Stay with me. Just stay with me," the dispatcher kept saying. "Help is almost there."

Then Mamie heard sirens. They were coming closer—getting louder—and then they were in the drive. Suddenly, people were in her house, and she was screaming... "In here! In here!"

Police were first on the scene, followed moments later by paramedics, who immediately moved Mamie aside and began examining Joel, then stabilizing him for transport.

Mamie stood against the wall, covered in blood, shaking so hard she couldn't catch her breath as she stared at all of the policemen in their kitchen.

One officer came in, eyed the masked man on the floor, then a knife and the iron skillet beside him.

"Where did the skillet come from?" he asked.

"I hit him with it," Mamie said.

His eyes widened. "You took him out with a skillet?"

Mamie nodded, still shaking.

A paramedic glanced up. "Are you injured anywhere, ma'am?"

"No. It's my husband's blood." And then her legs slid out from under her. "I'm going to fall down now."

The officer caught her before she hit the floor and got her to a chair. Within moments, there were neighbors coming into the house, yelling Mamie's name.

CHAPTER FOURTEEN

Gracie was still riding the high from her day, and when she got home and saw Lucy out on the back verandah, instead of going straight up to her apartment, she parked and walked across the driveway. They'd visited only briefly since she'd moved in, and usually when Gracie was coming or going—often then, just a smile and a wave. But Gracie liked her.

Lucy saw her coming and waved her up.

"Come join me!" she called.

Gracie strode across the grass to the garden path, and then up the steps.

"Sit with me, sugar. I'm having iced tea. Can I pour you some?" Lucy asked.

"Yes, please," Gracie said, and took the empty wicker chair and the tea Lucy offered. Gracie took a quick sip, and then another. "Mmm, so good."

"I always have Muriel squeeze fresh lime in my tea. Adds a little zip, and when you get my age, you need all the zip you can get."

Gracie shook her head. "You're not old. You're timeless."

Lucy sighed. "Thank you for that. So, tell me how your day has gone? Still job hunting?"

"Not anymore," Gracie said. "I took a job at Majestic Floral Design today. I start tomorrow."

Lucy beamed. "How wonderful! I love that place."

"I did a lot of that kind of work when I was in college. It's exciting to be able to go back to it."

Lucy eyed Gracie thoughtfully. "Donna Franklin has a good reputation and a huge business. She must have been impressed with you."

"She asked me to fill a couple of work orders so she could see my work, and she liked it."

Lucy clapped her hands. "Such good news."

"I had to fill out paperwork after she hired me. She recognized my address. I told her I'd recently moved into your garage apartment, and she said to tell you, hello."

Lucy smiled. "One can never have too many good friends."

"That's what they say," Gracie said, and then looked out across the grounds. "Your place is so pretty. I watch the birds in your water fountain almost every morning. There are so many in the water, or waiting to get in the water, that it makes me laugh. I don't know how they figure out who's coming and who's going, but they seemed to have a rhythm to it—like orchestrated confusion."

Lucy nodded. "They're my favorite things in the garden—them and the hummingbirds. I get a lot of songbirds at the feeders, but they have to fight the squirrels for the seed. No matter what I do, those little beggars get into them."

"I guess you'll have to put out squirrel feeders, too," Gracie said.

Lucy frowned. "Now why didn't I think of that? They're constant pests, but I love to watch them. Now I have a new project. Researching the best squirrel feeders and then getting them put up."

"Oh, I can put them up for you," Gracie said. "I'm pretty good with tools."

"Really?"

Gracie nodded. "Daddy died when us kids were all still at home. We learned to do a lot of things after that to pick up the slack."

"What happened?" Lucy asked.

"He had a wreck. Flipped his truck about a mile from home. No one ever knew why it happened." She blinked and then looked away.

"You said kids...you have siblings, then."

"I have a brother and two sisters, but they are not part of my life."

"I'm sorry," Lucy said. "I didn't mean to bring up—"

Gracie shook her head quickly. "Oh...it's okay. They removed themselves from my life when Mama lost herself. Her confusion made them uncomfortable. They were crushed when she didn't remember who they were. They couldn't bear to see her that way, so they never came back."

Lucy's mouth was open, but for the life of her, she was so shocked, she didn't quite know what to say.

"What did you do when she got that way?" Lucy asked.

Gracie shrugged. "I took care of her."

"For how long?" Lucy asked.

"I was there nine years. They quit coming after the second year."

Lucy's heart broke. She knew what that disease looked like. She knew the toll it took on caregivers, too.

"I'm so sorry," Lucy said.

Gracie set her tea down. "You don't need to apologize on their behalf. They abandoned us. In every way. They no longer exist in my world, and that's okay. It's actually a relief not to hold that anger anymore. Thank you so much for the tea. It really hit the spot. And thank you for your kindness. I guess I better get about my business. I still have some phone calls to make before it gets any later, and I have a dinner date tonight."

"Ooh! May I be so nosy as to ask who with?"

"John Gatlin. He mows your—"

"Girl, I know who he is. He's a good friend, and a good man. I didn't know you two had met."

"On my first day in Branson," Gracie said.

"Small world," Lucy said. "Before you go, I want to send something with you. I made blueberry muffins today," she said, and took off into the house on the run.

Blueberry muffins sounded amazing. And Gracie had nowhere

else to be. A couple of minutes later, Lucy was back carrying a pretty little gift bag and a small jar of jelly.

"I like jelly on my muffins," Lucy said, and handed them over.

"This is homemade jelly!" Gracie said.

"Yes...strawberry. I get it from Silver Dollar City. Their craft stores are amazing."

"Thank you," Gracie said. "Such an unexpected treat."

"Any time," Lucy said, then watched until Gracie went into the garage, closing the door behind her. "Bless her heart," Lucy muttered. "Just bless her heart."

COOL AIR WRAPPED AROUND GRACIE LIKE A HUG AS SHE ENTERED THE kitchen and set her gifts on the counter. Of all the welcome changes in her life, having a cool place to come home to was best. She danced herself down the hall doing a two-step, and then dropped her purse on the bed and kicked off her shoes.

"I, Gracie, am now a productive member of society!" she announced, flopped down on the bed, and got her phone to send Darlene a text.

I have a job at Majestic Floral Design, and I'm going to dinner tonight with John.

Within moments, she got a reply.

Yay for you, and who the hell is John?

Gracie laughed.

A nice guy who owns his own landscape business. That is all.

She hit Send, and then got up to change into shorts and a t-shirt. She was full of pent-up energy from the excitement of her success, so she got the lemon oil and a dust rag and began going through the apartment, wiping down the woodwork. Next, she took a dust mop to the hardwood floors.

When she was through, she ate half a blueberry muffin because they smelled too good to wait for breakfast. As she was eating, she thought about dinner tonight with John and shivered. The unknown was unnerving, but she felt happy—really happy—for the first time in a very long time.

JOHN GOT THE CREWS IN EARLY AND LOCKED UP THE OFFICE AS SOON AS his men drove away. Satisfied, he headed home to shower and change. He wanted tonight to be special for Gracie because she was so special to him.

Traffic was frustrating, and by the time he got home, he drove fast enough down the drive to his house that it sent the little rabbit into a race to get beneath the deck.

"Sorry, little guy," John said, as he slid to a stop, then got out on the run.

He stripped, leaving his dirty clothes in the floor of the utility room, and took off upstairs. One quick shower and a change of clothes later, he was back out the door. He got in the car, then glanced in the rearview mirror, combed his fingers through his still damp hair, backed up and drove away.

GRACIE WAS DRESSED AND IMPATIENTLY WAITING. SHE HADN'T SEEN John Gatlin since the day he'd given her back the angel she'd lost, and she was wondering if the image she had of him in her mind was real or exaggerated. What she remembered was dark hair, high cheekbones in a very handsome face, and eyes that flashed when he smiled.

She also knew that if this was going anywhere, then she wasn't hiding one thing about herself, including the scars. She didn't dress to exhibit them, but she also didn't choose clothes to conceal them.

The black slacks and sandals she had on were comfortable, and the turquoise-colored blouse she'd picked to wear with them had three-quarter length sleeves with a scoop neckline. She knew her scars were going to show, but it was now or never. If he was going to bolt, she wanted it to happen before it mattered.

She kept glancing at the time, and then getting up to go to the window, but when she finally saw a big SUV pulling up at her apartment, she almost panicked. Then he got out, and the wide set of his shoulders and his easy stride as he jogged toward the outer stairs made her heart skip a beat. She hadn't embellished any of her memory of John Gatlin. He was all that she'd remembered and more.

She stepped back so he wouldn't catch her watching, then hurried to the door to wait for his knock. When it came, she had to make herself wait just a little—just long enough to hide the fact that she wasn't standing there with her hand on the knob. Then she took a deep breath and opened the door.

The look on his face did not disappoint.

"Gracie...you look beautiful," he said.

"And you're looking fine for a guy your age," she said.

John blinked. "Uh..." And then the grin on her face gave her away, and he laughed. "You got me. Are you ready to go?"

"Yes," she said, and grabbed her purse from the little table beside the door and then turned to set the security alarm as she stepped out onto the landing, forgetting at that moment about the scars.

But it was a moment John would never forget. He didn't know what the hell had happened to her, but it didn't matter. Hopefully, one day soon, she would tell him when it mattered to her.

By the time she turned around, he was already talking as if he'd noticed nothing.

"The stairs are too narrow to go down together, So I'm going down first, and you follow. That way, I can catch you if you fall."

He gave her hand a quick squeeze then turned around and started back down, leaving Gracie to follow with his words still echoing in her heart.

Catch you if you fall.

The stuff heroes are made of, she thought, and followed him down, measuring the width of his shoulders, eyeing the way his hair grew in a swirl at the crown of his head.

She was already falling for him.

He waited for her at the bottom of the stairs with a ready smile and his hand out. She wasn't unsteady on her feet, but it was a good excuse to touch him.

Lucy was out on the veranda at the back of her house, having a glass of wine and watching the birds. She'd seen John drive up, and she'd watched them coming down together. There was something brewing between them. Witnessing love bloom was a gift, even if it was happening to someone else.

Then John saw her and waved.

She waved back. "Have a good time. Do something fun for me!" she said.

John gave her a thumbs up, and then they were in the car and driving away.

"We're going to the Saltgrass Steak House here in Branson. It's one of my favorite places, and since you're starting your new job tomorrow, I didn't want to keep you out late.... this time."

"I like a man who's always looking toward the future," she said.

He smiled. Gracie had wit and wasn't afraid to use it.

It was the dinner hour in Branson. Traffic was heavy, so he focused all his attention on driving.

By the time they reached the steakhouse on Branson Landing, they'd talked about everything except family. He'd keyed in quickly that was a topic she didn't intend to address.

Gracie was having such a good time, that she didn't realize she'd telegraphed her tension about it. John was fun and funny, and she had lost her nervousness about the evening.

As they were waiting to be seated, Gracie soon noted that John had a large circle of acquaintants. Some, she learned, were customers, while others were just people he knew from years of living here. And every time someone he knew saw him, he introduced her.

"This is my friend, Gracie Dunham."

The words echoed in her heart by the time they were seated. She tossed her hair back as she sat and picked up the menu. As she did, she caught the last few words from a woman seated at the table behind them.

"...all those hideous scars."

She glanced up. John was glaring at the people behind her. She laid her hand on his arm and then laughed.

"There's no accounting for ignorance. Some people were raised by wolves. Ignore them. I do."

John saw the reaction on the woman's face and realized she'd heard everything Gracie said, including being laughed at.

He took a deep breath.

"Yes, ma'am. Now...how do you feel about appetizers?"

"I feel kindly toward appetizers," Gracie said.

He chuckled. "As do I."

Gracie smiled. "You choose, please. I like surprises and remember I'm from Texas. Hot and spicy are my friends."

"Then Range Rattlers, it is," John said, and gave the waiter their drink and appetizer orders.

After that, the awkward comment from a stranger had lost all power.

When the stuffed jalapeño appetizers came, Gracie took a big bite, then rolled her eyes in delight as she chewed and swallowed.

"Houston...we have lift-off," she said.

John was in delight, moving slowly toward love, and he knew it. But he also knew this intriguing woman had secrets, and she'd been hurt in ways he could not fathom. He didn't yet know the way to her heart, but he was willing to take all the paths he needed to get there.

And so the evening went. After the appetizers, came salads, then steaks grilled to perfection, and baked potatoes dripping with butter. And laughter. So much laughter.

Gracie Dunham had her mother's drawl and dry wit, and John was the best thing that had happened to her in so long she didn't even know how to say thank you to the Universe without crying. So, laughter buoyed her when she faltered, and the look in John's eyes steadied whatever fears she had of being too happy, too fast.

It was nearing 9:00 when they left the steakhouse arm in arm. John seated her in his SUV, and then got in and reached for her hand, lifted it to his lips, and kissed it.

"Cinderella, I do not want this night to end."

She sighed. "It's been the best time I've had in so many years. You are such fun to be with."

"For my age?" he asked.

She sighed. "I was just teasing you. I'm the one who's been on the shelf."

"Any time you want to talk about that, I will be a compassionate witness," he said, then started the car and headed back to her apartment.

Her silence worried him. If he had offended her, it was going to bother him all night.

When they reached her apartment, he got out and walked her up the stairs. She had the door open and was turning around when he reached for her hand.

"If I overstepped a boundary, I'm sorry. It's just that I really like you, Gracie, and what hurts you, hurts me."

She sighed. "Come inside with me for a few minutes," she said, and then took him by the hand and led him to the sofa.

"I didn't answer you because my life is full of secrets I don't want to talk about, but the last nine years of my life have been hard. And pity is the last thing I want or need."

"You do not evoke pity. All I see when I look at you is a quiet warrior. Am I wrong?"

Words caught in the back of Gracie's throat. His intuition had caught her unaware. She took a breath, then shook her head.

"No, you're not wrong."

"When we first met, I asked you if you were okay, and you said, 'not yet, but I will be.' Are you there yet?"

"I'm getting there," Gracie said.

He reached for her hand. "Holding onto pain just makes it worse."

Gracie shuddered. "I know."

"So, let it go. I won't betray your confidence if that's what you're worried about."

"I wasn't trying to keep secrets about my life. I just didn't want to turn you off before you—"

"Well, that's unlikely, since I carried that angel you lost for days in the hopes that I'd see you again," John said. "And by admitting that, I've just bared myself to instant rejection."

"Then know that isn't going to happen. You cared enough to hang onto it and to look for me to give it back. That means everything to me. My mother gave it to me when I went away to college. I would have been devastated to lose it."

"Understood," John said. "So, you're still grieving her loss. It's understandable to—"

"No. I'm not. Not like you mean," Gracie said. "I lost my mother years before she died. Her death released the both of us."

"Then what?" John asked.

Gracie sighed. "It's an ugly story."

"I'm a big boy," John said.

She sighed, glanced at him, and then leaned back on the sofa and started talking.

"I'm the baby of four children. They are quite a bit older than me. Our world came undone when I was twenty, just out of college and only days away from leaving for Denver to a brand new job as an event planner for a big hotel. We were all home for Easter. My brother and sisters and I were visiting when Mama interrupted us. Said she had an announcement to make, and that she'd been diagnosed with dementia. She was scared, and my brother and two sisters sort of freaked and started talking about how busy they all were, and they couldn't walk away from their lives to tend to hers. She looked so lost and scared that it broke my heart, so I quit a job I hadn't even begun, and I stayed.

"They only came to visit twice after that...both times at Christmas.

By then, Mama didn't know who they were. She didn't remember her grandchildren, and she was loud and defiant. It scared them, so none of them ever came back until I called to tell them she'd died."

"Wait. What? But they helped you, didn't they?"

"No. And everything at the ranch began falling apart. Money got tight, and I sold everything that wasn't tied down to make ends meet. Mama set the kitchen on fire, then she began hoarding stuff. She wandered off onto the five hundred acres of prairie on our ranch and got herself lost."

John flinched. "How did you find her?"

"Buzzards. Daddy always said if there was flesh on the ground, there would be buzzards in the air. And there were."

John tightened his grip. "I cannot imagine living this...let alone living through it."

Gracie shrugged. "Thinking of it all together, it is a lot, but remember, it was just me and Mama, taking it one day at a time. Besides the day she stabbed me, the worst time for the both of us was losing air conditioning. It quit working four years before she died, and if you have ever spent a summer in West Texas, you would wonder how anything can live in that heat. But we did. And we would have gone hungry, but for my brother's ex-wife sending us her alimony every month."

John was holding onto both of Gracie's hands now, still locked onto that casual comment that had stopped his heart.

"Stabbed you? As in tried to kill you?"

Gracie nodded. "I never saw it coming, and it was certainly nothing she'd ever tried to do before. She liked to put up the clean flatware. I laid a handful on the table, then turned my back on her when, all of a sudden, she's screaming at me and stabbing me in the back and chest. I fought her, knocked her down, then called 9-1-1 before I passed out. I nearly bled to death.

"I stayed in the hospital a week. They put her in a psych ward for a month. When I got well enough, I brought her home because there were no safe places for people like that, and no money to put her in one of the fancy ones. And life went on. I have scars...all over my back, on my chest, and in my soul. She didn't mean to hurt me. She just didn't know who I was, and I guess she got scared."

"Why didn't you call your brother and sisters?"

And that's when he heard the rage in her voice.

"Because they'd already quit us, and I don't beg."

Within seconds John was on his feet, and she was in his arms. He felt her tense and try to pull away, so he started talking, his voice shaking—needing to get this said before she decked him.

"I'm hugging you because you need it. And because I need to fix the horror in your life, and I can't. I'm sorry. I'm so sorry this happened to you, and I'm so sorry that happened to your mother. She would have been horrified, wouldn't she?"

It was that simple statement of understanding that shattered Gracie's resistance, and she melted against his chest, his shirt fisted in both her hands.

"Yes."

And so they stood there in silence. John with his chin resting on the crown of her head, and Gracie with her cheek up against his chest. Then he tipped her chin until she was looking at him.

"Okay. So, here's what you have to remember. You shared your pain, so from this day forward, it is no longer yours alone. I'm helping you carry it, and one of these days, I'll help you bury it, just like you buried your mother. Understood?"

Gracie's eyes welled. "Understood."

John wanted to kiss her so bad he ached, but all he did was wipe tears off her cheeks. Lord have mercy, she was breaking his heart.

"I'll call you tomorrow to hear all about your first day at work. I'm excited for you, Gracie. Tomorrow is the first day of a new path, and knowing you, you'll be running, not walking." Her smile was wobbly, but a smile nonetheless. "This was our first date, but I'm hoping for more."

She nodded.

"Count on it," she said.

And then he was gone.

~

Long after Gracie had gone to bed, she kept going over the day in her head, and the one thing that stood out was what it felt like to stand within the circle of John's embrace. It should have been awkward, but all it had felt was right. Like it was where she belonged.

~

It was after midnight, and John still sat on the back deck in the dark, watching the stars, listening to the night birds, and thinking about Gracie. She was the most broken soul he had ever known, and he already knew he would love her.

Forever.

Even if she never loved him back.

CHAPTER FIFTEEN

*J*oel was out of surgery and in a room, and Mamie was at his side, listening to all the machines hooked up to his body, beeping out pulse rates and heartbeats. They were talking to Mamie, telling her about him, while she kept watching his every move as if it might be his last.

The police had taken her statement.

The assailant had been transported to another hospital. She had no idea if he was alive or dead and didn't much care, as long as she never had to see him again.

Neighbors had helped clean her up and then had brought her to the hospital. One had stayed with her until Joel came through surgery, and now Mamie was alone.

She'd called her "best" friends, thinking they would flock to her, but she'd been wrong. They'd voiced sympathy, offered prayers, and then nothing. She kept thinking of what Joel had said. *Maybe you need new friends.* Maybe he was right.

What she did know was that right now, at this moment, she would give up every luxury they had to get Joel well and healthy, and the guilt was killing her. This was karma. Her karma for what she'd done to Gracie. And Joel was paying for it. It had yet to dawn on her that she'd saved both their lives.

She kept asking the police, even after they'd taken Joel away, how had the man gotten inside without setting off the security alarm? When they told her it had never been set, guilt ate at her again. Joel always set it, but they'd been fussing when they'd left to go to counseling. So, their discord had added to the chain of events that had let a monster into their home.

She had also not missed the coincidence of two people in the Dunham family suffering stabbings.

Mama had stabbed Gracie, and she'd fought back and saved herself.

A stranger had stabbed Joel, and Mamie had fought him, and because she had, she and Joel were still alive. She raised her chin and straightened the slump in her shoulders. Maybe she wasn't as useless as she'd believed herself to be.

Her phone vibrated. She glanced down at the screen. It was Daphne. Finally, she thought, and pulled up the text.

Oh my God! Mamie! I'm just catching up on messages. I ran over my phone at noon. Destroyed it. Spent the whole afternoon getting a new one and trying to transfer data, and your message pops up and I nearly had a heart attack. I'm texting instead of calling because I'm guessing you're in the hospital. Is Joel okay? Are you okay? Do you need me to come to Austin?

Mamie sighed. So, the question of why Daphne had never responded was now cleared up, and once again, she was reminded of how alone Gracie must have felt, going through one crisis after another alone. She took a deep breath, and then messaged her sister back.

He's out of surgery. No organ damage. I wasn't injured. Yes, I'm in his hospital room. He's sleeping. I'm not leaving here without him. No, don't come. After what I did to Gracie, I do not deserve the considera-

*tion of family to keep me company. I will let you know when we go
home. Love you.*

She hit Send, then dropped her phone back in her purse. Daphne
sent another message, but Mamie didn't read it, and she didn't
respond. This was her redeeming moment, and she wasn't going to
screw up again.

～

DAPHNE WAS STUNNED BY MAMIE'S REFUSAL. GROWING UP, MAMIE HAD
never been able to do one thing on her own. She'd always had to have
company along, telling her what was right and what was wrong. And
she'd been just selfish enough to ignore anyone who told her something she didn't want to hear.

Daphne wasn't sure about Mamie assuming all of this was the
hand of God smiting her for her sins, but if that's how Mamie read it,
who was Daphne to argue the point?

Still, she felt the need to let James know what had happened, but
instead of texting, she called.

～

IT WAS LATE, BUT JAMES WAS STILL UP. HE'D HAD A COUPLE OF BEERS
with the pizza he'd had delivered and had gotten caught up in a
movie. So, when the phone rang, he almost let it go to voicemail, but
then saw it was from his sister.

"Hey, Daffy. What's up?" James asked.

Daphne rolled her eyes. The old childhood nickname had always
been a bone of contention between them, and she had not changed
her opinion of it. However, she chose to ignore it.

"Did Mamie call you about Joel?"

James hit mute on the TV and sat up.

"No. What about Joel?"

"They walked in on a robbery in progress in their house at noon.

Joel was stabbed, and the robber was coming at Mamie with the knife when she crowned him with a cast iron skillet."

"Oh my God! Are you serious? Mamie did that?"

Daphne sighed. "That's kind of what I thought. I would have expected her to scream and run. I think there's more of Mama in her than she knew."

James groaned. "Is Joel okay? Please tell me he didn't die!"

"He didn't die. Mamie said he came out of surgery. No internal organs were injured. She's at the hospital with him. I asked if she needed me to come be with her, and she said the strangest thing. She said, after what she did to Gracie by abandoning her, she did not deserve the consideration of family coming to comfort her. She told me to stay home! Can you believe? If I hadn't heard her say the words, I wouldn't have believed it."

James was silent for a moment, but the knot in his stomach was there and tightening.

"She's right, you know."

Daphne was trying not to cry. "Whatever. I can't change what I did. None of us can. And since I'm not going to cut my wrists for being an asshole, then my only other option is to keep doing what I do and try to never hurt another human for as long as I live."

"Agreed. I'm working on resolving my sins as we speak," James said.

"By doing what?" Daphne asked.

"You'll know soon enough. Thanks for letting me know about Joel. And since she doesn't want company, I'll send her my prayers. It's the accepted standard to fix everything these days."

"Isn't that the truth?" Daphne said. "Take care."

"You, too," James said, and then she was gone.

He sat staring at the television screen, but the sound was still muted. The thoughts that had been hanging onto his conscience took root. His eyes narrowed, and then he dug the heels of his hands into his eyes to keep from crying. He was so fucking tired of crying. This had to be the answer. Or he was done.

GRACIE SHOWED UP FOR WORK AT 7:45.

Donna was smiling as she let her in the back door.

"I have a walking boot. My world is back on track. Come in. Are you ready for all this?"

"I am so ready," Gracie said, and followed her through a hall, past storage rooms and a bathroom, and then past Donna's office into the workroom.

"Girls, this is Gracie Dunham. Gracie, you met Reba yesterday, and these two are sisters. Their names are Laura and Michelle."

They waved and smiled.

"Welcome to the Majestic," Reba said.

"Thanks. Any advice is welcome," Gracie said.

Laura, the redhead, laughed out loud. "I don't think that will be necessary. We all saw your work from yesterday. I am in awe."

Gracie smiled. "Thank you."

"Now, down to business," Donna said. "I have your worktable set up and a clean apron. We have more orders for that same funeral that have to go out before noon today, and most of them are sprays. We're working on those right now, so start there, card them, and put them in the cooler for noon delivery. The details of how this place works will become evident as you go. Never hesitate to ask questions. Never hesitate to ask me for advice, So... okay, then. Let's get to work!"

THE MORNING FLEW BY FOR GRACIE. STAYING BUSY HELPED. SHE HAD A crash course in ringing up sales, while Donna was the one who waited on walk-ins, and wrote up work orders.

They began staggering lunch breaks at eleven. Donna sent Reba and Gracie off first, which meant Gracie was going to have to talk girl-talk and chit-chat. Something she hadn't done in years.

"Where do you want to go to eat?" Reba said.

"You pick," Gracie said. "I haven't lived here long enough to know which places have the quickest service and best food."

"How about Subway. Good sandwiches, quick service, and tables to sit at."

"Sounds good," Gracie said.

"I'll drive. Hop in," Reba said, and off they went.

A short while later, they were standing in line, waiting to order. Reba was texting on her phone, leaving Gracie absently listening to the chatter of diners around her.

Then suddenly, there was the slam of cars colliding, the crunch of metal, and the sound of shattering glass, bringing every conversation to a halt.

Outside, two cars were crushed with steam rising from both of them, and people were running to their aid, while inside, a good number of the diners were rushing to the windows.

The low tone of conversations had turned to excited exclamations, and then dozens of people grabbed their cell phones and started videoing while others all talked at once.

Within the cacophony of voices, Gracie heard another sound—one she'd heard dozens of times when she'd still been home with her mama. Someone was choking.

She turned, quickly scanned the people still seated, and within seconds, spotted a middle-aged man sitting alone at a table. He had a frantic look on his face and was grabbing at his throat, desperately gasping for air.

Gracie bolted toward the table.

"Are you choking?" she asked.

He nodded, his wide-eyed gaze fixed upon her face.

She dragged him up from the chair, bent him slightly forward, and with her arms around him and her fists below his ribcage, she began squeezing his stomach with quick inward and upward thrusts, until all of a sudden, the bread stuck in his throat came flying out of his mouth, and he was able to breathe again.

"We're going to sit back down now," Gracie said.

The manager had been alerted by one of her employees, and came running out of the office, concerned for her customer and praising Gracie.

"I didn't see him," she kept saying. "He could have died. Thank you. Thank you."

But Gracie's focus remained on the man as she took his pulse.

"Sir, do you take blood pressure medicine?"

He nodded shakily, still drawing in one deep gulp of air after another.

She looked at the manager. "I think you need to call an ambulance. His pulse is irregular and racing."

The manager grabbed her phone and called 9-1-1, while Gracie pulled up a chair and sat down at the table with him.

"My name is Gracie. What's yours?" she asked.

He was sweating profusely, and both his hands and his voice shook.

"Edward."

"So, Edward, is there someone we can call for you?" Gracie asked.

"Nobody to call," he mumbled.

At that point, Reba appeared.

"What can I do to help?" she asked.

"Get my food to go," Gracie said, and handed her a twenty.

"Good call," Reba said, but the manager had other ideas.

"No, ma'am," she said. "It's on me." The woman called over to a girl behind the counter. "Comp these ladies' orders, please."

"Thank you," Gracie said.

"No, thank you."

Reba got back in line. Emergency vehicles were everywhere now. Police cars arriving. Ambulances arriving. The fire department was out in the street with the Jaws of Life, trying to extract a victim from one car. Finally, the ambulance they'd called for arrived. When the EMTs ran inside, Gracie stepped back. Adrenaline was crashing, and she was starting to shake. Reba handed her a to-go cup of Coke, and a sack with her sandwich, then grabbed her by the arm and out the door they went.

Reba said nothing until they were in the car and driving.

"We're going to the park. We can sit in the shade and relax while we eat."

"Fine with me," Gracie said, and then leaned back and closed her eyes, trying to pull herself together.

"You were amazing," Reba said. "How did you learn to do that?"

"My mother had dementia. One of the problems people have as the disease progresses is choking on everything from their own spit to anything they might put in their mouths. I learned to do that for her."

"Wow," Reba said. "Did she live with you?"

"I lived with her," Gracie said.

"Is she still alive?" Reba asked.

"No," Gracie said, and then reached for her Coke and took a drink. "Thank you for getting my food."

"Of course," Reba said.

Gracie nodded. "It smells good. You made a good choice."

Reba was silent as she pulled up in the shade of some huge oaks, stopped the car, then left it running.

"I keep thinking if I'd picked another place, that man might have died today. You had to be there for him," she said.

Gracie just nodded.

"Life is weird like that. You do things for one reason, and then wind up on a whole other path. I quit questioning it years ago."

But Reba couldn't let it go. "I felt so helpless, watching you. I want to learn how to do that. I'm going to look on YouTube tonight."

Gracie grinned. "The world has surely changed since I was last in it. It appears there is an answer for everything on YouTube."

Reba grinned. "Pretty much," she said, and began unwrapping her sandwich, then so did Gracie. After that, they talked as they ate, and by the time they got back to the Majestic, Reba had decided Gracie Dunham was the coolest woman she'd ever met, while Gracie was beginning to think she might have just made another new friend.

Reba immediately began telling everyone what had happened, while Gracie washed up, put her apron back on, and went to work.

Laura and Michelle left to go to lunch, leaving Donna there with Gracie and Reba.

"Good job," Donna said, as Gracie was putting the finishing touches on an FTD order.

"Thanks," Gracie said.

"And good job saving a life today."

"Just in the right place at the right time," Gracie said.

Long after Donna had walked away, Gracie began thinking, as she kept working, about all the times Mama had choked. She'd never thought about those instances as saving her life. She was just helping Mama catch her breath. And then she thought of the nights she'd gone to bed and prayed for the Lord to take Mama home because of how she was suffering.

So, Lord...all those times I kept praying for Mama to be released from her hell, and then she would choke, and I'd save her? Was that you trying to answer my prayers, or were you just testing me, making sure I was still the faithful daughter?

She struggled the rest of the afternoon, trying to make sense of something that no longer mattered. It was going to take more than leaving Texas for Texas to leave her alone.

JOHN MASHED HIS FINGER ON THE JOB A COUPLE OF HOURS BEFORE THE end of their day. It bled under the nail for a solid hour before it stopped, and he knew the nail would definitely come off. It wasn't the first time this had happened, and in his line of work, it likely wouldn't be the last. But right now, he was pissed off at himself, and by the time he'd locked up for the night and headed home, also miserable.

He thought about Gracie on the way, wondering how her first day on the job had gone, hoping it had been better than his. By the time he got home, he had a headache of major proportions, and his whole hand was throbbing.

He showered, dressed in a pair of sweats, then doctored his finger again, popped some over the counter pain pills, and laid down on his bed with his hand in a bowl of ice.

He thought about watching TV but decided to call Gracie instead.

"Hello?"

"Hi, Gracie. It's me."

There was a moment of silence. John wondered if he'd lost the connection, and then she spoke.

"What's wrong?"

He frowned. "Why would you ask that?"

"Because your voice sounds stressed," she said.

He sighed. "You heard all that in 'Hi, Gracie. It's me?'"

"You still haven't answered me, which means something *is* wrong."

"Does mashing the holy hell out of my finger count?" he asked.

Gracie groaned. "Oh no! I'm so sorry. Is there anything I can do? Where are you?"

"I'm home feeling sorry for myself, and no, honey, there isn't anything you can do. I guess I just wanted to hear your voice, and to tell you again what a wonderful time I had last night."

"Oh... So did I."

"How was your first day at work?" John asked.

"It was good. Everything went well. I like the people I work with. I like my boss. I love the work, too."

John smiled. "Awesome. I knew you'd do great."

But Gracie wasn't buying his chatty conversation act.

"Are you icing your finger?"

"Yes, as we speak, in a whole bowl of ice."

She sighed. "I'm sorry. I shut my hand in a car door once. Well, the wind blew the door shut on my hand, but however it happened, it sure didn't change the pain. I empathize. Did you take painkillers?"

"Yes. It'll kick in here in a bit. I just wanted to touch base with you before I fell asleep."

"Then consider the base as having been touched. Close your eyes and rest."

"Was it first base or second base," John asked.

Gracie laughed out loud. "If you have to ask, then you need to try harder."

She was laughing as she hung up.

He grinned, then winced and shoved his hand deeper into the ice.

She still had the best laugh.

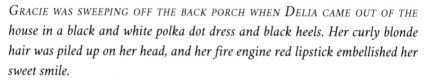

Gracie was sweeping off the back porch when Delia came out of the house in a black and white polka dot dress and black heels. Her curly blonde hair was piled up on her head, and her fire engine red lipstick embellished her sweet smile.

"Mama! You look beautiful!"

"Your daddy is taking me dancing."

Gracie stopped sweeping and looked toward the back door.

"Daddy's here, too?"

Delia laughed and turned just as the screen door opened again.

"See? Where I go, Tommy goes, too. He wanted to say hello, sweetie."

Gracie's heart was racing. "Daddy! You look so young...and handsome!"

He grinned, then slipped his arm around Delia's waist.

"You did good, Gracie Jean. Be happy."

And then he turned Delia into his arms and began dancing her around the porch, spinning and spinning, until they were gone.

Gracie woke up with tears on her face.

It was almost sunup.

She threw back the covers, went to get a Coke from the refrigerator, and then walked to the east windows overlooking Lucy's garden.

The horizon here was blocked by trees, and the streetlights and security lights blinded her to the darkness of night.

There were no coyotes here to sing her to sleep. And she might not get the full value of the color blast of a new day, but she was at peace.

She took a drink of Coke, thinking about Mama and Daddy. The feeling within her now was a sense of peace.

That wasn't just a dream.

They had paid her a visit—to let her know they were well and happy, and proud of her for a job well done.

She took another sip of Coke and then focused on the sky.

Mama used to say that the sun in the morning and the moon at night were God's lights. So, she stood watch, looking above the city lights, waiting for God's light to arrive. And when it did, the pastel wash of pink and yellow that finally appeared above the treetops was enough to make Gracie smile.

Today was here...and so was she.

It was time to make the most of it.

She picked up her phone and sent John a text.

Look to the East, John. It's a beautiful morning.

She waited, wondering if she'd texted him too early. Wondering if he was still asleep, she turned away from the window and went to get ready for work.

She was in the closet picking out something to wear when she found the old note that she'd packed.

I, Gracie, lost Mama today.

She sighed. "Nobody is lost anymore, Mama. Not you. Not me. And that reminds me. I need to email Decker's Funeral Home and give them my new address so they can mail me your death certificate. I'm not going to lose track of the life insurance you set aside for me. Not when it meant so much to you that I had it."

She slipped the note beneath a stack of t-shirts, the grabbed her laptop and sent the funeral home her updated address with the reminder about the death certificate, then she ran to get dressed.

John hadn't slept worth a shit.

His finger was still sore and achy when he'd finally given up on sleep and gone downstairs for coffee, which he'd then carried out to the front deck.

It was so quiet here. Watching night give way to a new day was a ritual, just as it was for him to salute the end of the dying day on the back deck.

191

The little rabbit was noticeably absent. Likely still hiding under the deck from the night owls.

He was thinking about Gracie when his phone signaled a text from her. He pulled it up, read it, then smiled.

Damn. What were the odds? Both of them already up. Waiting for sunrise. It was almost like sharing it together.

He texted her back.

Already here, waiting. Wish I was watching it with you.

CHAPTER SIXTEEN

*J*oel came to before nightfall, confused and in pain.
Mamie was instantly at his side.

"Sweetheart! Thank God you're awake. Are you in pain?"

"Hurts. What happened?" he mumbled, as he began feeling his belly.

"You were attacked. You're in the hospital, and you're going to be okay. I've been so worried. I love you. So much."

"Love you... Don't remember," he said.

"It's okay. You will," Gracie said.

"Tell me."

Gracie sighed. "We came home from counseling, remember?"

He was struggling to focus.

"Yes...counseling."

"You went in the house ahead of me and walked in on a robbery in progress. The man stabbed you. You had surgery. You're going to be fine. Just lie still and rest. I'm going to call the nurse."

Then Mamie rang for the nurse and told them he was awake and in pain.

"I'll be right there," she said.

Joel reached for Mamie's hand.

"Hurt you?"

"No. He did not hurt me at all. I hit him on the head with my cast iron skillet. He was still unconscious when the police and ambulance came."

Joel's eyes widened. "You fought?"

She frowned, her eyes flashing in anger.

"Yes, I fought. He invaded our home. He tried to kill you. No way was I letting him get away."

Joel closed his eyes, but he was smiling.

"Holy shit, baby. Holy shit."

Mamie sighed. For the first time since all this awful thing began, she was feeling hopeful that they would be okay.

And then the nurse came in, checked all his vitals, and gave him his next dose of pain meds in his IV.

"Just relax, Joel, and breathe easy. The meds will take effect in a couple of minutes," the nurse said.

"Thank you," Mamie said.

"Of course," she said. "That's what we're here for."

And then she was gone.

Mamie pulled her chair closer to Joel's bed, then sat with her hand on his leg, patting it as he fell back to sleep.

Joel would heal.

They would heal.

Mamie Freemont had been given a second chance to do the right thing, and she'd done it without thinking of the risks. For the first time in her life, she'd thought of someone else before she'd thought of herself.

THE NEXT FEW DAYS PASSED IN A FLURRY OF FLOWERS AND DEADLINES. Gracie had found her rhythm. She and John talked every night, and she was anxiously awaiting Saturday because he was taking her to his home for dinner.

He'd already warned her it was barbecue casual and to wear whatever was most comfortable for her because he was grilling on the deck.

She hadn't actually seen him since their dinner at Saltgrass and was coming to understand the meaning of absence making the heart grow fonder. She had been within the center of his embrace. She'd felt his empathy and his strength, and she wanted that again, and more.

When she'd woken up this morning and remembered it was Saturday, she'd bounced out of bed with a smile on her face. Half a day at work and then John!

She raced around the apartment getting ready, ate a toasted waffle while standing up at the sink, then took off down the stairs to her car.

Lucy was outside at her bird feeders in a peacock-blue caftan. She had a scarf tied around her hair, a hammer in one hand, and some kind of feeder in the other. But it was her bare feet that made Gracie smile.

Then she remembered! The squirrel feeder. She glanced at the time and took off across the drive.

"Is that your squirrel feeder?" Gracie asked.

"Yes, and I'm trying to decide where to hang it," Lucy said.

"Where the squirrels live," Gracie said, and took the hammer, nails, and the feeder out of Lucy's hands. "Pick a tree."

Lucy giggled. "I think that big one, the farthest away from the bird feeders."

"Good choice," Gracie said, and loped across the grounds with Lucy a short distance behind her. Once she reached the tree, she turned and looked back at the house, making sure to put it in a location Lucy could see. Watching squirrels was almost as entertaining as watching birds. She eyed the size of the feeder, then drove a nail into the tree and hung the feeder at a height Lucy could reach. "How's that?" she asked.

Lucy came up behind her, breathless, but smiling.

"Perfect, and just the right height for me to refill it. Thank you, darling!" she said, and gave Gracie a big hug.

Gracie hugged her back. "You're welcome," she said. "Have a good day," she said, and jogged back to her car.

Lucy turned and waved as Gracie drove past.

Gracie honked, and so her day began.

THERE WAS A STEADY STREAM OF CUSTOMERS IN THE MAJESTIC ALL morning, which Gracie loved. Work made time pass twice as fast, and she wasn't having to "learn" a new job. She was doing something she already knew.

It was about an hour before closing, and Gracie was working on a bouquet that was going to be picked up soon. She was laser-focused on getting it done and had zoned everyone and everything else out.

Donna was up front. The last customer had just left the building when the door dinged and another walked in. She smiled at him as she approached.

"Good morning! Can I help you with anything, or do you want to look around a bit?"

"My name is Edward Rollins. I'm looking for a young woman named Gracie. They told me at Subway she might work here because she was there the other day with someone who does. Work here, that is."

Reba had just put a new bouquet in the display cooler and over-heard enough of the conversation to realize who he was.

"Oh my gosh! Donna, this is the man Gracie saved. The one who was choking."

Edward nodded. "Yes, that's me. I don't want to interfere with her work. I just wanted to thank her."

"Of course. Reba, go get Gracie," Donna said.

Reba went straight back to Gracie's table.

"There's someone up front who wants to speak with you."

Gracie frowned. "Who?"

Reba grinned. "It's the man you saved from choking. Now go!"

Gracie was surprised, but pleased to know he was okay. She wiped her hands and headed up front. She recognized him instantly, but he looked much better than he had when she'd last seen him.

The moment Edward locked eyes on her, he smiled.

"There you are," he said. "I hope you don't mind that I'm here, but I just needed to find you—to thank you for saving my life."

"I was just in the right place at the right time," Gracie said.

"No. It was more than that," Edward said. "You did more than save me from choking. You really called it on my blood pressure problems. I spent a day in the hospital until they got it leveled out. I was bordering on a stroke. You didn't save me once. You saved me twice. I know the hug you gave me was life-saving, but may I be allowed to give a real hug as a gesture of my sincerest gratitude?"

Gracie didn't hesitate. "Absolutely," she said, and threw her arms around his neck.

He grinned and hugged her, then stepped back, still holding her hand.

"We haven't been formally introduced. I'm Edward Rollins."

"And I'm Gracie Dunham. It's a pleasure to see you in such good health."

"Yes, well... I just wanted you to know how much I appreciate you. I wish you a long and blessed life, Gracie Dunham. And now, I'll be on my way."

He nodded at Donna and then walked out of the store, got into a black Jaguar, and drove away.

Gracie went back to the workroom, with Reba right behind her.

"He was driving a Jag," she said.

"I saw it," Gracie said.

"I always wanted one of those," Donna said.

"I never was into sports cars," Gracie said. "I was a rancher's kid. If our vehicles weren't big enough to pull a loaded cattle trailer, they weren't worth having."

The girls all laughed, and Gracie smiled as she put the final touches on a bouquet of roses.

The door dinged again. Donna glanced up, then smiled at the young man who'd just entered.

"Good timing, Gracie. Here comes the new daddy after his bouquet of roses."

"I'll carry it to the counter for you," Gracie said, and followed Donna, who hobbled up to the register in her walking cast and set the roses down on the counter.

"Oh wow! Those are beautiful," the man said.

"Thank you," Donna said, as Gracie went back to the workroom and glanced at the clock.

It was twenty minutes to twelve.

Donna came back, smiling.

"We've done prom flowers for that young man. We did the flowers for his wedding, and now we've done flowers for his wife at the birth of their first child. I feel like an honorable auntie, or something. Girls, finish what you're doing, and then clean up your worktable. When you're done, go on home. If we get a last-minute customer, I'll handle it."

They didn't have to be told twice. A short time later, they were gone, and Donna locked up the front door, turned on the Closed sign, and began counting out the till.

GRACIE WAS SITTING AT A STOP SIGN WHEN A WHITE VAN DROVE through the intersection. She saw the sign and the logo on the side and grinned.

COYOTE CONSTRUCTION.

The logo was of a coyote running at full speed. What made her laugh was that the coyote had been painted to appear as if it was running toward the back of the van, while the van was moving forward.

She watched it passing, and then laughed out loud at the coyote they'd painted on the back doors. It was sitting on its haunches, facing the traffic behind it, tongue hanging out, as if it were too tired to go any farther.

Someone had a sense of humor.

But the irony of seeing a coyote in Branson was not lost on her. They'd been with her daily back home, and this felt like a bit of a hello from her past.

She drove back to her apartment, changed out of her work clothes, and got something to eat. Going through her mail, she found a letter from Decker Funeral Home. It was a "thank you for letting us serve you," letter, and a certified copy of Mama's death certificate.

Now she could file for the life insurance, and she did.

After that, the rest of the afternoon sped past until it was time for her date with John.

She stood in the bedroom, staring at herself.

With eyebrows and eyelashes as black as her hair, makeup was rarely on the agenda. She'd washed her hair over an hour ago, but it was still damp, so she just left it down to finish drying.

John would be here in less than thirty minutes, and she began to second guess herself about what she would to wear.

It had been a hot, humid day, and it would be a hot, sticky night, so decided to wear denim shorts and a red sleeveless top.

It was 5:00 when she heard a vehicle coming up the drive. She peeked out the window. When the SUV stopped and the driver got out, her heart fluttered. It was John, in jeans and a t-shirt that fit his body like second skin, and he was coming up the steps.

She got the keys from her purse, and when he knocked, she opened the door.

JOHN DROVE INTO TOWN WITH HIS HEART POUNDING. THE ANTICIPATION of spending a whole evening at his home with Gracie was like birthday and Christmas all rolled into one.

When he pulled up to her apartment and got out, he had to make himself walk up the steps because he felt like running.

He knocked.

The door swung inward, and she was standing in the doorway,

smiling, and all he could see was that beautiful face and legs that went on forever.

"Well damn," he said. "We match."

She laughed. He was wearing a red shirt and jeans, too.

"My jeans are a little shorter than yours," she said.

"Yes, thank you, God, and your Uber awaits."

Gracie smiled and followed him down the steps. After they'd gotten buckled up, he reached out to start the SUV, and she saw his finger. The one he'd mashed.

"Oh my God! Your finger!"

He glanced down. "It's a mess, isn't it, but it actually looks worse now than it feels." He started the car, backed up, and then headed down the drive and out into the street. "I'm not going to lie. I've been looking forward to this all week."

"So have I, and I can't wait to see your home. All I've seen of Branson is the city, except for driving out to The Beef Master interview. I come from flat prairie. All of these trees and mountains and green spaces speak to my heart."

"And you've been speaking to mine," John said, and then grinned to ease the seriousness behind his words.

Gracie gave him a side-eye. "Mama always said watch out for those sweet-talking men."

"Nothing but the truth," he countered.

Gracie laughed. She was excited, and anxious. This was more than nightly phone conversations, and she already knew she wanted more than a phone-a-friend.

As they drove, John pointed out the hiking trails, the signs leading to Table Rock Lake, and the different hotels in the area. When they passed The Beef Master Grill, it wasn't mentioned. For Gracie, it was mostly a case of been there, done that, and didn't need a t-shirt to prove it.

Traffic was heavier than she had expected, but it moved along at a steady pace. And then all of a sudden, John was turning from the main road onto blacktop leading up into the trees.

"This is all mine," John said. "Ten acres, including the house, and the property all the way down the shore to the lake."

Gracie was staring, trying to take in everything at once. The birds flitting from tree to tree, and others flying across their line of vision. Something small and furry slipped beneath some underbrush as they passed, and then the two-story log home appeared, nestled among the trees as if it had grown there.

The evening sun cast long shadows across the grounds as John drove around back and pulled up into a detached garage. He jumped out on the run, then opened Gracie's door and held out his hand.

Gracie grasped it and got out.

The air was still. Heat and humidity ruled. But she was used to heat, and the abundance of shade more than made up for it.

"Welcome to my home," John said. He led her up the steps of the back deck, into the house through double French doors. "This is the Great Room. Typical of log homes like this, it's all open concept downstairs, except for a guest bathroom down the hall. The kitchen is behind you. The living area before you. And the door leading out to the front deck."

"It's beautiful," Gracie said. "What kind of wood is this?"

"Spruce. There are four bedrooms and three bathrooms upstairs. My folks, and my sister and her family, stay here with me on Labor Day and Christmas. They'll be coming again this year. You are officially invited."

She smiled, eyeing the rooms and imagining them decked out in evergreens with a giant Christmas tree in the corner.

"Really?"

"Yes, really," John said. "Now. Let me start the grill so it can be heating, and then I want to show you upstairs. Help yourself to a cold drink from the fridge. I'll be right back."

Gracie watched him lope out onto the back deck, before moving into the kitchen area, which was all stainless-steel appliances, rustic cabinetry, black granite countertops, and light fixtures hanging from forty-foot ceilings. It was so beautiful she couldn't quit staring. She couldn't imagine living in anything this grand, either. Then she glanced out the window over the sink.

John was lighting the grill, so she opened the fridge, got a Coke, and popped the tab. It was cold and fizzy, and the first sip burned the back of her nose all the way down her throat, just like she liked it.

She scooted onto a stool at one end of the island and was drinking her Coke when John came back inside. He stopped, giving himself a moment to enjoy the pleasure of seeing her in his space.

"What?" Gracie asked.

"Just enjoying the view," John said. "Ready to climb a few stairs? If not, there's an elevator at the end of the hall."

"Stairs are fine with me," Gracie said, and as they were walking up the staircase, she paused halfway up, to look back at the view below. "It's even bigger from this perspective."

"I don't clean it," John said. "I have a good cleaning service who keeps it up for me. I do good to get my dishes in the dishwasher and my laundry done."

Gracie nodded. "I wouldn't argue with a cleaning service either if my house was this big."

John smiled. "Mom gives me grief about it, but she's also irked that at thirty-five, I am still single, too."

Gracie nodded. "Once Mama forgot she ever had kids, the scolding stopped, but she would have had a fit if she'd known about my brother cheating on his wife."

"Yikes," John said.

She grimaced. "That's not what Darlene said when she found out. She's a sweetheart. James is a self-centered ass, and I'm sorry I dragged my sordid family into this wonderful evening. Show me the upstairs, please."

"Not sordid. Just a typical family," John said. "Besides, there's you. You make up for a whole lot of other people's mistakes."

Gracie let the compliment soak in, and then set it aside for when she needed to remember she mattered, and someone cared.

"Here we are," John said, and began moving through the upper hall, opening doors, pointing out special features, working his way down to the master.

Gracie stepped across the threshold, then stopped just inside the door, staring in disbelief at the height and the size of the bed.

"Oh my lord! I have never seen a bed that big in my entire life," Gracie said.

John grinned. "It came with the house. It's a pain in the butt to make. But take a look at the view from my bedroom windows."

Gracie looked out. "Is that the lake?"

"Yes, an arm of it. We're high enough up to see a bit of it through the trees."

Gracie stood in silence for a few moments and then turned.

"I'll bet this place is gorgeous when it snows."

He nodded.

"I'd like to see that," she said.

"Then consider it done. First snow, I'm coming to get you."

Gracie's eyes widened. "Promise?"

"Absolutely," John said. "Now, let's go doctor up some steaks and get them on the grill. Are you hungry?"

"I'm starving," Gracie said.

He remembered the day he'd first seen her in the Hard Luck. How she'd picked up that burger with both hands and taken that big bite right down the middle.

"Awesome. So am I."

After that, whatever uneasiness Gracie had come in with was gone.

John kept up a running commentary as he first put steaks in to marinate and then potatoes in a convection oven to bake.

Gracie noticed he was favoring his finger, and when he began trying to cut up raw veggies for a salad, she gently took the knife from his hand.

"Let me," she said, then scooted him aside.

John stood there a moment, and then leaned over and kissed her cheek.

"Thank you, Gracie."

She smiled. "Of course."

He sat down on a barstool, watching the intensity on her face. She was truly one of the most complicated women he'd ever met, and one of the most compelling ones, as well.

"So, tell me about work. Anything interesting happen on your first week?"

"I went to lunch with Reba the other day. She's one of the girls who works at the Majestic. We went to Subway, and while we were there, there was a big wreck on the street out front."

"I saw that!" John said. "It was a mess. If I'd known you were inside, we could have spent a little time together."

Gracie dumped a handful of bell pepper slices on top of the lettuce in the salad bowl and then reached for tomatoes.

"As it turns out, a diner began choking on a bite of food while everyone was standing at the windows checking out the wreck. I saw him choking, did the Heimlich, and out popped a piece of bread."

"Gracie! You saved his life?"

"Someone else probably would have seen it, too, but nearly everyone was watching the fire department trying to cut one of the victims out of the wreck. By the time he was breathing again, his blood pressure was too high, so they called an ambulance for him, too. After all that commotion, Reba and I wound up eating in the car at a nearby park."

"You're amazing, lady. Is there anything you can't do?"

A tomato squished beneath the knife as she was trying to quarter it.

"It appears I cannot cut up tomatoes without making a mess," she said, and grabbed a couple of paper towels. "Is this enough salad?"

"I'd say yes," John said. "You can put it in the fridge for now. I'm going to put the steaks on the grill. The potatoes have another fifteen minutes or so, and the steaks will have to rest after they're done. I think our timing is good. Grab your Coke and come outside with me."

Gracie followed, then sat in a nearby chair to watch him cook. The air was warm and sticky, but there was just enough of a faint breeze slipping through the trees to keep her hoping for more.

She held the can of Coke against her neck, savoring the cold against her skin, then took another drink.

The meat sizzled and smoked as John laid it on the grill. When the juices began dripping, flames flared upward.

Gracie inhaled, relishing the scents and the company, then looked off toward the lake just visible through the trees.

Back home, she would have been sitting out on the back porch in the wind and the heat, maybe throwing a rock at the curious coyote or dodging a rattler. There wouldn't have been steak. And she would have been alone.

The tragedy of being the one left behind was having to find a new life in which to live. Nothing worked like from before. The rules were new. And Gracie was still finding her way.

She was sitting now with her feet up on the railing, her long legs stretched out, watching the end to this day. Birds were coming into roost, while other night creatures began to prowl. It was a little piece of heaven.

"Oh look!" she said, as a huge owl took flight from a nearby tree. "We had an owl in our old barn. He roosted in there during the day and came out at night to hunt the prairie."

John caught a glimpse of it, and then turned, saw her legs stretched out and her feet propped up on the railing, thought about them locked around his waist, and him deep inside her. At that point, he took a deep breath and looked away.

"Do you miss it? Home, I mean?"

She shrugged. "I don't have a home anymore. James inherited the ranch. I don't belong anywhere yet... But Missouri suits me, and I think I'm getting there."

You're going to belong to me.

John knew it. But he didn't say it.

The minutes passed as he turned the steaks, while Gracie watched the changing expressions on his face. Men weren't supposed to be beautiful, but in her eyes, he was.

Maybe it had something to do with the deliberate gracefulness of his movements, and that profile of his face.

"John?"

"Hmmmm?"

"Do you have any Native American heritage in your family?"

He paused, then turned, the tongs still in his hand.

"Why do you ask?"

"I see it in your face. In your profile most of all. Without the intention of giving you the big head, it's quite stunning."

He grinned. "Dad's people are part Choctaw. So, you're saying I'm good looking?"

She rolled her eyes. "Oh, Lord. I have created a bit of a monster."

He threw back his head and laughed, and she pointed to the grill.

"I like my steak medium."

"Oh, yeah. Steaks!" he said, and began taking them off the grill and putting them onto the platter.

CHAPTER SEVENTEEN

*J*ohn carried the steaks into the house.

A few minutes later, they had a mini buffet laid out at the bar and were sitting across from each other, eating and talking about nothing in particular.

Gracie was in heaven. After a week of telephone conversations, spending real time with John was the best. And, she couldn't remember the last time she'd had steak. The whole evening was her best ever in a long, long time.

"Is the steak done to your liking?" John asked.

Gracie nodded. "Yes, thank you. You are a master at grilling."

"And I'm pretty, too," he said.

She waved her fork at him.

"Now you are a man fishing for compliments. I have given you two tonight. Don't be greedy."

John grinned. The woman delighted him in a thousand ways, but her dry wit and quirky sense of humor might be the best part about her—that and those legs.

"You do know you are bewitching, don't you? I'm already lost," he said.

Gracie paused. "Don't worry. I am really good at finding lost people," and then took another bite.

"Like your mother?"

She nodded. "Yes. She managed to lose herself more than once. But I found her before much harm was done."

"Do you ever get lost?" he asked.

She glanced up. He was no longer smiling. She laid down her fork and took a drink.

"I'm trying hard not to be," she said.

"If you do, I'm a really good tracker."

Suddenly, Gracie's eyes welled, and John reached across the bar and took her hand.

"I didn't mean to make you sad."

Gracie shook her head. "Not sad. Just not used to having anyone for backup."

He gave her fingers a quick squeeze.

"Whether you like it or not, whether you want it or not, you are already a fixture in my life. I adore you, Gracie Dunham. You are a formidable, amazing woman. I won't push. But I'm not a man good at pretending. I dream about you. I think about you at the most random moments of the day. You are under my skin." Then he sighed. "If that just scared the shit out of you, I'll back off and never say another word. I'll take being 'just a friend' over losing you."

Gracie didn't hesitate. "I don't scare easily. Don't back off. I have been alone in a house with a crazy woman for the last nine years of my life. So, if you want the task of putting up with me and whatever comes with that, then I'm in."

John tugged on her hand.

She ceded to the urging, circled the bar, and walked into his arms.

"You give the best hugs," she said.

"I've got more to give," he said.

She slipped her arms around his neck and closed her eyes.

The kiss was perfect—just like him.

It went on until both of them were breathless and shaken just enough to know where they were. It was stop now, or there'd be no turning back. And so they stopped, and when they did, John pulled her close.

"Lord have mercy, woman."

Gracie sighed. "I knew it would be like this."

He cupped her face, rubbing his thumb along the edge of her lower lip.

"Like what, darlin'?"

"Like standing too close to the fire. One step more, and we go up in flames."

"Oh, we will combust, but not today," John said, then gave her a quick hug before letting her go.

He glanced at the time. "Come out on the deck with me for a while. The night is beautiful here."

She followed him outside, then settled down beside him in a two-seat glider. The moment she looked up at the sky, she saw the same constellation that she'd always seen back home, and something anchored within her.

Those stars—those constellations—they never moved. They never got lost. No matter where she went, they would always be with her.

John put his arm around her and pulled her closer. Her head was on his shoulder when the first deer came out of the woods, and within moments, a second followed.

She stilled.

John knew she'd seen them.

And so they sat, mute and motionless, watching them graze across the back of John's property, until they finally disappeared into the trees.

"They were so beautiful," Gracie said. "Thank you for this. For the food and everything else about this evening. It was perfect."

"What are you doing tomorrow?" John asked.

Gracie shrugged. "Laundry, unless you have a better idea."

"I have a better idea," he said. "Do you have a swimsuit?"

"Yes."

"Want to go swimming?" he asked.

She nodded. "Where?"

"There's a place called Moonshine Beach that's not far. Sandy beaches all the way to the water, and the water's clear and blue as the sky. It's a pretty perfect place to spend some time, and there are picnic tables."

"Yes, I would love to go."

"Great! I'll pick you up around ten, if that's not too early, and get picnic stuff. We can swim a while before we eat."

"I'm in, but I'm warning you ahead of time. People will stare at my scars."

"Do you care?" John asked.

"No. I'm used to it."

He frowned. "Then I don't care, either. All they are to me is proof of how hard you fought to stay alive. And I promise you now. You will never have to fight another battle alone."

~

GRACIE WAS LYING IN BED, BUT STILL AWAKE, LONG AFTER JOHN HAD brought her home.

They were going to make love. And she was going to give her heart to him forever when that happened. She had long since given up believing there was anything good left for her in this world, but he was everything she'd ever wanted in a man. When he'd appeared like the miracle he was, her course had been charted. All she had to do now was commit.

She fell into a deep, dreamless asleep, until long about morning when a memory slipped in for a visit.

MAMIE AND DAPHNE WERE OUT ON THE BACK PORCH SKIPPING ROPE. GRACIE *wanted to join them, but there were only two jump ropes, and they wouldn't share. So she sat, watching their feet dancing between the turn of the ropes, listening to the rhythm of their steps and their rhyme.*

"Daphne loves Melvin—Mamie loves Guy.

Easy peasy—puddin' and pie.
Cross my heart—and hope to die."

"Can I have a turn?" Gracie asked.

They ignored her.

Gracie got up and wandered back into the house, her shoulders slumped, her feet dragging.

"What's wrong with my baby girl?" Delia asked, as she looked up from *the peas she was shelling.*

"They won't share. They won't let me play."

Delia tossed a pea pod back in the bowl and wiped her hands.

"I'll play with you," Delia said. "What do you want to play, sugar?"

"I can't swim, Mama. I want to learn how to swim."

Delia frowned, and then nodded. "Let me go change my clothes."

"But we don't have a pool," Gracie said.

"We have a great big water tank now, don't we?"

Gracie nodded.

"Then that's gonna be our pool."

Gracie shivered with delight as her mama hurried off to change. She came back wearing old shorts and one of Tommy's t-shirts, and out the back door they went.

Daphne looked up. "Mama, where are you and Gracie going?"

"To play," Delia said.

"We want to play, too," Mamie said.

"Sorry. You wouldn't play with Gracie...now you don't get to play with us."

"But Mama! That's not fair!" Daphne wailed.

Delia paused, then turned around.

"No... You two are the ones who weren't fair to your little sister. You just go on with what you're doing."

Mamie threw down her jump rope and started bawling.

Delia took Gracie's hand and kept walking, paying no attention to them.

They reached the big stock tank at the far end of the corrals. Delia eyed the water level, then started the pump to add some water.

Gracie looked over into the tank. Unlike the bathtub in the house, she could not see the bottom.

"Is this water clean, Mama?"

"Not for us to drink, so keep your mouth closed. But it's good enough to learn to swim in. Are you ready?"

"Yes, ma'am," Gracie said.

Then Delia lifted her up in her arms, hugging her close for just a moment.

"Love you forever, baby girl," Delia said, and then kicked off her shoes and climbed into the tank with Gracie in her arms.

GRACIE WOKE, ROLLED OVER ONTO HER BACK, AND LOOKED UP AT THE canopy over her bed. This was not the stock tank, and thanks to Mama, she already knew how to swim.

"I'm sorry John didn't get to know you, Mama. He would have loved you as much as I did," Gracie said, and then got out of bed.

She didn't want to waste a minute of this day.

JOEL FREEMONT HAD BEEN HOME TWO DAYS, AND HE COULD ALREADY see his wife was a changed woman.

The day they'd come home from the hospital, he'd had to lean on Mamie's shoulder as they'd walked into the house. Unlike Mamie, he had almost no memory of the attack. It was such a relief to be home.

The house was clean, spotless as always, because Mamie had made sure their house cleaners came the day after the attack. She already felt like she was walking in Gracie's shoes, but she hadn't wanted to come home to a stain on her floor that never went away, and so it was gone.

Mamie catered to and babied Joel to the point of distraction, and for the first time in his life, he let her. She wanted him to know that he mattered to her and hoped to God she still mattered to him.

This morning they were sitting at the breakfast table, sharing sections of the Sunday paper as they ate.

"Joel, honey, do you want another piece of toast?" Mamie asked.

"No, thank you. I'm stuffed. That was a delicious breakfast, though."

Mamie beamed, and then got up and refilled their coffee.

"Do you want to take a little walk today before it gets too hot? Just down to the end of the block and back?"

"Maybe this evening, closer to sundown," he said.

"Whatever you say. You just let me know if you feel like it later."

"I will," Joel said, but he was looking at Mamie's face now, and he knew she had something else on her mind. "Mamie?"

"Yes?"

"What's wrong?" he asked.

Mamie sighed. "Nothing is wrong. But I've been thinking we don't need to go to any more counseling sessions. I know and accept that I am at complete fault for everything that happened. I was a selfish, self-centered bitch, and I don't much like myself right now. But I'm getting past it. If you can forgive me, I swear on my life, I will never let you down again, and I will hold myself accountable for my words and actions."

Joel reached across the table.

"I'm good with that," he said.

She nodded. "Thank you. Now, you go rest...take the Sunday paper with you. I'm going to clean up the kitchen, and then I'll check on you later."

Joel got up slowly, gathered the papers, and kissed her cheek on his way out of the room.

Mamie watched him leave, then began cleaning. Some days, if she didn't focus on something else, she still saw blood on the floor. As long as she lived, she would never get over it. No wonder Gracie was mad. If she hadn't saved herself and Mama, her own siblings would have let the both of them die.

She began cleaning off the table and loading the dishwasher, and when she was through, she ran a dust mop over the floor.

Mama had always told them cleanliness was next to Godliness, and Mamie needed to be as close to God as she could get.

DAPHNE CELEBRATED BY HAVING BREAKFAST OUT WITH ONE OF HER realtor friends. Yesterday, she'd made the biggest sale of her career, and was going to net nearly fifty thousand dollars as her broker's fee.

She wanted to call Mamie, but ever since Sweetwater, Mamie had changed. She wasn't as much fun to talk to anymore, and always serious. Mamie told Daphne that what happened to Joel was karma for what she'd done to Gracie, and she had to be better and do better.

Daphne had let her talk, listening and agreeing, and then after sending Joel her love, she'd hung up.

Mama was dead. Gracie was dead to them. And Mamie had gotten religion. The world she thought she'd known had all come undone. All she could do was keep working, and making sure when she got old, she had enough money to pay someone to take care of her, because it appeared that she'd put money and career ahead of life and loving, and now she was too set in her ways to change.

JAMES WAS WAITING ON WORD FROM THE LAWYER IN SWEETWATER THAT Delia's will had cleared probate. He couldn't put any property up for sale until it was legally in his name, and he needed to get rid of it. It was the weight on his soul that kept holding him down.

He had nightmares almost every night now where his daddy stood at the foot of his bed, shouting at him for abandoning Mama and Gracie.

Every time, he'd wake up sweating and crying, promising over and over he would make it right. He'd lost the chance to help Mama, but he could make sure Gracie was not suffering.

He didn't know where she was, but he knew Darlene would. When the time came, he'd grovel and eat all the crow it took to find out. But for the time being, he was on hold.

~

GRACIE WAS WEARING HER SWIMSUIT BENEATH A T-SHIRT AND A PAIR OF shorts. She packed everything else she thought she might need in a big tote bag and was now anxiously awaiting John's arrival.

The dream she'd had last night was still with her. That first swimming lesson had been scary and funny, and one of the best days of her life. At the time, she hadn't realized how many times her older sisters had left her out or pushed her aside. But looking back, it was obvious how easy it had been for them to push aside their responsibilities to her and Mama later. They were just doing what they'd always done.

As she was waiting, she texted back and forth with Darlene, but when John drove up, she stopped.

Gotta go! John is here.

She dropped her phone in her tote bag and went out onto the landing, locked up, and ran down the steps to meet him.

"Hey, honey!" John said, as he gave her a quick hug and a kiss. "Ready to go get your feet wet?"

"Can't wait," she said.

"Me either," John said. "Buckle up."

She buckled herself in as he got back behind the wheel, and then they were gone.

The drive to Moonshine Beach was further from Branson than she'd been before. And, as she was discovering, everything was scenically beautiful. Then she remembered John said he was from Kansas, which was just about as flat as West Texas, and she got curious.

"Um...John, you said you were from Kansas, so what brought you here?"

"Silver Dollar City," he said.

"I've never been there," Gracie said.

"I'll take you one day. My parents used to bring my sister and I here every year. Mom and Dad liked the music shows, and we liked Silver Dollar City and all the rides, crafts, and the candy makers. After I grew up, I kept remembering how pretty it was in Missouri. Kansas is flat and green. I wanted mountains and trees. I had a degree in horticulture when I came here, but I couldn't pay someone to give me a job, so I created my own."

Gracie nodded, letting the story of John settle within her, picturing their lives all moving toward this point where they'd finally met, and wondering how that all worked. Was there really a bigger plan in the cosmos, or was this all random chance?

"What are you thinking?" John asked.

"In a nutshell...what a miracle it was that you and I ever met."

"Meant to be, darlin'."

She smiled. She'd always wanted to be somebody's darlin'.

"We're here," John said, pointing to the signs directing them into the parking area. He paused to pay for parking, and then moved on into the lot.

"Got your suit on under your clothes?" he asked.

She nodded.

"Me, too. As soon as we park, we can strip down, grab our towels, and I'll lock everything up in the SUV."

Stripping down, as John called it, didn't take long. Within minutes, they were striding across the sand on their way to the water—John in his blue and yellow board shorts, and Gracie in a green and white two-piece. She'd braided her hair to keep it out of her eyes, and it was all she could do not to run.

John saw the excitement in her eyes and gave her braid a gentle tug.

"The roped off area is safe for swimming. Go ahead. Make a run for it," he said.

She dropped her towel and took off running, her long legs flying as she loped toward the water. As she ran, she left her cares behind, feeling like a teenager without a care in the world.

He laughed, left his towel with hers, and took off after her, catching up when she was waist-deep, then moved past her a few feet before sliding into the water and disappearing beneath the surface.

"You are one beautiful man," Gracie muttered, and waited for him to surface before going in farther.

He popped up a few yards away, shaking water out of his hair, and wiped his hands across his face, then waved her out.

She slid into the water with barely a ripple and swam toward him, straight into his waiting arms.

"You swim like a fish, barely disrupting the water. How do you do that?" John asked.

"Long body, long legs and arms. Not a lot of flopping and splashing, I guess."

After that, they swam, and floated, and talked and swam some more. When they finally got tired, they walked out of the water and back up the beach, spread out their towels, then knelt.

The hot sand all around them was calling Gracie's name. She leaned forward, smoothed out a space above the top of her towel, and then wrote, "*I, Gracie, am here.*"

John watched the whole ritual, smiling to himself, and when she had finished, he smoothed out the sand at the top of his towel and wrote, "*John sees you.*"

Gracie watched. With every word, with every action, she kept letting John Gatlin a little farther into her world, anchoring her ever deeper into this place. Satisfied that she'd left her mark, however fleeting, she went belly down on the towel.

John stretched out face up on the towel beside her, and as soon as he was sure she was okay, he relaxed.

Kids played nearby. Gracie could hear their squeals and laughter. The sun warmed her back and dried the suit on her body. John was so close she could hear him breathing, and she felt safe, and closed her eyes.

John watched her, thinking what it would be like to wake up beside her every morning. Wondering, as Gracie had, what magic in the Universe had thrown them together, grateful as hell that it happened.

A yellow beach ball came flying through the air, straight toward Gracie's head. Reacting on instinct, John slapped it away just before it hit her, and then sat up to look around for the owner. It didn't take long to see a woman and two little girls running their way.

"We're so sorry," the woman said. "Girls, apologize please."

Gracie raised up on one elbow and looked over her shoulder. "What's going on?"

"Just a runaway beach ball. All is well," John said.

"We're sorry," the girls said in unison, and then one of them moved closer to Gracie. Before her mother could stop her, she touched Gracie's scars.

"What happened?" she asked.

Gracie sat up. "I had an accident. What's your name?"

"Bronwyn. My sister's name is Bridgette. We're twins."

Gracie smiled. "I'm Gracie. It must be awesome to have a twin."

The mother was embarrassed. "Girls, get your ball and let's go. We're bothering."

But the twins were too fascinated by the scars on Gracie's chest and back to pay attention.

"Do they hurt?" Bronwyn asked.

"Not anymore," Gracie said.

"I'm not a very good kicker. We didn't mean for the ball to come toward you," Bridgette added.

"It wouldn't have hurt even if it had hit me. But it appears John saved me," Gracie said.

"Do you have to put medicine on them?" Bronwyn asked.

"I did when it happened, but not now."

The little girl jumped up and ran to her mother, dug through the beach bag she was carrying, and then came back with something clutched in her hand. She handed one to Bridgette and kept one.

"Mom puts these on us when we get hurt. They have medicine on them. It will make your booboos well, too."

And without hesitation, both girls peeled the wrapping off their Band-Aids, picked out a scar apiece, and gently stuck them on.

"There!" they said in unison.

"Thank you, so much," Gracie said. "I'm sure I'll be good as new in no time."

Satisfied with their good deed, the girls ran to get their ball.

Their mother smiled sheepishly at Gracie and quickly herded them away.

John leaned over and kissed Gracie square on the lips.

"What was that for?" Gracie asked.

"For being you," he said. "Let's go get our picnic stuff. I'm getting hungry."

They grabbed their towels and headed for the parking lot. John put his t-shirt on, and Gracie was reaching for hers when John stopped her.

"Want me to take the Band-Aids off?"

Gracie shook her head. "No. They're still full of love and good intentions."

"Just like you," John said, then got the ice chest, locked the car, and led the way to some shaded picnic tables.

Gracie sat on the bench as John began sorting out the food.

"Two kinds of cold sandwiches from Subway. Chips. Cookies. And cans of pop," he said.

Gracie popped the tab on a can of Coke and took a quick sip. Being happy was presenting problems she hadn't expected. Tears were always on the verge of erupting, and today was no different. The emotional shift from utter despair to pure joy had yet to settle.

"Thank you. This is so fun...and such a drastic shift from what my life was. Sometimes I'm afraid I'll wake up and this will have all been a dream."

John leaned over and kissed her again, this time with feeling. Her lips were cold, and they tasted slightly of Coke.

"Is that real enough for you?" he asked.

Gracie sighed. "Yes, and thank you," then reached for a sandwich and a bag of chips.

CHAPTER EIGHTEEN

The sky started getting cloudy as they cleaned up from their meal.

"Looks like our day at the beach is going to be cut short," John said.

Gracie glanced toward the gathering clouds. "I will never complain about rain. Back home, we never had enough."

John didn't want to take her back this early and offered a different option to extend their day together.

"Want to come home with me for a while? We can watch a movie, maybe nap if you're tired. Or...and I say this with regret...I *can* take you home. It's your call."

"We're closer to your place, aren't we?" Gracie asked.

"Yes, but either way is no problem," he said.

"Then let's just go there. You can take me home later, after the storm has passed," she said.

"Deal," he said.

Happy she wasn't ready to end their day either, he grabbed the ice chest as she dumped the last of their cans into recycle.

The sky was still sunny with building clouds in the distance, but the wind had already changed as they made their way back to the parking lot.

As soon as John stowed their things, they wasted no time leaving. And they weren't the only ones. Other beachgoers were already hurrying to their cars, loading up their kids and their coolers, hoping to beat the thunderstorm home.

Tired from swimming, sated from the food and the sun coming through the windows, Gracie leaned back in the seat and closed her eyes. It never occurred to her to keep up a running commentary with her date.

John was...John. He accepted her for who she was. He made her feel comfortable and safe.

When John reached the main highway again and paused for traffic, Gracie opened her eyes.

He gave her arm a quick pat. "We're not there yet, honey. Go back to sleep. I'll wake you when its time."

She sighed, then scooted farther down in the seat.

John accelerated, merging into traffic, and headed for home with precious cargo aboard. About fifteen minutes later, he began slowing down again, and when he turned off the road and up the drive, Gracie woke again, this time to a sky full of darkening clouds.

The wind was whipping the treetops as he parked in the garage. They got out on the run, Gracie grabbing her bag from the back of the SUV, as John aimed the remote to deactivate the security alarm at the house.

"I unlocked the door. I'm right behind you," he said.

She ran ahead, and then held it open.

The first raindrops hit as he came hurrying inside. She shut the door behind him, and then moved to the window looking over the back deck. The tree limbs were thrashing as the rain blew against the windows.

"It sure is blowing," Gracie said.

John walked up behind her, slid his hands around her waist, and pulled her close. "It's just rain. Don't be scared."

Gracie leaned against him. "I have great respect for storms, but I do love to watch it rain. The sound of rain on a roof makes the best sleeping weather."

John kissed the back of her neck. "Ever make love to the sound of rain?"

She paused. "No."

"I want to make love to you, Gracie."

She sighed. The inevitable moment was here.

"I don't play games," Gracie said. "Making love is serious."

"I couldn't agree more," he said, and held out his hand.

She took it and walked with him up the stairs, then down the hall to his bedroom.

Uncertainty came off with her clothes.

Nothing about John felt unfamiliar as he stretched out onto bed beside her. They had surely come this way before, in other centuries—in other lifetimes. And the moment he slid into her body, she knew him. The way he moved. The whispers. The promises.

She was finally alive, feeling everything, hiding nothing of herself with no more need for caution. No more holding back.

Making love with him was wild abandon—a growing madness within the storm above them and the one within her.

And then it happened.

The climax—breaking her into a million little pieces.

She was falling, falling, too fast, and then John's arms were around her, and he was whispering her name. She wrapped her arms around his neck and closed her eyes.

Loving John was going to save her.

THE STORM PASSED NEAR SUNDOWN.

They'd made love again and were still lying in each other's arms, counting down the moments they had left before he had to take her home.

John felt peace in a way he never had before. They were lying face to face, legs entwined, hands still mapping the shape of—

His chin.

Her brow.

Tracing the shape of his nose.

Cupping the side of her face.

"Love you, Gracie," he said softly, and then kissed the palm of her hand.

"I, Gracie, love you more," she said, and then threw back her head in laughter when he nipped the hollow at the base of her throat. But that soon turned to a moan as he kissed his way down to the valley between her breasts.

"One more for the road?" John asked, as he slid between her legs.

"Yes, please," Gracie said, as he swelled within her.

Taking Gracie home and then driving away without her was harder than John could have imagined. Their relationship was new, but the depth of his feeling for her didn't feel that way.

She was in his blood.

Gracie stood in the darkness of her apartment, watching from the window as John drove away. For nine long years she'd buried every personal wish, every emotion she'd had, to be focused enough to do what had to be done for her mama.

Until today.

She'd felt it happening—this coming back alive.

But never would she have believed it would be this sudden, soul-gripping, gut-wrenching bond to a man she barely knew.

It was the scariest, best thing that had ever happened to her, and watching him drive away had been the hardest.

He was in her blood.

GOING TO WORK THE NEXT DAY, GRACIE WAS CERTAIN THE GIRLS IN THE
Majestic would see her rebirth as she entered the shop. She felt
awkward and uncertain, like a baby learning to walk. But it didn't
happen. They waved. They smiled, and their chatter continued.

She got her apron, and as she got settled at her workstation and
picked up the first order, the uncertainty faded.

Understanding there were layers to a life was a relief. She could be
strong and vulnerable. She could be happy and sad. She could be a
fabulous floral designer, and the woman in John Gatlin's bed. What
she never had to be again was her mama's nurse—her mama's advo-
cate—her mama's voice.

THE DAYS FLEW BY.

One day, a check for twenty-five thousand dollars from Mama's
life insurance policy was in her mail when she came home.

The moment she saw it, she burst into tears, remembering the day
her mama had bought it.

You're gonna earn it, Delia had said. And she'd been right.

She turned around, got right back in her car, and took it to the
bank to make a deposit. Her salary was supporting her. Her nest egg
was growing. She was still taking care of business.

EVERY DAY BEFORE JOHN LEFT TOWN, HE STOPPED BY GRACIE'S
apartment. Sometimes just for a hug. Sometimes he brought food.
And sometimes they made love in her canopy bed.

Labor Day came and went with the same heat and humidity.

John's family arrived to spend the holiday, pulling her into their
silliness and their world.

She saw John in his father, David.

Tall, dark hair sprinkled with strands of gray, eyes crinkled up
from smiling, big hands callused from a lifetime of work.

She adored him.

His mother, Nola, was the peacemaker. Always soothing over misunderstandings, loving on her grandchildren, backing up the people she cared for. And without pushing the issue, she pulled Gracie into the mix as if she'd always been there.

John's sister, Linda, was a sweetheart. Gracie found companionship with her that she'd never felt from her own sisters, because they'd always had each other.

John's nephews were funny, little versions of their father, Lee, and they kept everyone busy trying to keep track of them.

Gracie thrived on the feminine influence she'd been missing like rain soaking into dry ground.

Life-giving.

Life-saving.

By the time they left, Gracie knew she belonged to someone and his people. She had the beginnings of a family again, and that began to mend a tear in her soul.

~

After that, Gracie spent every weekend with John at his home. It was beginning to feel like her home, too. She had clothes there. And a toothbrush there. And Coke in the fridge.

He loved her.

She loved him.

It should have been so simple. But there was a feeling within Gracie that made her uneasy. Like the world couldn't inhale. Like it was holding its breath.

Some nights it left her sleepless, almost afraid to close her eyes. Like something was too good to be true.

The feeling usually faded with the sunrise, but it was never really gone.

~

JAMES DUNHAM WAS A SHADOW OF HIS FORMER SELF.

He'd lost nearly fifty pounds in the months since his mother's death. He took sleeping pills to knock himself out at night. He couldn't face the torment of his dreams. Time, and the legal system, had come close to breaking him as he went through the steps to finally become the legal owner of the family ranch.

Five hundred acres of land in Texas cattle country, with a going rate of over $3,000 an acre was a nice chunk of change, and without an inheritance tax for anything less than $5.4 million, it was all his.

And then he sold it.

The day that money finally hit his bank, he went home and cried. It was over. Done. Now he had to find Gracie. And that meant talking to Darlene.

He sat down on the sofa with a beer in one hand and his cell phone in the other, then called her. She answered, and as always, sounded pissed that he was bothering her.

"Hello."

"Darlene, it's me. Don't hang up."

"I already know it's you... Caller ID and all. If I didn't want to talk to you, I wouldn't have answered. What do you want?"

"I need Gracie's address."

"Why?"

"Because I finally sold the ranch, and I need to give her the money." There was a long moment of silence. "You mean her share."

"No. All of it," he said, and heard Darlene gasp.

"You're serious? What about Daphne and Mamie?"

"Daphne called it blood money and rejected it the day of Mama's funeral. Mamie and Joel rejected it, too. And I can't keep it. I don't want to keep it." His voice broke, and he began to cry. "I think I'm dying. Daddy is in my dreams, shouting at me. Mama looks at me from the foot of the bed with tears on her face. I can't sleep. I've lost weight. I need to make all this right. Gracie is the only one who stayed. We all walked away from home and Sweetwater years before Mama got sick. But Gracie stayed. We deserted Mama and Gracie when they needed us most, and Gracie still stayed. The money is hers

—by everything that's good and holy. I just need a way to get it to her."

For the first time in years, Darlene felt sorry for him.

"I know where she is. I have her address. And I do know the name of her bank because she mentioned it a couple of times. But that's all. And I don't want to be in the middle of this, but I also don't want you injecting yourself into her life to assuage your guilt."

"Don't worry. I have a lawyer. He'll know how to get the money deposited in her account. I'll write her so she'll know where the money came from. She has to take it. She's the only Dunham who deserves it."

There was dead silence. And then, "Do you have a pen and paper?"

James put down his beer.

"Yes."

Darlene began talking, giving him Gracie's home address, the place where she worked, and the name of her bank.

"Normally, I wouldn't help you across the street," Darlene said. "I'm doing this for Gracie, because she deserves it."

"Is she okay?" James asked.

"Mostly."

"Is she happy?"

"She's damn sure trying to be," Darlene said. "Don't go and fuck this up for her. If you do, your mama and daddy won't be the only people haunting your sleep. Do you understand me?"

James shuddered. "Yes, ma'am."

Darlene ended the call without saying goodbye, but it didn't matter. All he wanted now was to get that money into Gracie's hands before God struck him dead.

IT WAS LATE SEPTEMBER. A HEATWAVE HAD BEEN HANGING OVER THE area for days, highs close to the nineties, with enough humidity to soak the clothes on your back within minutes.

Even the tourists filling the city were either at Table Rock Lake and in the water, inside the music shows, choosing air-conditioned entertaining, or lining up for the water rides in Silver Dollar City.

Because of the heat, John and his crews were out at the crack of dawn, working hard to finish up yards and landscape jobs before mid-afternoon. He made the rounds every day to his crews, taking them cold drinks and snacks to keep them hydrated, and because he wanted to see Gracie, he took drinks to all the girls in the Majestic, too. Just seeing him coming in the front door with a carrier full of icy drinks or frosty malts, put smiles on their faces. Gracie took their jokes in stride because she always got a kiss with hers.

THE MORNING DAWNED WITH THE HEATWAVE STILL IN PLACE.

Gracie woke before her alarm went off and checked her phone. As always, she had a good morning text from John.

Have the best day, sweetheart. See you this evening. Stay cool. Love you.

As always, Gracie sent back the same reply.

Love you more.

She turned on the TV as she got dressed, hoping for a little rain in the weather, and noticed there was a cool front coming across Kansas and the northern part of Oklahoma. Part of it might sweep their way, and it might not. Nothing to count on to cool anything off.

She dressed for the weather, and after downing a bowl of cereal, she headed to work, and walked into all kinds of drama.

A couple of weeks back, Donna had taken a request from the Wisteria Inn Hotel to redo the display piece in their front lobby. It would be placed on a massive four-foot tall table in the middle of the lobby using one of their own urns. They'd requested that the new display be at least five-feet tall and reflect the name and ambiance of their hotel. They'd left the design up to Donna. But they didn't want fresh flowers. They wanted high-end artificial flowers that would stay in place until the holidays rolled around.

This morning, the entire order for the Wisteria Inn had arrived, and Donna and two of the girls were going through it, making sure everything she'd ordered had arrived in the right colors and quantities.

"What's happening?" Gracie asked, pausing to keep from stumbling over the massive boxes all over the place.

"The order came for the Wisteria Inn," Donna said. "If everything is here, I'll have our delivery guys get the products to the hotel. I'm sending you and Reba to do it."

Reba's eyes widened. "Uh..."

Donna grinned. "Don't worry. Gracie is in charge of the design. But she's going to need an extra pair of eyes and hands."

Reba grinned. "Oh. Thank God. I love my work, but I also know my limitations."

Gracie began poking around inside the boxes. "Good stuff, Donna. This will be fun to do."

"They have their own urn. It's squat and heavy. It won't topple. Just make it Old South elegant. The wisteria will make it showy."

"I can do that," Gracie said. "When do we start?"

"My delivery guys are on the way. I'll load up two of the vans and send them out to the hotel with the flowers. You two grab your own tools and follow. Take a picture for me when you're done."

"Will do," Reba said.

"Am I supposed to be working in the middle of the lobby, with everyone coming and going?" Gracie asked.

"No. I told them that wasn't safe, and to give you a space all your own. They'll probably set you up in one of the empty banquet rooms on the second floor. They can move the finished piece on their own. All you'll need to do is follow to make sure nothing jiggles loose or falls off, and then you two are done."

The buzzer sounded at the back door.

Donna jumped. "That will be the drivers. Someone get the door. The rest of you, let's load these boxes."

A short while later, the vans were gone, and Reba and Gracie were on their way to the hotel. Reba turned the blower up on the air conditioner as she drove.

"Lord, but it is hot out today. And it's too still and muggy. Something weird is gonna pop with our weather before this day is over. You mark my words."

Gracie frowned. She thought about the weather report she'd seen earlier. Maybe it wouldn't be bad. Maybe it would just be rain.

They arrived at the hotel and were soon ushered up into an empty banquet room on the second floor. The urn she was to use sat on a table in the middle of the room, and an employee from the hotel was approaching.

"Good morning, ladies. My name is Paul. If there is anything you need, I'm here to assist you."

Gracie eyed the setup and then began pointing.

"I will need some tables placed around the one with the urn, arrange them like a platform we can stand on while we work."

"Absolutely," Paul said, and grabbed his radio. Within minutes, he had the makeshift platform in place, and ice water and glasses nearby. "Cell service isn't very good up here. I'm going to leave you with a two-way. Just press the button and page me if you need anything. Or at least let me know when you're done."

Gracie nodded, and as soon as they were gone, she and Reba got to work building the infrastructure first. Artificial stems were basically wire with rubber or plastic coatings, and since the flowers and greenery here were huge, everything was heavier. That meant whatever Gracie put them in, needed to be strong enough to keep them upright and in place.

They spent two hours building infrastructure inside the urn before they were even ready to begin the piece. Then once they did, the work went faster.

Gracie had a vision in her head of how she wanted it to look—having the multi-colored clusters of hanging Wisteria evoke the images of Spanish Moss dangling from Live Oaks and hot steamy days in the south.

About halfway through, Reba jumped down from the table and stepped back to look.

"Oh, Gracie, this is glorious!"

Gracie paused and smiled. "I need some more Wisteria vines here. Bring me a few bunches, will you?"

Reba dug through the boxes on the floor, then came back with an armful, and the work continued.

NOON HAD COME AND GONE, AND GRACIE'S ARMS WERE ACHING FROM reaching up so high. Despite the air conditioning, a river of sweat ran down the middle of her back. She was doing final touch-ups, covering up the bits of base structure with flat pieces of dried moss and pinning it into the wiring and Styrofoam with floral pins.

She was on her knees now, working around the base when she reached back for another piece of moss and realized there wasn't any.

"Hey, do we have anymore dried moss? I just used up the last of it, and I need at least another three feet."

Reba looked, then frowned. "No. All of the boxes we brought in are empty."

Gracie rolled over and sat down, rubbing her aching knees.

"Does this hotel have a flower shop?"

"No. Just a gift shop, but there's plenty at the Majestic. I'll just run and get some. It won't take me more than thirty minutes to get there and back. Go get yourself something to eat and drink. I won't be long."

Gracie nodded and slid off the table. "Okay, and thanks. While you're at it, go ahead and take a picture for Donna. Then we can take another one after it's in the lobby."

"Ooh, good idea," Reba said, and snapped a couple of pictures, then left on the run.

Gracie thought about going to get something to eat, and then didn't want to leave the piece alone, but there was nowhere to sit. She had the floor, or a table, so she got back up on the table, pulled out her cell phone, then sighed.

No cell service at all up here, and the two-way radio wasn't going to serve her purpose, when all she wanted was to call John, so she rolled over on her back, pillowed her head on her arms, and looked up at the piece she'd just finished. It was floral elegance at its finest.

THE WEATHER CHANNEL WAS ALREADY ISSUING WEATHER BULLETINS FOR Branson and surrounding areas. Tornado warnings in some places; tornado watches in others.

John had called in his crews and was waiting for the last one to come in so he could lock up. The longer he waited, the more antsy he became. Clouds kept piling higher and higher, with a tinge of green to their color—a sure sign hail was in them.

He tried to call Gracie more than once, but the calls kept going to voicemail, which was worrying. She always answered when she was at work, but then he told himself it was just the weather messing up the cell service in the mountains.

When the last crew finally came wheeling into the yard, John ran out to meet them. They unloaded tools and mowers for servicing and headed home. He locked up everything, and then jumped in his truck. The need to check on Gracie got stronger. By the time he hit Main Street, the sky looked worse. Wall clouds were rolling over the mountains, bringing low, airborne rotations threatening more than rain.

"Shit," John muttered, and sped up. All he needed was to see her face and know she was okay.

He pulled up to the Majestic and got out on the run. The Open sign was still on, but the streets were almost empty. He came inside yelling Gracie's name. He could see Reba crying, and then Donna met him at the register.

"Where's Gracie? I've been trying to call her all morning."

"She and Reba have been working in a banquet room on the

second floor at the Wisteria Inn all day. The room is soundproofed, which makes cell service spotty."

John grabbed Donna by both arms. "But where is she now?"

"She's still there," Reba said. "We ran out of some stuff. I came back to get it, and now Donna won't let me leave. We tried to call the hotel, but no one is answering the switchboard."

Donna waved toward the windows. "You can't! Look outside!" The hail was falling like bullets. "Listen! They're already blowing the storm sirens. Do you want to die in that?"

"No," Reba wailed. "But Gracie..."

John's heart sank, and then a calm came over him.

"Gracie isn't going to die. She'll get herself to a safe place, and when it's over, I'll go get her. It's okay. It's okay. All of you. You're doing the right thing."

"And so are you," Donna said. "Get in the cooler with us and don't argue. It's the safest place to be."

John had talked a good game, but he was scared. Walking into that cooler with all of the other women, without knowing if Gracie was safe, made him sick to his stomach.

And then Donna shut the door, and the decision was made. They began moving canisters of flowers so they could get up against the walls and into the corners, huddling together to wait out the storm.

GRACIE WAS FLAT ON HER BACK AND HALF-ASLEEP IN A SOUNDPROOF room. She didn't hear the wind, or the sirens that were now blowing in the city. But when the walls began to pop, and the table she was stretched out on began to shake, she sat up with a jerk, jumped off, and ran out into the hall.

The moment she stepped out of that room and began hearing screams and sirens, and seeing people running, she knew something terrible was happening. She started to go back to get the two-way radio, then looked out across the second-floor lobby to the massive glass windows on the other side, and all the hair stood up on the back of her neck.

Hail was hitting the glass in rapid-fire motion. The sky was black, and the tornado spinning out of the belly of the storm was on the ground and coming this way, chewing up and spitting out everything in its path.

Gracie panicked. Not only was she not underground, she was on the second floor, facing a wall of glass, and she needed to move. She jerked as if she'd been slapped, and bolted for the stairwell, knowing her life depended on getting down.

Glass was already shattering behind her as she reached the Exit— the roar around her so loud she couldn't hear her own screams. She leaped into the stairwell, then began vaulting down steps, two and three at a time. Even within this windowless tube, the roar of the storm was deafening, but she couldn't slow down.

She was almost to the first-floor landing when the power went out, leaving her in a complete absence of light. She fumbled for her phone, trying to get it out of her pocket to light the way when the walls came down around her.

CHAPTER NINETEEN

$\mathcal{T}$he tornado plowed through the north side of Branson, leveling homes, damaging buildings, and leaving downed trees and broken power lines in its wake.

As soon as the sirens stopped blowing, John and the women left the cooler and ran outside.

All the windows in the buildings on the opposite side of the street were shattered because they'd been facing the storm. But it had come in from behind the Majestic, and by a stroke of fate, their storefront was sound. The hail damage on roofs and vehicles were a whole other thing. They had been hammered by the hail, and it showed.

"I'm going to find Gracie," John said, and jumped into his truck, quickly leaving the old part of the city and heading north.

He kept calling her as he drove. All he needed was the sound of her voice, but she never answered.

Twice he had to stop and take a longer route because of scattered debris, and the closer he got to the hotel, the more frantic he became.

The damage here was worse. Many homes and business were total losses. They'd had enough warning. Hopefully, everyone had taken shelter. Things could be rebuilt, but people were irreplaceable.

He was still a couple of blocks away, but he could see roof of the

Wisteria Inn now, and it didn't look right. It took a few seconds for him to realize that both the roof and the top floor of the hotel were completely gone. The sight and the shock were so startling, that for a few seconds, he couldn't breathe.

Then he began to drive faster, coming up behind fire and rescue vehicles, then stopping to let ambulances pass. It was a nightmare. He drove up in full sight of the hotel, not knowing if she was still there, or if she was even alive.

Forced to park almost a block away, he got out running, then once he reached the location, joined the gathering crowd already combing through the exterior wreckage for victims.

～

"Gracie. Wake up, darling. It's time to wake up now."

Gracie groaned. "No, Mama. Not yet. My eyes don't want to."

"You have to, Gracie Jean. John is looking for you."

John? John was now. Not from before. Mama didn't know him.

"Gracie! You need help. Wake up now!"

It was the phone ringing in her pocket that yanked Gracie back to consciousness. She was opening her eyes and trying to reach for the phone when she realized she couldn't move.

The first thing she saw was debris all around her, then the sky above her. After that, pieces of walls, broken concrete, and twisted rebar—and water dripping somewhere near her head.

This is a dream. This isn't happening.

But it was happening because she wasn't in bed. She was lying on her side on stairs, wedged beneath some kind of debris, unable to move.

Panic hit, hard and fast. She began to shout for help—the sound echoing back to her in the stairwell, until something wet rolled down her face and her mouth.

What the hell?

Something coppery—salty on her tongue.

Blood! Her blood!

And then it hit her!

The tornado!

She was trapped...but she was alive.

"Help me! Help! Help! I'm here!" Gracie cried, and then everything around her started spinning, and she was spinning with it, and the world went black.

RESCUE WAS BARELY UNDERWAY WHEN JOHN REACHED GROUND ZERO. Utility crews were frantically turning off the power so searchers could get inside.

Firemen were hosing down a few hotspots that had sparked up after the storm, and people had started to emerge from the hotel. Some staggering, others walking out with a look of shock and disbelief on their faces.

John ran up to each of them, asking, "My girl...Gracie Dunham! Did she take shelter with you? Do you know her?"

But they just shook their heads and kept walking, and he kept searching among them, asking the same thing over and over until no more came out, and he was still standing, staring at the hotel.

When the firemen got the okay to go inside to search, John stopped them.

"My girl, Gracie Dunham, was working on the second floor. She hasn't come out. Call her name. She might be trapped. Maybe she will hear you."

"Yeah, will do, buddy," the fireman said, and gave John a pat on the shoulder.

After that, he was sent back behind the roped off area. All he could do was keep calling her number. Praying she'd eventually hear it—or that a rescuer would hear it ringing in her pocket and find her that way.

~

GRACIE DRIFTED IN AND OUT OF CONSCIOUSNESS. NO DREAMS. NO sound. Just going in and out from dark to light.

Then that sound woke her again. Someone's phone was ringing. It made her head hurt, but it finally stopped.

She was starting to feel pain. Her head. Her shoulders. Her arms. Her legs. She kept telling herself that had to be a good sign. As long as she had feeling, she was good.

When that phone began to ring again, she was conscious enough this time to know that it was hers.

In her pants pocket.

Just beyond the tips of her fingers.

She could feel it now, vibrating against her leg as it rang, but she couldn't lift her arms—she couldn't reach it. And so it kept ringing, and ringing, and in a moment of sanity, it hit her.

John. It was John.

He was looking for her. She needed to let him know she was trapped. He would get her out.

Her left arm was folded across her breasts, completely immobile. But her right one was flat against her side. She could feel the seam in her pants, even the edge of the pocket where the phone was. Maybe she could pinch just enough of the fabric to tug it upward—to pull the pocket closer to her. It was worth a try.

The phone rang again as she began pinching at the fabric and pulling it up. Pinch then pull, pinch then pull. Hoping to get it high enough to get her fingers in the pocket.

She was making a little progress, but not enough. When the ringing stopped again, she burst into tears.

"Don't quit me," she sobbed.

And just like an answer to a prayer, it began ringing again, and this time, she was pinching and pulling harder and harder, inch by inch pulling the fabric of her pants up her leg until her fingers were in her pocket, and she could feel the surface of her phone.

"Don't stop ringing. Don't stop ringing," she cried, and began swiping, and swiping as far as she could reach. But it kept ringing, and then she screamed.

"Dammit all to hell! I will not die this way!" she said, and swiped all of her fingers across the face in a last-ditch effort to connect.

Then the ringing stopped, but this time, she could hear a voice—John's voice.

JOHN HAD BEEN CALLING FOR SO LONG THAT HE ABOUT TO LOST HOPE. A part of him knew she could have blown away in the storm, but he kept thinking of all she'd survived before and couldn't believe God would let this happen. So, he kept hitting redial and praying.

When her Caller ID suddenly appeared on his screen, and then he couldn't hear her, his heart stopped. He forgot he was standing in the crowd and began shouting.

"Hello? Hello? Gracie! Gracie! Can you hear me?"

And then he heard her voice. It sounded faint and far away. He started running to get away from the noise and put the call on speaker so he could hear her better.

"Trapped. Can't move! Don't hang up. Don't lose me!"

"I hear you!" he kept shouting. "Are you in the hotel? Do you know where you are?"

"Yes. Hotel. Stairwell...between first and second floor. Can't move."

"I hear you! I hear you!" John said. "The firemen are in there now. I'll tell them. Are you hurt?"

"Yes."

"Are you bleeding?" John asked.

"Yes...head. Hurts."

"Don't quit on me, baby. I'm here. I'm going to find some rescuers right now so I can let them know where you are."

"Don't leave me. Keep talking," Gracie begged.

"I'll never leave you. Just hang on. I need to tell the men where you are."

Gracie moaned. "Dizzy...can't focus."

"Gracie?"

She didn't answer.

"Gracie!" he shouted...but she was silent, and he was already running toward the nearest rescue crew.

Within minutes, they had radioed a search crew inside the building, directing them to begin searching stairwells between the first and second floors.

It was the longest fifteen minutes of John's life before the fire chief turned, giving John a thumbs up and a grin.

"They found her. Trapped, but alive. She's covered in debris. It might be slow going getting her out, but they'll do it."

"Let me be with her," John said.

"I'm sorry, son. There's barely enough room for the rescuers. Just hang in with us. Let us do our job."

John's heart sank, but he wouldn't argue. She was alive.

The fire chief saw the look on John's face and relented.

"If you stand on the tailgate of my truck, you'll see us bringing her out." And then he was gone.

Grateful to be this much closer to her, John crawled up in the back of the truck, his gaze fixed on the front of the hotel, the phone still clutched in his hand, waiting for her to wake up again. Waiting for the sound of her voice.

"Ma'am! Can you hear me?"

Gracie opened her eyes. She was surrounded by firemen. The relief was overwhelming.

"You found me," she mumbled, and then started to cry.

"Yes, ma'am. Just lay really, really still for us. We're going to start removing debris so we can get you out."

"Yes, I will," Gracie said. "Did John send you?"

"Yes, ma'am. He told us right where to look, and we found you."

Then she remembered the phone. They'd been talking. She could still feel it beneath her fingertips.

"John! Are you still there?"

And then she heard him.

"Gracie! Gracie! I'm here, baby!"

"They found me, John! I'm not lost anymore."

"I'm just outside. I'll be waiting. I love you, Gracie."

"Love you more," she said, and then the noise got too loud to hear him any longer.

They covered her face to keep dust from falling into her eyes, and then they began her extraction.

Outside, John could hear everything—what they were saying, the sounds of their tools—but he could no longer hear Gracie. The sky that had been so dark and deadly was now bathed in sunshine, easily marking the path the storm had taken.

Thirty minutes passed...and then more. He was starting to worry when the fire chief walked up to the truck.

"They're bringing her out. She's banged up, but she's talking."

John was on his feet in seconds. Watching. Waiting. And then he saw them coming out, and the stretcher they carried.

"Thank you, God," he whispered, and started running toward it.

His first sight of her was shocking. She was covered in some kind of white powder and blood. But her dark eyes were flashing, and he could see her lips moving.

He reached the stretcher, grabbed her hand, and ran with them as they hustled her to a waiting ambulance. Her gaze was fixed on his face, her fingers clutching his hand, and then they were putting her in an ambulance.

"Stay with me," she begged.

"I'll be right behind you. Don't be afraid."

She blinked, then they closed the doors and she was gone.

John turned and ran back to where he'd parked his truck. It felt like a lifetime ago since he'd driven up on this scene. He plugged his phone into a charger, and then called the Majestic as he drove to the Medical Center. He wasn't sure if they'd still be open, but it was the only contact he had for any of them. It rang and it rang, and then Donna finally answered.

"Majestic Floral."

"Donna, it's me. We found Gracie. She was trapped in a stairwell under a lot of debris. Don't know the extent of injuries, but she was awake and talking when they put her in the ambulance. I'm on the way to Cox Medical now."

"Oh my God. Thank you for calling. I have been so scared, not knowing if she was even still alive. Thank you so much for letting me know. I'll contact the hospital about her worker's comp insurance. Tell her not to worry about that."

John disconnected, and kept driving, forced to make two short detours due to debris, but finally reached the parking lot. He parked near the ER entrance and ran inside.

The ER was full of storm victims bringing themselves to the hospital, and ambulances coming and going. It was a waking nightmare. People crying. People bleeding. People in shock, wandering the halls.

He ran straight up to the desk.

"I'm Gracie Dunham's next of kin. She is one of the victims from the Wisteria Inn Hotel. Where is she?"

The clerk was harried, and it showed, but she managed to find Gracie's name and location, and pointed.

"She's in Bay 4."

Moments later, John was in the Emergency Room, walking past bays, looking at the room numbers as he went, and then he saw it and walked in.

She was on a gurney. Naked but for a towel they'd thrown across her hips. They'd cleaned off the blood and powder from her face and arms.

A doctor was in the act of stapling shut a gash on her head, but paused as John walked in.

"Whoever you are, you can't be in here," he said.

"He's mine, and I want him here," Gracie said.

John's vision blurred. "She's mine, and I need to be here."

The doctor sighed. "Fine. Just stay out of the way."

And so John watched, and listened, and learned.

The blood had come from a deep cut in her head. She had a concussion, a couple of cracked ribs, and her body was a mass of bruises and contusions. They were keeping her overnight for observation, and when they finally moved her from the ER to a room upstairs, John made the trip with her, holding her hand as he walked beside her bed.

It felt like forever before they were finally alone, and then John leaned over the bed and kissed both cheeks, before brushing his lips across her mouth.

"I have never been as scared as I was today, not knowing if you were still alive."

Gracie reached for his hand. "I knew you would find me. I kept hearing the phone ringing, but I couldn't reach it. Every time it quit ringing, I would panic, thinking it might never ring again. I finally got my fingers far enough in my pocket to answer, and then I heard your voice. After that, the panic ended for me. I wasn't lost anymore." Her voice broke, and she started crying. "I thought I was going to die without getting a chance to tell you what you mean to me. I love you forever, John Gatlin. So much I'm afraid to be in the world without you. And if that scares the shit out of you, then get over it."

John grinned. "The storm scared the shit out of me, but you don't. I only need one thing in my life to make it perfect, and that's you."

"Okay then," Gracie said, and closed her eyes. "I feel dizzy again."

"Concussion. Rest."

Her eyes were closed, but she kept talking.

"How bad was Branson hit? Is the Majestic still there? Was it on my side of town? Did it hit your business? Is your home okay?"

"It hit the north side pretty bad. The Majestic is okay. I don't know about your place or mine."

She opened her eyes again. "Then will you do something for me?"

"Anything," John said.

"Will you please go check on Lucy, and see if my apartment is still standing? And after that, go check on all your stuff?"

He sighed. "I don't want to leave you."

"I'm right where I need to be, and I'm not going anywhere. You've already taken care of business today, helping get me found and rescued. Now, go do you."

He kissed her again. "I'll be back."

"I know that," Gracie said, and then closed her eyes again as he walked away.

The room was spinning—to the point that it felt like she might take flight, and that couldn't happen, because she was too sore to launch.

CHAPTER TWENTY

*J*ohn's business was the nearest, so he stopped there first. Even as he approached the area, he guessed the tornado had missed it. Power outages and some broken tree limbs seemed to be the only problems in this area.

He stopped long enough to make a quick sweep inside the office and then down to the building where all the vehicles were housed. No broken windows, and all locked up tight.

He went from there to Lucy Bedford's, and when he pulled up in the drive, he saw wind damage, but little else. He was getting out of the truck to do a quick check of the windows in Gracie's apartment when Lucy hailed him from the back garden.

"John! John!"

He stopped and then jogged toward her. She had a bandana tied around her head and held a rake. She'd obviously been rained on and looked a little frazzled.

"Are you okay?" he asked.

Lucy leaned the rake against a garden bench and pointed at the broken limbs down near her back fence.

"Yes. The roof is sound. My old house is sound. But some of the big trees lost a few limbs."

"I'll get the boys out to clean those up for you," John said.

"Thank you, honey. Is your shop okay? Did the Majestic make it through the storm okay? I was worried about Gracie and the girls."

"The shop is fine, and the Majestic is, too, but Gracie isn't. She was at the Wisteria Inn on a job for the shop when the storm hit."

Lucy's pink cheeks went pale. "Oh no. Wait! That's one of the places that took a direct hit! Is she hurt bad?"

"She has some injuries, none of which are life-threatening. She got trapped in a stairwell beneath a pile of debris. It took a while to figure out where she was and if she was still alive. Scariest damn hours of my life," John said.

Lucy hugged him.

"Where is she?"

"They just moved her from the ER up to a room at Cox Med Center. She's staying overnight for observation. She has staples in her head, a couple of cracked ribs, and a concussion. She's going to turn black and blue all over before she's well. But she's still Gracie. Still a survivor. Still my best girl. I'm here because she wanted me to check on you and her apartment. And then I have to go home and check on my place before she'll hush about it."

"Bless her heart," Lucy said. "We still have power here. Tell her that. And if she can get up the stairs to her apartment, I'll look after her as she heals."

John nodded. "Yes, ma'am. I'll tell her. Is there anything I can do for you, other than send the boys to clean up?"

"No, I'm fine," Lucy said. "Now, run on along and check on your home. I've already checked the windows in the apartment. They're sound."

"Thanks. I guess I'll see you tomorrow then," he said, and went back to his truck and headed out of town.

There were hardly any vehicles on the road, and the ones he encountered were few and far between. The road leading to his home was southwest of Branson, and the further he went, the more apparent it became that the storm had stayed true to its path and kept moving east across the northernmost part of the city. There was nothing out here to note but water in the road ditches.

By the time he got home and pulled up in the garage, adrenaline was crashing. The place still had power. Walking into it, with everything like he'd left it that morning and nothing out of place, felt like a miracle.

He stripped in the laundry room, then walked through the house and up the stairs to his shower, moving now on autopilot. He couldn't focus on anything but getting clean and back to Gracie.

He turned the water on full force, then stepped beneath the spray, bracing himself against the walls as the water pelted his head, his face, and then his chest. But when he closed his eyes, the sight of all that devastation returned and he shuddered.

Seeing Gracie on the stretcher again, coming out of the hotel, then Gracie in ER and the wounds and the bruises, and the intensity in her voice: "He's mine. And I want him here," she'd said.

His shoulders slumped, and then his legs went weak. He'd almost lost her. But now that she was safe, he was losing control. Tears came swiftly, blinding in their intensity. He moved deeper into the shower, standing fully beneath the spray as they came faster—lost within the water pouring down on his head.

GRACIE WAS ASLEEP WHEN JOHN CAME BACK, AND HE'D COME PREPARED to stay. He nodded at the nurse who walked in behind him. He set his bag beneath the windowsill, and then stood at the foot of the bed, watching as she checked Gracie's vitals.

"Is she still okay?" John whispered.

The nurse nodded, gave him a thumbs up, and walked out.

He moved a chair close to her, then touched her arm. It was warm, soft to the touch, and so bruised it hurt him to even look at it. Her eyes were moving beneath her lids—her fingers twitched, but he could see the steady rise and fall of her chest. Likely, she was dreaming.

All the nights they'd made love—all the passion and the lust with all the magic of new lovers—and none of it had prepared him for the gut-wrenching fear of losing her.

She sighed.

He watched a tear roll from the corner of her eye. Her fingers twitched again. He couldn't stand it any longer and took her hand.

"Gracie, don't cry, baby. You're safe."

She moaned, and then opened her eyes.

"Johnny, you're back. Is everything okay?"

He hadn't been called Johnny in a good twenty years, but coming from her, it was perfect.

"Everything is fine. Lucy sends her love. Donna and the girls send their love. And you already have all of mine."

"Never too much of such a good thing," she said. "Oh, Lord. What I wouldn't give for a Coke."

John got up, unzipped his bag, and pulled out a little cooler.

"The Good Lord's busy. I got this," he said, opened the cooler, took out a can of Coke, and popped the tab. Then he pulled the straw out of her water, put it in the can, and held it to her lips.

Gracie took a little sip, swallowed, and then took one more. "I've been wanting this all day. I kept putting it off at the hotel, and then..." She took one more sip, then stopped.

"Enough?" John asked.

"For now."

He set it aside. She was drifting again. But he wasn't going anywhere. He wasn't leaving here again without her.

GRACIE WAS IN THE PORCH SWING WITH DELIA, HOLDING HER HAND AS THEY swung back and forth.

Delia was silent, her glassy eyes staring off into the distance into a world beyond anything Gracie could see.

She was worried. Her mama had quit eating. The doctors had told her this would happen, and yet now that the time was here, it was frightening.

She felt like she was letting her mama go hungry, even though they'd said this was part of the end.

And so they rocked. Delia saying nothing, while Gracie cried.

"I love you, Mama. I'm sorry this is all so hard. You've been the best mother any little girl could ever want. You taught me everything I am ever going to need to know. So, I want you to know that I've got this. I, Gracie, know how to take care of business because of you."

A fly buzzed around Delia's face.

Gracie shooed it away, and kept rocking, and wiping her own eyes, and blowing her own nose.

"If only it would rain. This dry-assed, God-forsaken land needs a drink of water, Mama. You need a drink of water. But I can't get you to swallow anymore. God should be ashamed this disease exists. I don't understand the need for all this suffering, so I want you to talk to Him about it when you go home. It's wrong. There is nothing to be learned from this kind of pain. There is nothing to be gained from even witnessing it. It is the utmost betrayal of a good woman's life...that it's coming to this end."

The sun was slipping from the sky like a pat of melting butter, and Gracie had a headache from crying now. She let the swing come to a stop, and then laid her head down in her mother's lap and closed her eyes.

"I love you, Mama. Bigger than the sky. If I didn't, this would have killed me." And then she sighed.

Delia hadn't spoken in weeks, but now her hand was on Gracie's head, and she was humming.

Gracie was afraid to move. Afraid to break the spell.

⁓

GRACIE WAS CRYING IN HER SLEEP AGAIN.

John heard it and got up.

He didn't know if she was sad or in pain. He didn't want to wake her, so he slipped out of the room and went across the hall to the nurses' station.

"Good morning, John. Is everything okay?"

"I was wondering if Gracie could have something for pain now?

She's crying in her sleep. I don't know whether it's from what happened, or if she's hurting."

"I'll check her chart and be right in," she said.

He nodded and hurried back into the room. She was still sleeping, still crying.

He felt like crying, too.

A few minutes later, the nurse came in carrying a syringe.

"She was due something for pain. This will give her some ease," she said, and then after she'd injected it into Gracie's IV, she checked her vitals.

Gracie roused. "What's happening?" she asked.

"You were crying," John said. "I was afraid you were hurting."

She sighed. "It was an old hurt," she said.

John brushed a long strand of her hair away from her forehead. He felt helpless. She'd been leveled by life before he'd even met her, and now this.

"Is it morning yet?" she asked.

"In a manner of speaking. It's just after four."

She wrinkled her nose. "I wish this bed was big enough for two. I know you haven't slept a wink."

The nurse chuckled. "That bed is barely long enough for you, Gracie. This long-legged guy of yours wouldn't fit."

Gracie laughed softly, then winced. "Ow. Hurts to laugh."

John let them talk, satisfied by the smile on her face. And when the nurse was gone, and Gracie had drifted back off to sleep. He walked to the window.

Part of the city was in darkness, still without power. He knew this hospital was full, and the more serious victims had been air lifted to Springfield.

Like Humpty Dumpty, a big part of the city had taken a great fall. It was going to take time and energy to put it back together again.

$\sim$

THEY GOT GRACIE UP AFTER BREAKFAST, WALKED HER DOWN THE HALL and back, and then gave her a bath. John went by the Majestic to get Gracie's purse, then, following her instructions, let himself into her apartment to get some clothes for her to wear home.

One of his crews was already at Lucy's house cleaning up storm debris when he arrived. There was so much to clean up in Branson, that it was all they would be doing for the rest of the week.

Lucy was waiting by his truck when he came down the stairs with Gracie's clothes.

"Is she coming home today?" Lucy asked.

John nodded. "I had to get something for her to wear. They cut her out of her clothes yesterday."

"Bless her heart," Lucy said. "Looks like you and your boys will have your hands full this week with storm debris. Don't worry about Gracie. I'll tend to her during the day."

John hugged her. "Thank you. You're the best."

Lucy sighed. "I think you're pretty fine, yourself. You two haven't known each other long, and you're sure stepping up in her time of need."

"It feels like I've always known her. She's my girl, and that's how I feel."

"Are you gonna marry her?" Lucy asked.

"Absolutely...if she'll have me. But Gracie came here with wounds that only time will heal. I'm just giving her a little space to deal with her past before I make me her future."

Lucy laughed. "I love that. Now go. I've kept you long enough, and I'll be watching for you when you bring her back."

"It'll likely be after lunch sometime. We're waiting on her doctor to release her," he said.

Lucy waved and walked back toward her house as John drove away.

❧

GRACIE GOT DRESSED WITH THE HELP OF A NURSE, WHILE JOHN LOOKED through the drawer in the table for anything that might be hers.

"There's a bag with her things in it in the closet," the nurse said.

Gracie frowned. "I didn't know I still had 'things.'"

"It's the clothes they cut off you, and whatever would have been in your pockets."

"My phone?" Gracie asked. "Is my phone in there?"

"I'll look," John said, got the sack out of the closet, and sure enough, soon found the phone. "It's here," he said, and pulled a charger out of his bag to plug in her phone to charge.

"When can I go home?" Gracie asked.

"Doctor has to sign off on your release papers. I'll see if he's still making rounds," the nurse said, and left the room.

Within minutes of her phone being charged, Gracie began getting dings from a multitude of texts.

"Oh wow... I kind of forgot about Darlene. She's my ex-sister-in-law. Pretty much the only person from before that I still care about."

"Don't text. Call her," John said. "She'll want to hear your voice." He traced the tip of his finger along the side of her face. "I want to kiss you like crazy, but there's no place safe to touch you."

Gracie frowned. "My lips don't hurt."

"Okay then," he said, and brushed a soft kiss across her lips. "Thank you, baby. I've been wanting to do that all morning. Now, I'm going to step out and give you some space to talk. I'll just be down the hall for a bit. Want me to bring you back a Coke?"

"Yes, please," she said, and then made a call to Darlene.

The phone rang twice, and Darlene answered, talking.

"Where the holy hell have you been? We saw the storm damage on TV yesterday, and I've been texting and calling, but you didn't answer and—"

"Darlene!"

"What?"

"I was in the storm. I'm just being released from the hospital."

Darlene let out a wail. "Oh my God...I knew it! I just knew it! What happened? Are you okay?"

Gracie sat down in the chair and started talking, relating the whole story from beginning to end. And by the time she was finished, she was in tears.

"It was kinda like back when Mama stabbed me. I thought I was going to die, and then I didn't."

Darlene was bawling. "I'm so sorry. Do you need me? I can leave the kids with my parents and come stay with you. Are you still in the hospital?"

"No, I don't need you, honey, but thanks. I have John. And I'm going home today. I'll stay at my apartment. It wasn't in the area that got hit. It still has power, and John will be in the city all day every day helping with clean-up. He'll always be available if I need him. He said my landlady has offered to help me during the day, and I'll be with him at night. So, I'm all set."

"Oh my God. Just, oh, my, God," Darlene muttered. "Okay...but you have to promise that if you need me for anything, anything at all, you'll let me know."

"I will," Gracie said.

"I love you, sugar. And I'm so glad you're going to be okay. Rest and know that you are loved."

"Love you, too," Gracie said, and then disconnected.

She was wiping away tears when John walked in.

He frowned at the tears, as he popped the tab on her Coke and handed it to her.

"Thank you, honey," she said, and took a sip. "Mmm...Just what the doctor ordered. You are a good man."

John grinned. "That's me, Doctor Johnny Be Good."

"I know that song! Johnny Be Good! It's an old Chuck Berry song! Daddy loved music, and the classics even more. He had a beat-up old guitar and played music and sang to Mama all the time." Then her voice softened. "She loved it when Daddy sang."

John sat down beside her.

"That's a great memory, darlin'."

She nodded and rested her head against his shoulder.

"I know. We made lots of good memories before he died, and Mama went crazy. I'm going to have to remember them more."

"We can make us some good memories, too," John said. "But after you lose your raccoon eyes and the staples in your head."

Gracie blinked, burst out laughing, then punched him on the leg.

"Oh, shit. You made me laugh. It hurts to laugh," but she was still smiling.

John sighed. Just when he thought he couldn't love her more, she proved him wrong. Growing old with her was going to be a blast.

THE NEXT THREE DAYS WERE A BLUR.

John got Gracie's car to a body shop to have the hail damage repaired.

Donna and the girls sent her flowers—a dozen yellow roses for the girl from Texas. And the next afternoon, a big bouquet of flowers was delivered to her from Edward Rollins, the man she'd saved from choking.

Gracie didn't know there had been video of the rescuers bringing her out of the Wisteria Inn on the news, but he'd seen it and wanted her to know she was in his prayers.

The third day, Donna came by after work with a pie from her favorite bakery. She kept telling Gracie how sorry she was, not to worry about anything but getting well, and that her job would be there for her when she felt like coming back.

John and his crews worked from sunup to quit, just cleaning up storm debris.

Gracie slept, and rested, and Lucy fed her, entertaining her with an ongoing jigsaw puzzle and many hands of Blackjack while they drank endless glasses of sweet tea and Coke and told stories. Lucy talked about her men who'd gotten away, and the ones she'd dumped. To Gracie's delight, Lucy laughed when she admitted to regretting none of it.

John brought them lunch every day and stayed long enough to

realize he never wanted to play Poker against Gracie. Her laughter was easy. She was healing from the storm, but she was also healing from what had come before.

He took her home with him every night and held her when the dreams turned bad. She talked in her sleep, revealing way more than she'd told him awake. Crying because they were hungry or cold, or hungry and hot. Crying when the last of the cattle were gone. Crying when her mama didn't remember her anymore. Crying because her siblings had abandoned them.

He was falling deeper in love, and at the same time, realizing how broken she was. The greatest gift he could give her now was time.

ON THE SEVENTH MORNING AFTER THE STORM, JOHN BROUGHT GRACIE back into Branson and settled her into her apartment for the day.

Gracie was feeling more confident about being alone, but he and Lucy weren't. They hadn't given her a choice. Not until she could at least stand up straight and walk without groaning.

John was just getting ready to leave, and Lucy had yet to arrive. Gracie got her morning Coke out of the refrigerator and he waited for her to settle.

"Gracie, honey, do you need anything before I leave?" John asked.

She paused. "My goodbye kiss."

John grinned. "You were going to get that, anyway," he said, and gently cupped her cheeks before brushing a soft kiss across her mouth.

Gracie sighed as he let her go. "That was exactly what the doctor ordered."

"I can do better when your bruises are gone," John said, and then there was a knock at the door.

"That must be Lucy," Gracie said. "Would you let her in?"

John strode to the door and swung it inward, but it wasn't Lucy. It was a man from FedEx.

"Special Delivery for Gracie Jean Dunham."

"She's here. I'll take it," John said.

"I'm sorry, sir, but she has to sign for it."

"Oh, sure. Hey Gracie, can you come here a sec?"

Gracie came out of the kitchen, a little bent over and walking slow. The messenger's eyes widened when he saw the bruises and the way she was walking.

"I'm so sorry, Miss. I could have come to you if—"

"It's okay," Gracie said. "Just went ten rounds with a tornado, but I'm still standing."

"Jesus! Oh wow. Uh..." Then he held out his delivery scanner and a stylus to sign the screen. "Sign here."

So she did.

He handed her the envelope, gave her one last horrified glance, and took off down the stairs.

Gracie carried it to the sofa to open, pulled out some papers, then frowned.

"What's wrong?"

"I don't know... It's from a lawyer."

"Just read it aloud, and then we'll both know," John said.

And so she did.

Dear Miss Dunham,

The attached letter is from your brother, James. He has instructed me to deliver this news, and the accompanying letter.

As of 8:00 this morning, the sum of $1,550,000 has been deposited into a checking account in your name, at First National Bank in Branson, Missouri.

It is the proceeds of the sale of a home, outbuildings, and five hundred acres outside of Sweetwater, Texas. (See attached paperwork for the plat map marking the land that has been sold and the price per acre.)

Gracie stopped reading. She was shaking so hard she couldn't breathe.

"Take a breath and read the rest," John said.

There are no taxes due on these monies. It is yours, free and clear.

Your bank has already been apprised and assisted in this transfer, and while it is presently in a separate account, it is now yours to do with as you wish.

My sympathies on the loss of your mother.

Roger Dean, Esquire

Dean, Dean, and Marshall, Attorneys at Law.

Gracie laid the cover letter aside, and then recognized James's handwriting on the letter beneath.

"This is from James. I don't think I can read it," she said, and burst into tears.

John took it from her, tucked her close against him, and read aloud.

GRACIE,

Nobody deserves this but you.

Daddy haunts me every night for what I did to you and Mama. It doesn't belong to me. I don't want it.

Daphne won't take it. She says it's blood money, and she will not profit from a sin.

Mamie and Joel have rejected it. They will not take from you since they basically left you and Mama to die.

It's yours by birth. It's yours by right.

You were still there when we all left home.

You were always with Mama then.

And you stayed with Mama after...when the rest of us betrayed you.

Please don't reject this because of us.

Accept it because you are the Dunham who deserved it.

Accept it in Mama and Daddy's name.

You kept the dream of who we were alive, even as Mama lay dying.

If I could change what was done, I would. But I cannot. I will not ask for forgiveness. I gain no respect for myself by doing this. Only the hope that in meting out this long-delayed justice, I will finally get a measure of peace.

—James

John laid the letter aside and then pulled her up into his lap, holding her as she shook, choking on harsh, ugly sobs. Even reading between the lines, the devastation done to her and by the people who were supposed to love her, was clear. He would have borne the pain for her if he could. All he could do was hold her and love her.

"That's it, darlin'. Let it go. Let it go," he said.

And so she did.

Nine years of fear, and pain, and grief came up—spilling over— pouring out. The letter hurt her heart; for all they'd been, and for all they'd lost. It had stripped her raw, in a frightening, soul-shattering way she had not seen coming, and she didn't know how to breathe without coming apart. Then John's voice had pulled her in, and she'd cried herself out in his arms.

When she could breathe again without wanting to scream, she went still. She could feel John's heartbeat beneath her hand. He was the faithful man. He was the loving man. Him she could trust forever.

She sighed.

"It's not enough that I have raccoon eyes, but now I've just about cried them shut."

"Hush your bad self," he said. "Don't say mean things about my girl."

"After all of this ugly family stuff, are you sure you still want me?"

He heard the uncertainty in her voice, and sighed. It was time for a little confession of his own.

"The day of the tornado, I was so scared I'd lost you that I couldn't see a tomorrow without you. And after we found you, I was so over- whelmed you were alive, that I went home and cried myself sick. So, yes I still want you."

Silence.

"You did?"

He sighed. "Yes, and if you tell anyone, I'll swear you lied."

"Tell what?" she said.

He grinned. "That's my girl."

"I guess I should get up and let you go to work," Gracie said.

"I guess... But can I ask you something first?"

She nodded.

"Now that you know how your brother and sisters feel about what they did, and that they wanted you to have the money, does that change how you feel about them?"

Her answer was swift and terse.

"Money doesn't make a sin go away. Money doesn't change a betrayal. And that money didn't come from them. It came from Mama and Daddy. So, I receive it in their honor. Not as hush money to make what my siblings did to me and Mama go away. I feel nothing for them."

John hugged her.

"Guts and brains. God, how I love you, girl. I wish I could stay, but I better get to work."

She got out of his lap, and followed him to the door, then hugged him again.

"I love you, Johnny."

"I love you more."

And then he was gone.

TEN DAYS AFTER THE TORNADO, GRACIE TOOK HERSELF TO THE DOCTOR and got her staples out, and then she stopped by the Majestic. Within seconds of walking in the front door, she was mobbed.

"You look great!" Reba said.

"Seriously? I have green circles beneath my eyes," Gracie said.

It made them laugh.

"Were you out shopping?" Donna asked.

"Nope. Making sure my brains were all tucked back in my head before they pulled out the staples."

They laughed again.

"When can you come back to work?" Donna asked.

"I can't lift or reach over my head yet. My ribs aren't fully healed. But I can sit on my butt and put flowers in a vase all day."

Donna cheered. "How about tomorrow from open to noon for the rest of the week? Just to ease yourself back into the routine. I don't want you overdoing anything. If that doesn't stress you in any way, then you can go back to your regular schedule."

"I would love that," Gracie said. "I am going stir crazy."

"Then we'll see you tomorrow!" Donna said. "Welcome back."

"Tomorrow," Gracie said, and left feeling better than she had in days.

Five people had died the day of the storm. Twenty-two were severely injured. All but four had been released from the hospital. Gracie was one of the lucky ones, and she knew it.

When she got in the car to go home, she ran her fingers gingerly along the tender, still healing gash on her head, grateful that the staples were gone.

She could almost hear her Mama's voice. *One step, one day at a time, baby girl.*

She glanced up at the empty passenger seat, half-expecting to see Delia riding shotgun.

"I know, Mama. I'm just takin' care of business."

~

IT WAS LIKE THE FIRST DAY OF SCHOOL.

Everything was an unknown.

Gracie had stayed by herself last night because she felt like a fake expecting John to take care of her now when she was perfectly capable of taking care of herself again.

She didn't really want to give up the nights at his home, but he'd offered her shelter because she was hurt, and now she wasn't. She was a Dunham, and Dunham women knew how to take care of themselves. She and John were still falling in love, but that didn't mean they were at the moving in together stage. She knew she was going to miss him, and she did.

The whole evening was both lonesome and eerie. After it got dark, she found herself jumping at every little sound, then thought she heard footsteps coming up the stairs. But every time she looked out, it was peaceful and quiet.

Then John called her, and everything was right in her world.

"Hey darlin'. I sure do miss you. Are you okay?"

Gracie slid into bed and pulled the covers up to her waist.

"I'm fine. I miss you, too...terribly."

"We can fix that," John said. "All you have to do is say the word."

"I know. But I don't want to come to you still broken inside. I want all of me to be present with you."

"I know. It's why I don't push," John said. "Are you looking forward to going back to the Majestic tomorrow?"

"Yes. I love the girls, and I love the work."

"Just half a day, though. Ease yourself back into the routine."

"I will. I'll pick something up for lunch on the way home, and then rest after I eat."

"Get enough for me, and I'll come tuck you in before I go back to work."

"Really?" Gracie said.

He chuckled. "Yes, really. I can stay long enough to eat and steal a kiss, and that's about it."

"Deal," Gracie said. "See you tomorrow."

"Sleep well, sugar. Love you."

"Love you most," she said, and hung up.

After that, the night sounds were just that—nothing scary, nothing ominous. Just the old garage settling, and a tired, wounded city trying to put itself to sleep.

For Gracie, going back to work felt like turning off a switch to being a victim. This was the second time in her life she'd cheated death, and she was getting the hang of it.

Within the week, September was over. She had dates with John that ended in her bed, and on Sundays, he took her out of town to his home and made love with her in his.

The trees were turning, the days were getting colder, and their walks along the lake got shorter. John made her laugh and feel beautiful, and she ached for him in the way a woman wants her man. When they made love, it wasn't just passion. It was healing her.

She knew John understood. She never saw impatience in his expression. Only the love, plainly visible in his eyes. He wouldn't ask. He wouldn't push. He'd already made the offer. It was up to her to say when, and so October came and went.

Then one Tuesday evening in early November, Gracie was sitting in the living room, watching the flames dancing in the fireplace, staring at a glass half-full of Coke and an uneaten cookie, when she decided she was tired of being independent. She missed John. She missed his voice. And she thought... *Why? Why am I punishing myself with his absence? Because that's all this is. I don't deserve to be punished, and neither does he.*

Even though it was already dark, she picked up the phone and called him. When he answered, he sounded tired.

"Hello, my love. What's going on in your world?"

"Nothing, and that's why I called. Remember when you said all I had to do was say the word, and this business of your place and my place would end?"

There was a brief moment of silence, and then he answered. "Yes, I remember."

"Then... Word! I am officially over myself and missing you something awful. What can we do to rectify this situation?"

He laughed, and the feeling that went through her was one of heat and want.

"Can this wait until tomorrow? I have a slow leak in a tire. I don't want to take off after you in the dark and then have to change a flat."

"Yes, of course it will wait. I just...I just wanted to see if the offer was still open, I guess."

"Well, it is, and you've just made me a very happy man. Is Lucy going to be okay with this?"

"Yes. She told me months ago that she'd let me out of my lease if the need arose."

"Can you ask off work at noon?" John asked.

"Yes."

"Then I'll see you at your place tomorrow and help you pack. I won't be able to sleep now for the excitement of knowing this is actually happening."

Gracie sighed. "Me either. Love you, Johnny."

And this time, it was John who had the last word.

"Love you more."

WHEN GRACIE CALLED LUCY THE NEXT MORNING TO TELL HER, LUCY laughed.

"I knew this day was coming. It's about time, girl, and I'm so happy for the both of you. I'll get the utilities switched back into my name and have them send you a final bill. I have John's address. Is that the one you want to use?"

Gracie shivered. "Yes. That's the one, and thank you for being the lifesaver you were. You were my first friend in Branson, and I hope I continue to see you."

"Oh, you will. You'll probably be doing flowers for my famous New Year's Eve party, but you and John will be getting an invitation, as well. And one of these days, I'm going to beat you at Poker."

Gracie laughed. "I'll leave the key and the remote on the kitchen counter. I won't lock up, so you'll have to come get them after we're gone."

"I can do that. And don't fret about cleaning anything. I always have it done professionally between renters anyway. I love, you, girl. Invite me to your wedding."

"Yes, ma'am," Gracie said.

She grabbed her purse and started to walk out the door when a blast of cold air hit her in the face. Without missing a beat, she made a U-turn, went back in the house, traded her jacket for a coat, and then tried that exit once more.

The wind was still cold, but Gracie was fine, and as soon as she got to work, she cornered Donna in her office.

"I hate to ask at short notice, but I need off this afternoon."

"Of course," Donna said. "Is everything okay?"

"It will be as soon as I get packed. I'm moving in with John."

Donna grinned. "It's about time! And whenever you have that wedding, I'm doing your flowers."

Gracie laughed. "One thing at a time. Right now, I'm just taking care of business, getting me where I'm supposed to be next."

Then she went to the workroom, and the morning flew, and when her lunch time came around, she didn't linger.

"Hey, where'd Gracie go so fast?" Reba asked.

"She had to go see a man about the rest of her life," Donna said.

Reba's eyes widened. "What?"

"She's going home to pack. John's moving her into his place today."

"Aw, man. She's so lucky," Reba said.

Donna thought of all the hell that girl had been through, and then shook her head.

"No... This isn't lucky. This is her coming out of a really dark place, and it's about damn time."

WHEN THEY DROVE UP TO THE BIG LOG HOUSE, THE SMOKE COMING OUT of the chimney was her own smoke signal, welcoming her home. John had all her things in his SUV, pulled over for her to park beside him, then walked her across the deck. She was about to enter the house as she always did when John stopped her.

"Wait," he said. He opened the door, then picked her up in his arms and carried her across the threshold. "Welcome home, my darling. Welcome home," he said, and sealed it with a kiss. "Stay inside where it's warm. I'll carry everything in, and then we can get everything where it needs to go afterward."

"I can help," Gracie said.

"I know...but I still don't want you carrying heavy stuff, okay?"

She nodded, and then walked toward the big fireplace and backed up to the fire, warming her hands, and then her feet as she turned.

She watched him scurrying in and out with her things, and when the last load was in, he kicked the door shut behind him and started up the stairs.

"I'll carry them. You can unpack and put away," he said.

Gracie was so happy, she all but danced up the stairs. She'd spent nights here plenty of times, but she'd never been "in residence" before, and it was exciting.

John had made room for her clothes in the big walk-in closet and had emptied three drawers in his dresser for her. He was excited, too. A huge milestone was taking place in his life, as well. From this day forward, he would be her protector and her partner. She would be someone to cherish, and the person he trusted who would always have his back. That someone he'd always wanted to come home to was finally here, and her name was Gracie.

THAT EVENING, AFTER EVERYTHING HAD BEEN CARRIED INTO THE HOUSE and Gracie's clothes were hanging in the closet next to John's, and her great-grandmother's cuckoo clock was hanging on the bedroom wall, and her Mama's quilt was on a trunk at the foot of John's bed, something wonderful happened.

It began to snow.

Gracie saw it first and came off the sofa with a squeal.

"John! Look! Look! Those are snowflakes!"

He got up and followed her to the window, looking out across the front deck to the yard and the surrounding trees.

"It sure is! It's the Ozarks, welcoming you home," he said, and hugged her.

She turned, her dark eyes shining. "I love that," she said. "Let's go out on the front deck. Just for a bit. It's falling so soft, floating down like feathers. And there's no wind. Oh my God, snow in Sweetwater didn't fall, it blew sideways."

"Sure," John said. "Let me get our coats."

Gracie was still at the window when he came up behind her and held out her coat. She slipped her arms into the sleeves, and then buttoned it up while he was putting on his coat. She missed seeing him pat the pockets before opening the massive front door.

"After you," he said, watching with delight as Gracie walked out.

She stood in the middle of the deck, completely silent, feeling the flakes melting on her skin.

"It's magic. The silence is magic, and everything is so beautiful. It's like standing in a snow globe."

John slipped his hand inside the pocket of his coat. He could feel the little velvet box against his palm. He'd had it for a long time, waiting for Gracie, and now she was here.

He walked up in front of her, suddenly blocking her view. Then before she could open her mouth, he dropped down on one knee with the open box in his hand.

"Gracie Jean, you are my love, and you are my lover. You are the voice of my conscience, and you are my best friend. I trust you to the depths of my soul and with all my heart. I need you in my life. Will you marry me?"

Gracie gasped at the size of the diamond solitaire, and then saw so much love and promise on his face. All she could do was nod.

"Is that a 'yes'?" John asked.

"Yes! That's a yes! A great big yes!" Gracie said.

"Thank God," John said, and slid the ring up her finger.

Gracie laughed from the sheer joy of it, threw her arms around his neck, and hugged him. Then she spun out of his arms with her hands in the air, shouting.

"I, Gracie Dunham, am engaged to John Gatlin,"

He laughed, then slipped an arm around her waist and started dancing her across the deck while the snow fell down around them.

"We have confetti, but no music," John said.

Gracie threw back her head and closed her eyes.

"I hear music. It must be Daddy. He's playing 'Johnny Be Good.'"

EPILOGUE

*I*n the floral business, when you are planning your own wedding, you plan it between holidays, with a nod to the season for certain flowers.

Valentine's Day was out. That was nonstop flowers for a solid week running.

Easter was out. Tulips, Easter Lilies, and baskets galore.

After that, it was one holiday after the other.

Mother's Day.

Father's Day and June weddings.

Fourth of July—with all the others too far away to consider.

Gracie was between a rock and a hard place, and so she chose the valley between: March 13.

IT WAS A SATURDAY WHEN THAT DAY ARRIVED.

The weather was beautiful.

The Ozarks were wearing their best spring greens as the guests began arriving at The Dogwood Chapel outside of Branson.

Gracie sat in the dressing room, staring at herself in the mirror. She'd spent forever picking out the dress.

It had a high neckline and long sleeves, but without the lace. It hid the scars, but not her shape. She'd had a childhood dream of being married in her Mama's wedding dress. This was the closest she could get.

She sighed.

"God, Mama, I wish you were here. Healthy and happy, and lining everybody out as to how to behave, and what to do, and how to do it. You would so be taking care of business."

She took a deep breath and then blinked away tears.

Today was not for crying.

And Mama *was* with her. She knew it.

So here she was, waiting for someone to come get her and take her to the preacher.

She wanted to be Gracie Gatlin.

She wanted to be John's wife.

She felt like she'd been practicing for this moment for most of her life.

And then the door opened, and she turned around.

Donna beckoned, then put the wedding bouquet in Gracie's hands as she walked out into the hall.

"You look so beautiful," Donna said.

"I am so happy, and the flowers are perfect," Gracie said.

The bouquet was magnificent in the fragility—magnolias in full bloom framed by their own thick, waxy leaves, like lilies on lily pads, gathered together with satin ribbon.

Gracie clutched it with both hands as a lady approached, then led her through the winding halls, all the way to the entrance to the chapel.

Her heart thumped. The seats were full. Recognizing people from looking at the back of their heads wasn't easy, but some were impossible to mistake.

Darlene and her fiery red hair. She'd driven all the way from Houston with Caleb and Joanie.

Lucy, with her white hair all fluffed out in every direction, was wearing a turquoise feather in lieu of a hat.

And down in front, John's whole family had filled up a row.

Those were the guests who mattered most to her, but she was looking for John.

And then she saw him at the altar, silhouetted against the windows behind the pulpit, and thought, *Thank you, God, for this man.*

A chord of music was struck.

The pastor lifted his arms.

The congregation stood, turned, and then a hush fell.

The music began, and Gracie started down the aisle.

John's heart was pounding.

Thirty-five years he'd waited for this day. For her.

He hadn't known who she would be for the longest of times, then once he'd seen her, he had held onto the memory of her face.

But for a tiny angel charm and the grace of God, he might never have seen her again, and yet here she was, and so was he, and nothing was going to stop them now. They belonged, and in a very few minutes, the rest of the world would know it, too.

Now she stood beside him, her shoulder almost touching his, both of them facing the preacher. The man kept talking and talking...and then he turned to face her.

Gracie saw her reflection in John's tear-filled eyes and tightened her grip on his hands.

She was on lock and load.

She knew the words by heart.

Her whole life had been in preparation for this day, for this man, for this moment in time.

Repeat after me, the preacher said, and so she did.

"I, Gracie, take thee, John..."

The End

ABOUT THE AUTHOR

Sharon Sala is a *New York Times* and *USA Today*, best-selling author.
First published in 1991, she has 127 books published in six different
genres – Romance, Young Adult, Western, Fiction, Women's Fiction
and Non-Fiction. Her industry awards include: eight-time RITA final-
ist, (romance industry award), the Janet Dailey Award, five-time
Career Achievement winner from *Romantic Times Magazine*, five-time
winner of the National Reader's Choice Award, five-time winner of
the Colorado Romance Writer's Award of Excellence, Heart of Excel-

lence Award, Booksellers Best Award, Nora Roberts Lifetime Achievement Award presented by Romance Writers of America, and the Centennial Award from Romance Writers of America for recognition of her 100th published novel. Sharon lives in Oklahoma.

Made in the USA
Thornton, CO
12/13/24 14:31:52